Praise for

REDEEMING BROTHER MURRIHY:

The River to Hiruharama

the debut novel from

ANTONY MILLEN

"A highly successful first novel ... a quest for self-discovery and redemption written by someone who has a deep understanding of what stirs the spirit." - Christodoulos Moisa, *The River City Press*

"Few can write anything that will cause a person to be still thinking about it days later. Antony can. Truly something extraordinary and special." - Sarah Knight & *The Drunken Druid*

"Absorbing and Lyrical ... Once begun I could not put this book down and was gripped to the end" - Tui Allen, author of *Ripple*

"Best read slowly so that you can savour the rich descriptions, poignant inner dialogue, and extensive cultural background that is so skilfully woven throughout."
— Tracy Krauss, author of *Wind Over Marshdale*

MAPLE KORU
PUBLISHING

antony.millen.wordpress.com

REDEEMING

BROTHER MURRIHY

The River To Hiruharama

Antony Millen

MAPLE KORU
PUBLISHING

Redeeming Brother Murrihy

The River To Hiruharama

Printed by CreateSpace

Cover photograph: The Meeting of the Whanganui and Ongarue Rivers, Taumarunui 2013, Antony Millen
Author's photograph: The Road to Whanganui, 2013, Mary Millen
Maple Koru Publishing logo, Leanne Reynolds

Note: For thematic reasons, different spelling systems have been used to further distinguish narrative voices.

Find more information at:

antonymillen.wordpress.com

Follow Antony Millen on Twitter and Facebook for updates on future projects.

ISBN-13: 978-0-473-24893-2
ISBN-10: 047324893X

CONTENTS

To my brother

PROLOGUE: THE RIVER'S MOUTH

We are te wai-tuku-kiri o ngā tūpuna—the river where our forefathers performed great rituals.

We flow out of Io-wairoa—the fountainhead.

We are te wai-herunga o ngā kuia—the river where our foremothers groomed the future.

We feed our children, give them life and draw them to us in times of need.

We are tūpuna kuia—grandmother of Te Atihaunui a Pāpārangi, the descendants of Haunui-a-Pāpārangi.

We   know   our   people   who   have   been   and   who   will   be.

A GOOD KIN MAN

I hold a memory of my mother's eyes clearer than any photograph, even the photograph I am developing now; the one that hung on our kitchen wall all my life. It's black and white, a picture taken by my father before any of us were born. She's looking at something in the near distance with a slight furrow in her brow. Her lips are thin and straight. Her nose is well defined with a lovely small rise at the end. On her forehead lives the mole that no longer exists. I remember this well, as if it was something I must have fixated on as an infant. She hated the mole. It looks lovely in this photo. It was that blemish I identified as distinctive to my mother. That and her eyes. Eyes that always seemed to be looking at something that's there, but not there; revealing, not a longing, but a pensive understanding that all is not as it should be, but that all can be good.

She's dying now. I have accepted that and am moving with it. This photo will be the centerpiece of a montage at her funeral.

Aging wooden floorboards creak above me at the top of the stairs.

"Conrad?" It's my father. "Can you come up and join us now? Your sister is here."

"Sure Dad." I listen to his receding footsteps return to the living room. As I hang my photograph to dry and wash my hands of the fixer, I look out the window at the autumn leaves falling in our backyard. Finishing, I switch on the lights in Dad's make-shift darkroom and open the door. Turning left, I climb the simple old staircase, two steps at a time as I have always done, as my father always does, as my brother always did.

It's warm upstairs. I can hear voices in the living room, each very soft, very somber. I dread this. Family gatherings are bad enough, but pow-wows are not our strong suit. My aunt will be melodramatic. My sister will be cold and unhelpful. My father will be perfectly PC. I'll say little in order to keep the peace, no matter how I feel.

Our living room, and I still call it our living room, is comfortable with plush carpeting and double glazed windows. Across the room, through the large front panes, I can see spruce and birch bending in submission to a wind that has been picking up all evening. At the far end, in the high backed chair, sits my sister Clio. We smile at each other before I greet my aunt who is settled on the floor by the coffee table. She brushes the top of the stack of photos I developed earlier this morning. More black and whites, consistent with a motif my father loves.

Dad is on the couch beside Clio's husband Daniel, a taciturn man who nods at me, obviously uncomfortable. I take my seat in the lounge chair by the front door, leaning forward as I can see my aunt is ready to take us through this.

"Hello Conrad darling. These photos really are lovely. She will love them."

"Thanks Mavis".

She reclines against the couch near Dad's leg. "Conrad, we were just talking about Francis."

I'm not impressed. I look at Dad, then at my sister. I squeeze my hands and sigh, shaking my head. "Frankie? Far out. What are you thinking?" My stomach rises, not so much from anger as from annoyance.

"Your mother has asked about him Conrad." It's still Mavis. Dad and Clio let her do the talking. We hear Mom cough in the bedroom next door.

"Far out," I say again. "What has she said?"

"She wants to see him."

I stand and walk behind my chair. "Well, I can imagine she does. But we've been through this before Mom's diagnosis. He's gone—he doesn't want anything to do with us. Open your eyes! We haven't heard from him in over two years for Christ's sake. We don't even know where he is!"

"We know that Conrad, but she's asking about him." She pauses. "She's asking *for* him."

Bloody melodrama. Does she ever get tired of listening to herself talk like this? I grip the back of the chair before sitting down again. I look to my father. "Dad, there is no time for this. There's no time for us to do anything about Frankie. We've tried, eh? He's gone - she even accepted that at one point. It's not going to change now because of a tumor." I canvass the faces in the room. "I mean, we're planning a funeral here. A month ago, the doctor told us we'd have eight weeks at the most and she's in there getting worse each day. What are you all thinking? Clio?"

Clio looks hard at me. I don't know why I called on her.

"Mom's asked for Frankie. We have to at least talk about that."

"Yes Clio, you're absolutely right," Mavis says. "That's all we're really doing Conrad, is talking about it. Your mother knows about Francis. She knows he's left us, but it's always been awful for her. She may not have shown that to you, but it's been so, so hard on her. He's her first-born and now she's dying without seeing him one last time. We do need to talk about it."

"Fine then," I say. "What's there to talk about? He's somewhere in New Zealand. We have no contacts there who might know where he is. No phone number or address. He told us nothing in his last e-mail and when we've tried replying to it, we've only received automated responses saying his address doesn't exist. Dad, you even flew down there and . . . and couldn't find him. There. What else is there to talk about?" I can't look at them now. We sit in silence listening to the wind outside.

"Conrad . . . ." My father finally speaks. "You're right. For some reason Frankie has stopped talking to us. We don't know how much time your mother has left. But we have to try something. I'm not going to ignore this request from your mother."

His voice composes me. Dad has spent his life trying to meet Mom's needs. Not that she's a needy woman or demanding. He loves her, I know that. I sigh, still not sure what is meant to happen next. "Dad, what do you want to do?"

Dad looks at me, his eyes shaking. "Son, I have waited to hear from Frankie for almost two years. I did the wrong thing. I should have kept looking for him when I had the chance. Now I can't. I need to be here with your mother."

Mom's eyes appear in my mind; eyes looking past me, looking at something or someone else. Looking at Frankie. In my heart I reach, hoping she will look at me, see me. She doesn't.

"Dad," I whisper, there's no-one else in the room now, "you know I'll do anything for Mom, but you also know what might happen if I go? You know what I might lose?"

Dad nods slowly. "I do son. I'm not asking you to do it. But I don't know what else to say or do. Can you talk to your mother?" He turns to Mavis. "I don't know what else to say."

I look at Mavis and Clio, even Daniel. Mavis says, "It's not right that you should go Conrad. But is it right that you don't?"

~

It's after midnight and I'm developing more photos. This one is a picture of Mom sitting on the living room floor with Jacob and Kim, Frankie's children, before they left for New Zealand. Jacob is three and Kim is one. Mom's head is full of her thick dark-brown hair. She's smiling at something silly Jacob is doing for the camera, probably held by Dad. Kim looks on from Mom's lap. We've always known this photo in color, but the black and white composition highlights Mom's smile and adds depth to her eyes.

I pin this up to dry with the others: a picture of Mom and Dad walking out of church, Mom wearing a mini-skirted wedding dress, Dad sporting the shortest haircut I've ever seen on him, showing his large ears; a photo of Mom and Clio, looking so much alike; another of Clio that I took in the same fashion as Dad's taken of Mom over thirty-five years earlier; photos of Mom with my own daughter, Jade.

I need photographs like these to help me remember. I can't explain why, but I tend to see the world like an impressionist painting. Even though I'm a journalist, I would make a terrible eye-witness to a crime, missing out important identification details, like hair color or clothing. If you ever want to know what happened when we were growing up, you'd be better off asking Frankie. He is a genuine eidetic—he literally has a photographic memory.

But I don't need a photograph to remember my mother's eyes.

I will talk with Mom tomorrow. I will try and get her to see that it's too much. Too much for her, too much for everyone, too much for me. It's crazy. She'll see. I can't believe we've even entertained it.

She'll see it's too much and that it's time for us all to move on with this.

As I finish for the night and switch the lights on, I stop in the door to look at a photo of Mom and Frankie. It's the night of his prom and he's wearing a tuxedo. Mom looks proud, her arms around his waist. She appears conscious of his awkwardness in the moment. His eyes are arrogant and his smile is forced. I miss him just now. In this photo, he didn't know what was going to happen. He didn't know what he was going to do. He didn't know what I would be asked to do. Looking into those eyes, I wonder if he'd care if he knew.

Closing the door behind me, I move into the porch and pull on my coat and boots. The wind has retreated outside but the temperature has dropped again. Jordan will know where I've been but I'm not sure what she will think of today's madness.

~

There's something about Nova Scotia in autumn that speaks comfort and warning. The leaves whisper colors, telling stories of beauty and death. Reds and ambers fill the hills and litter pathways and highways. Green spruces testify to longevity, promising their deciduous neighbors they will be waiting for them. Driving home from our house in Sutherland's River is one of the most stunning journeys in the area at this time of year. This morning, I leave it and the Trans-Canada highway behind as I reach the first exit for New Glasgow, making my way to Westville via Stellarton.

My parents still live in the house in which I was raised. The property has its own mix of beeches, birches and spruce. Two solid oak trees stand on either side of the driveway providing a natural gateway. There are no street numbers on our road; when ordering pizza, the delivery is made to "the fourth house on the left with the brown cedar siding". My father built this house, or that's the way I remember it. We moved in when I was three, just before Frankie started school. We lived in the basement for a long time, while Dad finished the upstairs. I vaguely remember pink insulation in the exposed walls and the black paper covering the space where our sliding glass door would go. It was the seventies and building codes must have still been in development.

As I get out of my truck, I look at the pond down the hill behind our house. Ice will cover it soon, and that will be covered with snow. No young neighborhood boys to sweep it for hockey these days. Today, it looks clean and quiet. The summer frog noises have stilled and the bull-rushes are limping. Frankie and I loved the pond. I loved the summer pond with the frogs and dragonflies—warm and living and wet. My brother loved the winter pond with the ice and skate-marks—cold and dry and only alive when used for risk and challenge.

At the top of the deck stairs, I see Dad sitting in the sun-room with a newspaper. It's Saturday morning so he'll be working on the crossword regardless of the pressures that enfold him. He stands when he sees me and is seated at the kitchen table when I walk in.

"Coffee's made," he says.

"Thanks Dad, I'll get some in a minute, eh?" I leave my shoes by the door and drape my coat on the chair opposite my father. He looks good today. Routine must subdue the turmoil, if that's what you'd call whatever is going on inside this man.

"How is she today Dad?"

"Well, you can go and ask her yourself. She's awake. Has been for most of the night."

I walk over to her door. Until a month ago I would never have walked into my parents' room while they were in bed, even as a child. I don't remember why. Now it's the only place I see my mother.

The room is dark, even at this time of morning when the sun is crisp and high on this side of the house. Dad built the adjoining sun-room as a way of capturing some solar warmth, but the bedroom has always been sheltered. Mom is lying in bed. Her eyes do seem to light up when I enter. I smell hair-spray and clean laundry.

"Conrad, I thought that was your voice. How are you?" Her voice is soft and tremulous, as it always has been.

"I'm OK Mom. Dad says you've been up all night. You alright?"

"Oh, well," she laughs airily, "you know, not great." She smiles and says, "Yes, I was up through the night. But you know, being awake doesn't bother me. I like to see and hear and think about things. A lot of memories mostly. I have good memories."

I sigh. "Yeah, you do eh Mom?" I hate this now. I thought I'd got through this part. When the cancer returned, Mavis has said a lot of things like that: "She's had a good life you know, we all have such wonderful memories together." It was so trite. Mavis seemed to skip any grieving process and move right onto greeting card platitudes. Mavis, our life-coach guru who had a phrase to smooth over any inconvenience from spilled Javex to her dying sister. I got through it and I got past it. I decided I wasn't afraid of her cancer and I wasn't afraid of her dying. I got it.

But I don't get this.

Mom's talking about Frankie. "He should have stayed. They should have stayed. We should have done more to help them to stay."

I listen, frustrated that I've heard this before and that I felt free from it only a few months ago.

"It must have been terrible for him. When your father and I got to him in Taumarunui, he had already buried so much. The funeral was so amazing. So many people we didn't know showing such care for our son."

I listen, remembering the reports about the funeral. Remembering my incomprehension that Frankie buried his wife, my nephew, and my niece so far away from home, with strangers.

"Frankie didn't come back. Your father and I didn't know what to say to him about it. He just said he needed to stay with them. What could we have said? We should have known what to say."

I listen, angry at this brother, this son who kept his reasons to himself but handed the guilt on to his family.

"When your father went back to find him, he just couldn't manage. As soon as he got there, we found out about my first tumor. Your poor father . . . ."

Dad had gone to New Zealand, a capable man but he had only managed to get to Frankie's school in Taumarunui when he found out about Mom. He was a mess and unable to generate any leads. Alone in New Zealand, carrying the second most devastating news he'd ever heard—I don't know how he managed to get back here on his own.

But that was in the past. Mom almost completely recovered from surgery. No tumor. No radiation or chemotherapy required. She has lived with short-term memory loss ever since, and this has changed her, but we've all just been glad to have her with us. I still want her, but I know I can't hold on to her. That's why it's so hard listening to this talk.

"Mom, please stop," I say. She does of course. Always polite. Those eyes focus on me for a moment and then find their usual way over my shoulder.

"We've got to wake up Mom. Frankie made his own choices you know. He chose to go to New Zealand. He chose to stay there." I hesitate because I don't want to hurt her. "He's chosen to live without us . . . without you."

Then my mother does something I have only once before seen her do. She cries. She's sobbing and shuddering and I worry that she's having a seizure. "Mom, are you alright?" I ask stupidly.

She moves her lips, pressing her fingers to her eyelids, but no words come out. I don't know what to do. I can't sit on the bed with my mother. I can't hug her. I don't want Dad to come in and see what I've done. So I wait.

She's gasping, but her sobbing eases. She stammers, "I . . . I . . . can't . . . ," several times.

"Calm down Mom, please. What can't you do?"

"I can't go."

I close my eyes and see my heart breaking, feel my fingers reaching, hear my voice saying, "I know Mom. I don't want you to go."

"No," she says, restrained now. "I don't mean that. I can go. But I can't go without seeing Frankie."

~

Sitting in my own driveway, I think about what I'm going to say to Jordan. She's so erratic but she's stronger than me. Things aren't always good with us, but she'll tell me to go. She'll say do what's best for your mother and for your relationship with your mother. But she better not say do it for your brother. I'm thinking about what I'm going to say that won't drive me mad, that won't change my mind.

She must have seen me sitting out here, as she's come out the front door. I get out of the car to meet her and in her eyes, I see she already knows. We hug and go inside.

PASSENGER

I have never been to New Zealand. I have never left Canada. I have never flown in an airplane. Jordan booked the flights and I am due back at the end of October. I can change the return date, but I'm giving myself one month to bring Frankie back. One month before my mother is due to die.

Getting time off from the newspaper was easy considering my situation, my tenure there and the fact that they can conjure just about anybody to cover stories on turkey stuffing and Hallowe'en escapades.

Fortunately, I do have a passport, acquired for an aborted attempt to visit a London job fair. I met with Dad two days ago to get maps, travel guides, contacts and old e-mails and letters from Frankie. He's only ever been to Auckland and Taumarunui and this is where I will need to start.

I didn't know how to say good-bye to my mother. I could tell she didn't want to concede our separation might be permanent. She spoke more of Frankie and was even up and moving about the house. I did give her a hug.

I have always wanted to travel but I've never wanted to fly. We are meant to live on land, not in the sky. Taking off from Halifax, I sit in the window seat and look down at the woods surrounding the airport filled with those gorgeous Nova Scotia leaves. I love my home province. Maple syrup runs in my veins and bagpipes play in my soul.

9

And it turns out I don't just dislike flying—I'm downright petrified of it.

Regardless, on this airbus to Toronto, I am seated beside a Newfoundlander heading out to Fort McMurray, in Alberta. I have only recently heard about the tar sands. This man is on his third trip out there to drive one of those monster trucks, leaving his wife and children three months at a time. Oh Canada. The Maritimes do be a hard place to make a living.

That's why Frankie left—no jobs. He graduated from university in 1993 or '94, about the same time his son Jacob was born. I know he tried to make a go of it in Nova Scotia, substitute teaching around the county, applying for every job he could. But what chance did he have when other teachers had been working part-time temporary jobs for over a decade, without landing anything near permanent? I didn't understand it then. I was too wrapped up in meeting Jordan and sorting out my own work-life along with our own unexpected child. I had dropped out of university and was working any job I could find, from insurance sales to wedding photography. Frankie didn't seem capable of doing that—working outside of teaching. I remember suggesting several jobs to him—just things that could help him pay the bills, pay his student loans. He just didn't seem to comprehend. I suppose he'd put so much into getting his degree, he needed to use it. Still, I always wanted to move away and work as a photojournalist, maybe for a magazine or a big city newspaper, but had to give up that dream to focus on my family, making it work any way I could.

So, no job in Nova Scotia led to searching elsewhere. It was a shock when he announced he was going to New Zealand. Mom and Dad told me he was looking outside the province but I never thought he'd go so far. He and I had lost touch a bit. He and Kathy, his wife, just seemed to cloister themselves away more and more and we hardly ever saw him. At one point, things got so bad that they declined their invitation to our wedding. Frankie never told me what was going on but I thought he'd sort it out somehow. Leaving the country wasn't what I had in mind, but then, I don't know what I had in mind. Our family has never been great at resolving conflicts. We usually avoid them in the first place and carry on being civil. Frankie wasn't being civil and he wasn't sorting it either.

He would have taken this same flight, now that I think of it. In fact, I guess it would have been his first time flying as well. Imagine that: your first trip on an airplane is to take your pre-school aged family around the world with a suitcase each.

Idiot.

After a bumpy flight and an unpleasant landing in Toronto, I'm happy to be reconnected with terra firma. The airport is interesting enough. After Halifax and here, I gather that airports are just glorified shopping malls with terminals and luggage carousels. Sitting in a cafe, people-watching, I note a fellow traveler on a bench outside a clothing outlet. He is wearing "the look". I know the look well because I invented the look—a gormless stare resting heavily on slouched shoulders, a mind filled with elsewhere-dramas. The look of a man waiting for his wife to emerge, unable to stem the tide of consumerism in his life. We watch programs like Les Stroud's *Survivorman* but we're too scared to venture out ourselves or push back against our civilizing, not only scared of the wild outside, but our wild inside and the destruction it would cause to our marriages and our pension funds.

I survey all these strangers around me. So many people I will never encounter again. For my intents and purposes, these people might as well be living in this airport with no other life outside of my contact with them here in this time and place. Thinking of Mom and the things that matter most to me, I couldn't care less if they all were dead tomorrow, it wouldn't impact my life one iota. Unless of course we share a plane together.

Three hours later and I'm boarding for Vancouver, putting my own newly discovered fears to the test, in the hopes that I'll get used to this flying thing.

Stashing my carry-on bag above my head, I hear a woman's voice from the seat next to mine. "Would you mind putting this up there as well?" She speaks with a foreign accent. I lean over and see a small Indian woman peering up at me through thick glasses that inflate her eyes to twice their normal size. "Hello," she says now that she sees me better, "It was too heavy for me and the stewardesses are busy at the other end. Thank you very much."

I accept the bag from her, tell her it's not a problem and laugh inwardly to myself about the way she pronounced her last words. She sounds like such a typical Indian from television shows. Nova Scotia, or at least Pictou County, still doesn't have a lot of ethnic diversity, so anybody other than our local Chinese restaurateurs are a novelty.

Everybody looks like me where I come from, a collection of white descendants from the UK.

I settle into my seat and fasten the safety-belt. "Thank you," she says again and offers me a pleasant enough smile. This woman is endearing and even adorable. She wears a sort of silky head-covering and I wonder if she is Middle Eastern instead of Indian. I don't strike up first conversations well, unless it's for a story, so we travel for a good hour without talking. I do ask her if I can sit by the window, but after that I focus on the sights below. If I can't keep my feet on the ground, at least I can try and keep my eyes on it.

I have never traveled this far west before. Our family only took trips by train as far as Montreal and Ottawa when I was younger. Ontario, and perhaps Michigan and Minnesota pass below us. Whatever the states or province, I see what must be the Great Lakes and am amazed at the terrain below us; endless rivers and hills west of Toronto.

Food usually creates a path for conversation and it's no different on an airplane. My companion and I finally speak to each other as we sort out handing over food trays which then leads to me hailing the stewardess several times to clarify arrival times for my co-passenger. It turns out she's as anxious as I am, though for different reasons.

"If you're nervous about flying, just remind yourself that the pilot must be well-trained and experienced if he's working for Air Canada. There's more chance of dying in a car crash than in an airplane crash," she advises me lamely.

"You've obviously flown before then have you?"

"Yes, though I've never enjoyed it. At first, I did feel a bit out-of-sorts, like I was part in the air and part still on the ground, but I suppose what we're doing is unnatural isn't it? We'll be fine. Do you want to talk about something else to take your mind off things?"

I imagine Jordan seeing this and laughing at me. She knows I hate talking for the sake of talking, especially with strangers. Why can't people just sit in a space together without submitting to the need to pollute the air with empty words? It's like eating rocket candy—crap carbohydrates—when what you really need is protein-rich steak. It's better to fast and wait for the steak than to fill up on junk. But here I am, in need of some assistance.

She offers to start and we're away. She's a nun and from India originally, not the Middle East. Her name is Sister Niranjana. I ask her if she had ever met Mother Theresa, but she hadn't. It was a stupid question anyway. What else would I know about Catholics in India for God's sake? She's from the north of India but moved to England when she was fifteen; entered a convent somewhere there and now works in India and sometimes Canada.

"Are you from Toronto then? Or Vancouver?"

"I am based in British Columbia, mainly on Haida Gwaii. Do you know of Haida Gwaii?"

"It used to be Queen Charlotte Islands?"

"Yes. I work with the people of the island. I am returning from my furlough in London."

"Furlough?"

"A furlough is a holiday from mission work. I have not had a furlough for three years."

"Sounds like a full-time job Sister." Unbelievable. Slave labor in the Catholic Church.

We talk some more about her work in B.C. I tune out at times, especially as she fills her speech with Catholic jargon. She does seem lovely but also programmed. Institutions like the Catholic Church are filled with terminology designed to unite members of the club, but make others feel inferior and stupid for not understanding. So much Latin and Greek-based vocabulary. I don't have anything against Catholics, but the signs of cult and exclusivity are rampant. No different from freemasonry and parliament. Someday religion's going to end.

My wife is Catholic and so is Frankie. He wasn't when he left home. When he left for New Zealand, he went to work at a Catholic school. I didn't understand that either. I guess he was allowed to work there because Kathy was Catholic. Actually, they did get married in a Catholic Church in the Valley and their kids were baptized. Still, the original Frankie was agnostic like the rest of us unless there was something else going on that I didn't know about. Some months before the accident, Frankie e-mailed us to tell us he was converting. After Mom and Dad saw him at the funeral, he announced that he was joining some order to be a priest or something. Maybe he wanted to be a monk or a monkey, I don't know. Dad says he had one letter from Frankie trying to convince him about some Jesus stuff, but soon after that, we lost contact.

But Sister Niranjana seems nice enough.

"So, what are you doing in Vancouver?" she asks.

"I'm not going to Vancouver Sister, I'm going to New Zealand. I have a relative down there."

"Oh, I see. That's a long way. Does your relative know you're coming?"

What a strange question to ask. "As a matter of fact he doesn't. It's been a long time since I've seen him, so I'm trying to track him down." I don't really want to talk about this right now. "Excuse me Sister, I need to go to the washroom."

When I return, my new friend has her eyes closed. At least the conversation worked in relaxing her. I slip into my seat, careful not to disturb her and look out the window, hoping for a quiet remainder of the flight and a steadier stomach.

Over the next few hours, the landscape parades below—miles of flat land, prairies whose only features distinguishable from the air are meandering rivers and oxbow lakes with occasional settlements along the banks. Eventually, the Rocky Mountains appear and the terrain changes dramatically, the flatland giving way to foothills followed by full mountain peaks. I can't believe how long we fly over the mountains. On maps, they appear as a small strip of dark coloring, running down the left hand side. But from here the range is an expanse of valleys, peaks, crevasses—it's massive.

Finally, we fly in sight of ocean and the on-board map indicates we are nearing Vancouver. Sister Niranjana has been asleep for hours and only stirs now, as we are told to fasten our safety-belts.

"Thank you so much for the conversation," she says with a smile. "I want you to have something." She reaches behind her neck and unfastens a small chain, then draws its cargo out from beneath her blouse. She wraps it in her hand and holds out a clenched fist, at the same time pulling my wrist under hers.

She locks her eyes onto mine as she says, "I sense there is more to your journey than you have told me and I won't pry. This relative of yours—is he your brother?"

I nod my head, and for some reason feel small in the gaze of this little nun. "Yes he is, Sister."

"Brothers are important. This trip must be significant for you and your family. You will need great strength. Please, take this." She opens her hand and I feel the chain drift into my mine. I look down at a small, copper-colored medallion with the figure of a North American Indian girl with braided hair.

"This is Blessed Kateri Tekakwitha. She will be a Saint one day. She will help you on your journey and perhaps you will help her on hers."

I wince, but resist the urge to scoff. "Sister, I have to be honest, I don't believe."

"That is OK. Kateri will look after you anyway. I will pray for you." She hasn't taken her eyes off mine. I look away and mumble my thanks.

~

Vancouver airport is different again. There is a terrific maze of languages and faces in the international wing. So many people from around the world, many whose origins I can't begin to guess. It still feels like Canada, but definitely not Nova Scotia. The presence of First Nations' art work dominates the panorama between Starbucks outlets and souvenir shops. A six hour wait provides time to read some material my father packed for me. Not the most meticulous of people, he's crammed papers inside a New Zealand travel guide which is now four years old. They don't seem to be arranged in any order except for a printout from an e-mail sitting on top with "Frankie's last letter" written in my mother's handwriting. It's dated 6 November 2001:

Dad,

Sometimes it's better when things are left unsaid. You and Mom taught me that.

Francis

That's all it says. There's no sign of any e-mail from my father that might have provoked such a reply. I have read it before and Dad says it may have been in response to a telephone conversation a few days prior, but he could never figure out what it was in reference to. He worried he might have said too much about Frankie's increasingly infrequent correspondence or that it may have gone back to his rejection of Frankie's admonitions about the place of Jesus in Dad's life. Either way, it's a shitty way to end a dialogue with your parents.

Looking though the papers, I find only a few e-mails between the date of the accident in November 2000 and his last one. There's not much to go on. Mainly via phone calls, we knew that Frankie had joined the priesthood, but in this package of correspondence he doesn't mention any activities related to this, other than to inform that he is well fed and meeting interesting people. I'm not surprised. We never talk religion in our family, so what could he have to say to us about it? We certainly wouldn't have much to say back.

I also find some old faxes with photographs on them; pictures of the house Frankie and his family lived in when they first arrived in New Zealand, including Jacob and Kim playing in the front yard. Frankie wrote captions beside each photo saying things like, *"The gardens are beautiful"* and *"The kids like visiting the donkeys and pigs in the neighbor's field."* There's a photo of his school, St Patrick's. No other people, just buildings and the school playground. These were all taken in Taumarunui and it's there that Dad aimed to visit in 2002 when he tried to find Frankie. We don't know where he went to study or train so it's there that I'll need to start.

After some sleep on a waiting-area bench, I hear my first boarding call. I find a pay-phone and call Jordan, letting her know that I'm OK and to talk to Jade. There's not much to say, just reporting in as if I was out of town for a story.

Checking in at the gate, I hear my first New Zealand accents from the stewardesses and realize I'm surrounded by a lot more of them. I locate my seat. This is a much larger plane—a 767. No window seat for me this time, though with hardly anyone else yet to board, it looks like there may be an empty seat between me on the aisle and the traveler by the window. I sit across from him and note a strange figure—an apparently handsome young man, probably middle-aged, with dirty blond hair cut in the style of the 1940s. He's dressed in an antiquated suit, complete with a vest under his jacket with what looks like a watch on a chain resting in a front pocket. He's ignoring me, staring out his window and worrying a small thin mustache, curled slightly at the tips. That suits me fine. I plan on getting as much sleep as I can during this thirteen hour flight.

We leave at night, so supper is served early in the piece, but I refuse the meal as I've eaten as much as I dare on the previous legs and while waiting in the airport. The traveler beside me merely waves his hand at the stewardess without a glance. He has yet to turn his face from the window. After the service is cleared away, the lights are dimmed and the plane begins to quiet. Most passengers wear headphones of some sort. The New Zealand accents are stilled and I close my eyes imploring sleep to visit me until Auckland.

~

I never dream, but I dream as I sleep on this plane, at least as far as Hawaii. I dream I am trapped in a burning house, searching for my father. The flames are in my peripheral vision but never in front of me, always down a corridor to my left or right, always outside of an open window. I call for him as I run from room to room and up and back down flights of stairs that are different each time despite remaining in the same location. I hear my father calling my name, but something is wrong in his voice. Instead of the cry of a father for his missing son, his tone is threatening. In my dream I realize that, as I am searching for my father intent on his rescue, my father is hunting me, intent on my death.

~

When I awake, the plane is still silent and darkened, but as I turn in my seat, I meet the eyes of the strange traveler watching me. I don't startle, but stare back at him accusingly and sit up. He reaches a hand out in the space above the seat between us.

"My dear friend, I am terribly sorry if I caused you any alarm just now," he says. His voice has a clarity and articulation unlike anything I've ever heard. His accent is completely foreign to me. I want to say it's British, but it is definitely not. It is both universal and uniquely individual at the same time. "I have not been staring at you, I can assure you." He laughs slightly. "In fact, it truly was you that startled me. You emitted quite a noise in your sleep just now."

"What do you mean? Did I shout or something?" I ask, remembering the horrible feeling I had at the end of my dreaming.

"No, no, no, nothing quite like that. It was more of a sigh, but really a most unusual one. It resonated with a deep antipathy."

Far out. "Well, I don't exactly know what that means, but I'm sorry if I bothered you."

"Please, think nothing of it. I myself have had cause to wake from a variety of unpleasant somnolence." He scans me with one eye. "In fact, sometimes I wait to wake with such a sigh from this dreamworld." He laughs loudly before lowering his voice with a look around the cabin at the sleeping passengers. Then he whispers, "You know, Captain Cook once said, 'I think it would be nice to be able to talk directly to the surface.'" Then he looks at me with that one eye again, nods and turns back to his window.

~

I spend the next few hours alternating between attempting to get back to sleep and monitoring the aircraft visual of the trip, ticking off kilometers. The flight is horrendously long, but delightfully capped near the end with a sunrise over the Pacific which, even from my aisle seat, I can appreciate as I see the crimson hues above the bed of clouds outside our window.

The Pacific. I never considered it while I was in Vancouver, but I am over the Pacific Ocean for the first time in my life. That massive ocean that touches countries like China and Australia. So much more exotic, seemingly, than our lobster-infested Atlantic, populated so long by North American and European traders and trawlers.

"The journey on the Hind was ferociously protracted, you know, especially after all the trouble in these parts." It's my strange companion again. "There was no stopping Drake however. All of them really, from Drake to Franklin, all of them, terrific knights of the sea. We have it so easy now don't we? Still, you have more to go don't you?"

His voice is amazing to listen to and he's speaking more freely now, as the other passengers are bustling through bags and the stewardesses are beginning to make their way down the aisles with breakfast carts. But I really don't know what he's talking about.

"I hope I won't be too much longer. I'm hoping to get back to Canada in less than a month."

"A month is it? Well, that would be grand then if that is what you are aiming for. It is a shame you won't spend more time exploring these islands. I hear they are still as stunning as when Cook found them here filled with all those beautiful Maoris." At this, he nods toward a gentleman sitting a few seats up and across the aisle from me. I had noticed him, but had assumed he was Hawaiian. I studied a bit about Maori people when Frankie first moved to New Zealand. He was teaching some Maori students so I read about them in some *National Geographics* in the New Glasgow library. Of course, I've seen the All Blacks rugby team perform their war dance on *TSN*.

"However, I can tell you're a man on a quest, not an exploration. You have that look in your eyes and in your jaw. Is it a great adventure you're on, or a somber mission? Never mind. Let me give you this little word from Drake: 'There must be a beginning of any great matter, but the continuing unto the end until it be thoroughly finished yields the true glory.'"

"I'm not looking for glory."

"Are you sure about that? Every man looks for it in some form, even if it's in the eyes of only one person."

~

We land in Auckland and I'm exhausted and nauseous. I know it's morning, but my body is sure it is late afternoon. I collect my bag from the overhead compartment. My companion and I have not spoken since our odd sunrise chat, but I feel I should thank him for what seemed to be well-meaning words. But before I can speak, he grasps me by my wrist, the same wrist once held by Sister Niranjana. For a moment, I see a desperate look in his eyes, a manic look that betrays his calm, if ranting demeanor of our trans-Pacific trip. "Please," he says. Then, as the look in his eyes eases, "Please remember me. Not for glory, but for simple remembrance."

"I will," I say blithely, "and thanks for your words. Would you like to get out in front of me here before the crowd pushes through?"

"No, thank you young man." He releases my wrist and folds both his hands in his lap and looks out the window. "I'll stay here awhile yet. I wish you well on your quest. Remember me."

As I shift with the crowd to the front of the plane, I look back toward our seats. The end of the line of passengers has passed our section and the traveler is still sitting, still staring out his window.

~

Haere mai, brother of our son. Come. You are welcome in this place, through gates of cloud, water and bush. None but we know of your coming, but those who know the son will not be surprised at your arrival. He is yours, though we would keep him as our own. We know these things here—his season has come, a time to return, a time to rest with his own.

You see things too, though your eyes are not as exacting, your memory unsettled by mystery. You will learn the value of mist, the purpose of myth and the treasure that is story. Come and be changed as your brother was changed.

We gift him back to you, our grief lapping our shores and singing with yours.

Learn of our aroha—our love.

Haere mai.

Haere mai.

WELCOME

Clearing customs is a breeze. I'm only challenged by a Polynesian-looking agent who asks me if I know the words to New Zealand's national anthem while she playfully holds my passport out of reach. What a difference between here and North America already. I offer to sing her a few bars of "Oh Canada" but she just lets out a big belly laugh filled with "hee-hees" and hands me my documents while glancing mischievously toward her co-workers. "Kia ora", she says, "Welcome to Aotearoa. Have a pleasant stay."

I left Halifax on Tuesday and today is Thursday. I've lost a day of my life crossing the International Date Line—I will never have a 29 September 2004 in my life. After ringing Dad to tell him I've arrived and to find out how he'd got on organizing a rental vehicle, I'm outside and enjoying my first breath of fresh air in twenty-eight hours. This is the cleanest air I've ever breathed.

As I exit the terminal and look for a taxi, I take note of the green trees with enormous leaves blowing healthily around the parking lot periphery. It's spring here. The temperature reminds me of the autumn I left at home and I am refreshed by that same feeling you find in a Nova Scotia spring; a feeling that something is around the corner and you're almost there.

I find a taxi driver who looks like the customs agent but without the long hair and breasts. He has the same wide-mouthed smile and twinkle in his eyes. I ask him if he is Maori. He laughs and says, "No sir, I am not. I am Samoan. Talofa! But, I have many cousins who are

Maori. In fact, the next Maori you meet will probably be my cousin!" He laughs again, but I don't get the joke. Still, I'm grateful for the friendly answer.

As we drive, I absorb my surroundings and adjust to seeing traffic on the wrong side of the road. From the airport to the rental agency, there is a lot of concrete, but I can see plenty of trees as well, many that look like palm trees, with long trunks and clumps of large leaves sprigging from the top. The cars are different, with names like Holden and Mitsubishi, but I also recognize Toyotas and Fords. I'm struck by the fact that no cars have rust on them. The buildings we pass are unrecognizable—a "tyre" outlet, and what looks like a supermarket called New World. At the same time, we pass various MacDonalds' and Pizza Huts. It all seems out-of-kilter, especially with what I assume is jet lag on top of my fatigue and stomach complaints. Why didn't I just book a hotel upon arrival? Because it was daytime?

We pass through many sets of lights, but also small rotaries, "roundabouts" Dad called them when he told me about driving in New Zealand. We have one rotary in Pictou County, but apparently New Zealand is filled with these.

I farewell my driver when we arrive at the agency. This is run by a small Asian man who sorts me out in a hurry. For the next month, tops, my wheels will be under a small red Ford Focus. My plan is to get out of Auckland and head south toward Taumarunui, but I need a pit stop as soon as I am able to find a place to stay. Driving in the city intimidates me, so I elect to head south and find a motel in a small town somewhere. Looking at the map, it seems that Auckland gives way to rural areas within forty kilometers or so.

Leaving the agency, I find the highway easily enough, so I'm soon on my way down the left side of the median. I have developed a coping habit of noting signed place names as I travel. You never know when it will be good to recall a location. I'm not sure how to pronounce names like Manurewa, Takanini and Papakura, but I love the look of these words. Easier to recognize are Drury and Bombay and I consider the mix of Maori and British influences that exist here. I wonder if Scottish or Irish ever settled here. Are there any Camerons or Reids? Any Murrihys?

The sun is brilliant today. It illuminates everything, making colors crisp—even the pavement glistens. As expected, I've left the concrete of Auckland behind and see plenty of greenery along the highway, but also in surrounding steep hills. It all looks very farmed. It is strange to not have names for trees. At home I can identify varieties of birch, beech, elm and oak, but here I can only describe what I see. More palm-like trees and others with the largest leaves I have ever seen; some iconic ferns which I recognize from magazines. Nothing like the spruce-lined highways of Nova Scotia. Everything looks deciduous here and I wonder if it all looks barren and dead in winter or if the trees retain a level of lushness, as the seasons here are surely not as harsh as in Canada. Here in the North Island, it is about seven to eight degrees closer to the equator, making it sub-tropical.

Despite my flowing adrenaline, I really do need to find a place to rest before traveling the four hours to Taumarunui. I leave the highway via the exit to Pukekohe, which is marked with a hotel sign, and make my way into what looks like a small town. I pull into the first motor lodge I find.

After entering reception, I need to ring a bell as there is no-one in sight for the first few minutes. Even then, I still wait a minute or two before a short woman with large, round, dark-rimmed glasses emerges from a back room. She wears, what looks like, a sailor-suit— a blue woman's pant-suit whose top bears large lapels with white trim. Her name tag reads, "Lerlene Murphy". I've found my first Irish descendant.

"Hello," she says with an unconvincing smile.

"Hello, I've just come from the airport. I know it's early, but could I check into a room for tonight?"

"I suppose we can do that for you. Standard rate applies plus extra since you're using the room for so long."

I'm a little stunned. I'm only asking for a few hours extra which surely won't put them out as long as the room is empty anyway. But I'm exhausted so I don't argue. Besides, maybe this is the way it's done here. "OK," I say. "Is the room available now or do I need to wait for it to be cleaned?"

"No, it's clean," Murphy says flatly as she turns back from the wall slots behind the desk and pushes a key with a sign-in form across the counter to me. I fill it in as she talks. "You have a standard room with a double bed. There's milk in the fridge. Check-out time is 10:00 tomorrow morning. Everything else is explained in the guidebook in the room." She retreats toward her lair, but I call her back asking, "Sorry, can you point me toward the room please?"

Did she just roll her eyes? She turns and points through the window next to the front door. "The motel's shaped like a courtyard," she says like a sarcastic robot, "You drive your car around that way until you see your unit." Then she looks at me as if to say, "Have you got that or do I need to actually take you there?"

I thank her and she swiftly disappears.

Despite the cold reception, the room is warm and clean. An attractive painting of Auckland's Sky Tower hangs above a mirror. The entire back wall consists of a sliding glass door concealed by a massive, velvety swath of curtain which opens onto the courtyard. Outside is a tidy piece of lawn complete with a bistro-style table and two chairs. A swimming pool acts as the central feature of the yard, but is barren and looks flaky and rusty in some parts.

I make myself a coffee and finally relax on the bed, content to call it a day. I don't set an alarm but hope that I can sleep until the next morning.

~

I do sleep and I sleep well, with no dreams. I wake up at 3:30 in the morning, but manage to stay in bed until 7:00 watching television, my plan being to get up at a normal time in order to beat this jet lag. New Zealand television offers me little contrast to North America. Infomercials are just as annoying, and repeats of *All in the Family* make me feel at home. The actual TV commercials are the most interesting, especially graphic ones aimed at combating drink driving.

I make some more coffee while I watch the news. Canada's made the headlines here in a story about ownership of the North Pole. Apparently Denmark and Russia are laying claim. Bush and Kerry have finished their last debate and it looks like Spain is going to approve same-sex marriages. New Zealanders seem to be mainly concerned about some issue with their coastlines.

But I've got to make a move. With check-out in just over two hours, I need to make a plan for today. I lay out the documents from my father's folder, scanning for references to Taumarunui. I set aside the photos of the house and the school. Then I find an envelope sent from Frankie marked with a return address. That would be for the house; the school is meant to be across the road. So far, so easy. The envelope is empty, but there is a hand-written letter from Frankie dated 21 June 1997. It's addressed to my mother.

Dear Mom,

As you can tell by the date, I am sending you your birthday present a little late—unless the New Zealand and Canadian postal services can pull off a major miracle and get you these in three days! Anyway, by the time you read this, you'll know when it arrived, but at least you know I was thinking of you at about the right time eh?

I hope you like the coasters. They show different animals here in New Zealand. One is a Kiwi bird (like the fruit). It is flightless and endangered. You can only see them at night and only if you're lucky. New Zealanders call themselves Kiwis as well. What a versatile word! Another one is the tuatara. It's like a lizard. It looks scary but I hear it's harmless and rare. The third one is a weta. It kind of looks like a grasshopper don't you think? It's got a harder shell and likes to eat ketchup. Kathy and I found one in the garden last week and fed it some. It was weird. The kids loved it. The last one is a sheep and, well, you know what sheep are. They're a big deal here in New Zealand. There are three times as many sheep as there are people here. I don't know who took that census. My principal says that New Zealand is really just one big farm and I can see what he means. Even here in the King Country, with its steep hills, the land is all cultivated. There are still lots of trees but it's amazing to see how much land has been cleared for farming.

Anyway, the kids are doing well. Kathy's been taking Jacob to kindergarten each day. It's hard without a car, but she walks some days and has met some other mothers who sometimes drive him there. Kim is doing well. She loves the tricycle you sent over for her. Thanks for doing that. Thanks for lots of things. School is hard work and I'm up late most nights, but you know what that's like. Say hi to Dad for me and I hope you had a great birthday (I'll have spoken to you by phone anyway).

Love,

Frankie

So frigging banal. But nice enough. Frankie was always "nice". He wasn't meant for conflict of any sort—not a politician or a debater, although a bit of a babbler and a rambler whenever he was buzzing about something new he'd learned and chasing Dad around the house with it. He didn't have a gift for holding people's attention and he would believe almost anything, invariably ending up with inconclusive experiences. It hurts to see him writing so affectionately to Mom back then, knowing how much pain he's caused in the last few years. I sound heartless, considering everything he went through, but nobody else seems to blame him for the grief he caused. Instead they romanticize him and make excuses.

Those first few years were weird, when Frankie went to New Zealand. Jordan and I got married just before they left and soon had Jade to think about. I wanted to be a decent uncle to Jacob and Kim, in fact I wanted to be a great uncle, but they shut me out and then moved so far away. I would really only hear news about my brother and his family through Mom and Dad. Frankie would phone on my birthday and at our grandparents' for Christmas, but other than that, lives were moving on back home.

It's strange to be in this place thinking about him living here. I wonder if he ever stopped here in Pukekohe, or if he knew this motel. He surely knew the drive from Auckland to Taumarunui.

~

These are the sorts of thoughts occupying me as I drive the highway south. I imagine Frankie, the young teacher from Canada with his young wife and very young children, squeezed into a car with their suitcases heading to a house and life they didn't know, far from home. A lot of pressure I suppose, a lot of worries. I can imagine Frankie handling it all stoically, not letting any stress show, but going through all the motions required to make it work. Or did he have breakdowns along the way? Were there tears and upsets between him and Kathy? Who knows.

The day is grey. Yesterday's sunshine is hidden now, behind a long white cloud stretching from north to south. The new lime-green leaves along my route are no longer glistening. The motorway is busy with morning work traffic heading to Auckland on the opposite side. I still feel queasy in my abdomen, but I am rested, and ready to get something of my mission done. I'm adjusting to driving on the opposite side and pass exits to places called Pokeno, Mercer and Meremere. Another sign tells me I'm leaving the motorway and am now on the Waikato Expressway, but I don't see any difference. It must be a regional custodial distinction. I drive through a small, run-down looking town called Huntly. The greyness of the day probably doesn't help its lack of appeal. The twinned highway is behind me and I drive through town slowly, looking at the backs of warehouse-type buildings, noting lots of peeling paint and out-dated signs. Its prominent landmark turns out to be the power station I passed at the north end.

After Huntly, I realize the highway has been following the course of a river for some time and I make the connection with the power station. It reminds me of Trenton back home, a town based along the East River. This river is headed north toward the sea and I wonder if I will get anywhere near its source. Lake Taupo springs to mind as do the mountains in the center of the North Island.

I look for a place to pull over to interrogate my maps. A hillside approaches on my left with a small bay for cars and it is only after I park the Focus that I see the cemetery on the slope. It's impressive—graves cover the hillside as far up as I can see; a variety of tombstones of all sorts of shapes and colors, some that look like coffins themselves sitting above ground. Every grave has flowers on it, real and artificial, with little windmills and some with photos of the deceased either built into the gravestone or in small picture frames leaning against vases. Out of habit, I turn to the back seat to retrieve my camera, but I haven't brought it on this trip. I'm not interested in playing tourist or recording this journey. There's nothing I intend to remember—just find my brother and return home to Mom.

I dig out my map and see that I am in Taupiri along the Waikato River. I also see that, regardless of motorway or expressway, I've been driving State Highway 1 from Auckland. The cars whiz by at speed through here and it seems odd to hear such traffic next to a cemetery. I get out to stretch and am immediately refreshed by the air. I walk closer to the cemetery entrance, passing another vacated car in front of mine, and read the names inscribed on the stones at the bottom of the hill. Surnames like Tamihana, Pirimoana and Tumata with first names like Te Whatahuhu and Pini tell me this must be a Maori cemetery. Everything about it feels old and regal. I look further up and see a gravestone with a photo of a Maori woman with an amazing tattoo on her chin. I push through the gate and make my way toward it, careful not to disturb the decorations and gifts adorning the graves in-between.

The gravestone is dark with bold white lettering—a quotation in Maori introducing readers to this lady as Mere Tuwhangai. She has been lying here since 1918, having passed away at the age of twenty-seven. Yet there are vases on her site, each filled with fresh flowers; a multi-colored windmill flits in the stuttering breeze. Her eyes in this black and white portrait are fierce, and the tattoo looks like flames rising from beneath her chin to lick at her lower lip.

"What's your interest there mate?"

I'm startled by the voice and rouse myself from my reverie to see an imposing old man standing about ten feet up the hill from me. His hair is grey and short and he wears my grandfather's suit pants and shirt with a blue windbreaker jacket. The gumboots on his feet seem out of place and they are muddy. In his hand, he holds an intricately carved walking stick which he seems to wield rather than rely on for support. Beside him is a small girl, about three years old, carrying a pair of hedge-clippers. She looks at me boldly, waiting for my answer.

"Oh, hello," I say with a smile. "I've just pulled over for a rest and thought I'd check out some of the fascinating graves here."

"This is a cemetery, not a tourist attraction," he snorts. His voice is deep and articulate with a New Zealand accent that differs from the ones I've heard on the plane and at the motel. It is earthy and sharp. The little girl continues to stare, holding her minder's hand.

"Of course. I'm sorry," I say, not sure what to do next. In Nova Scotia, cemeteries are easy places to visit. When I was eleven, we toured around the province visiting museums and cemeteries; they were another part of our education. And they were good places to play on Hallowe'en.

"Come with me," the man says and walks toward me, motioning his walking stick in the direction of the gate. He lets go of his ward's hand and uses it to guide me, without touching my back, away from Mere Tuwhangai.

As we approach the gate, he directs me to stop by a white plastic bottle half-filled with water, hanging from a piece of wire on a tree branch. He lifts the bottle from its mooring and says, "Hold out your hands." I hold them out to him and he pours the water. Then he does the same for the girl who stands waiting with hands outstretched. She wipes them on her pants so I do the same. The old man finishes the ritual by washing his own hands and musters me though the gate with a nod.

"This mountain is sacred," he says. "It is the home of our ancestors from our most revered and ancient at the top, to our most special and honored at the bottom. It is tapu and so we must wash ourselves of any death we have encountered while we have visited. These people," he says, sweeping his walking stick toward the hill, "are my family." He places his hand on the girl's shoulder and says, "They are the family of my mokopuna here. They are not exhibits." His words make sense and he doesn't exactly sound angry, but I can't help feeling like I'm being told off.

"OK, well thanks for that. Like I say, I'm a visitor so I didn't know."

"Ka pai, it's all good mister. You have a good visit then eh? Kia ora." The old man turns back through the cemetery gates, his miniature charge trailing behind him.

I hit the road again, stopping in Ngaruawahia for coffee and gas at a gas station. The drive to Hamilton is uneventful. It's a river city, apparently, and a busy place, but a straight-forward drive through, even with multiple roundabouts to contend with. These do seem to keep traffic moving without much stopping and starting again. According to my map, this will be the only city between here and Taumarunui. I recall Frankie telling us this was their major center for shopping when they could get out of town.

From Hamilton to Te Awamutu to Otorohanga. The traffic thins the further south I drive. Somewhere along the way, the hills have closed in. No more open spaces. In a way, it reminds me of Nova Scotia—you can't see very far in any one direction—but the hills here are much steeper. They are also filled with sheep and some cattle. At times, it's difficult to tell if it is sheep or grey boulders on the distance slopes.

Te Kuiti is the last town before Taumarunui and, as I exit the southern end, I see the road sign telling me it is another eighty-four kilometers further. I remember this sign from a photo Frankie sent us, remarking that there were no places to stop for gas beyond this point.

Now I really ascend to the interior of this country. The hills flank one another as far as my eyes can see. They are green of course, but sore looking. New Zealand is a young country, geographically speaking, and the hills look scarred with deep and intense grooves; as if a glacier had not finished its work before melting. Fences line multiple fields like stitches holding the injured land together, still waiting for completion or healing. Many barns are covered in moss instead of paint. Occasionally I see an immaculate home, well positioned in one of the many valleys, far from the noisy highway.

If you can call it a highway. The speed limit signage tells me I can drive up to one hundred kilometers per hour, but the twists and dips of this road discourage me. Other cars overtake me when a passing lane appears, always going uphill, or when a straight stretch emerges from this maze of bends, which is a rarity. On one particularly steep and sharp bend, I pass a small hillside waterfall that reminds me of the spring on Green Hill back home. A car is parked by the spring and a woman is collecting water. Oddly, there is also a small blue monument there with more plastic flowers surrounding it. But I drive on.

After climbing for another thirty minutes or so, I reach a place called Mapiu and from there it seems it's all downhill. Road signs count down my journey to Taumarunui from thirty-eight kilometers to twenty-five. Another river appears to my left, but smaller and running south alongside me so I am certain it is no longer the Waikato.

Finally, around one final hairpin, I see the fifty kilometer speed sign that tells me I must be arriving at a town. On my left, I see a picture of a foreboding looking Maori warrior complete with a full-faced tattoo and a hairstyle like a North American Indian, including a feather. Beneath the painting it reads, "Taumarunui Welcomes You". With a face like that, I'm not so sure.

~

Te wahine lives beyond Hawaiiki, where all Māori go in the end; across the oceans and across great lands, lands far larger than this island, Te Ika a Māui; with far larger awa than us. We see her, but she knows nothing of us, our whakapapa or our mokopuna.

Today, we see another vision of te wahine. She flows down from Io-wairoa though we know not why—that is His way sometimes. He flows where he wills, revealing aspects of His mystery to some and during some times. We are patient and eternal.

Today, te wahine is crying. We cannot see her eyes, but we can see her tears fall on an image of a man in her hands. The tears wash over the image until it reaches the ring on her finger causing the metal to glisten under a dim light.

We are Te Awanui-a-rua, the second teardrop of Rangi-nui, a gift of compassion. We are a river of tears and know both the sorrow and companionship they bring. Despite our many tributaries, we are formed at our mātāpuna—our source—by the tears of Rangi-nui. He is our sky father, who placed one of two teardrops near the summit of mount Tongariro to bring comfort to Matua Te Mana, the mount Ruapehu. In the beginning, after Māui pulled this island out of the sea, Ruapehu was charged with the task of subduing this great fish, but he was lonely. Rangi-nui is with him now as are we. And in us, Rangi-nui is reunited with our great ancestress, Papa-tū-ā-nuku who lays as our bed.

Te wahine removes her ring and places it, along with the photo, at her knee-side. She is going back—to a time of freedom, to a time of chaos—to follow her tears and see what might have been.

TE ROHE PŌTAE

I haven't eaten since breakfast in Auckland so I head into town before looking for St Patrick's school. The town resembles Huntly, Otorohanga and Te Kuiti. From the north end it appears the southern exit is in sight. I pass two gas stations and a New World supermarket before parking in front of a grassy picnic area on my left. Exiting my vehicle I meet another strange sight: a giant boulder taller than me with an enormous top hat leaning jauntily from the apex. There's a plaque attached to the stone's belly and I read:

THIS IS A COUNTRY
BEYOND THE MEANS OF TIME TO A STRANGER
TO KNOW IT YOU ARE BORN

FROM A TABLE TOP MOUNTAIN
TO THE JOINING OF THE RIVERS
LIES THE HEART OF THIS LAND THAT
GIVES US OUR SOUL

I really can't be bothered finishing it. Instead, I walk across the road to look for a restaurant of some sort. It's a strange thing when you don't know the usual markings of things like restaurants. I have to read signs carefully to try and determine their purpose. A garish sign for "Super Liquor" makes me laugh and is tempting. In Nova Scotia, the liquor stores all look the same and are run by the government in buildings that are difficult to distinguish from the post office or the unemployment agency.

After passing a video store, I see I've parked well as I've already located a cafe-style restaurant. It's probably a non-descript place really, if you're a local. But to me, everything is different and, as a result, it all appears jumbled and blurred. I have to study everything even to determine whether I'm meant to get food myself or sit down and wait to be served.

I collect a sandwich from a cabinet and a Coke from the fridge. At the counter, I order a slice of carrot cake from an intelligent-looking, white haired gentleman. I sit by the front window so I can observe passers-by and acquaint myself with these surroundings. Outside, three teenage boys with one skateboard cross the road to our side; one lays the skateboard on the sidewalk before motoring past two elderly ladies who don't seem to pay attention to the fact they were almost sideswiped. The other two boys yell out to their friend but don't chase, instead jumping up to knock and swing the signs suspended outside the adjacent stores.

A series of classic cars drives by, six or seven in all, an unusual sight for a Nova Scotian. I'm not a car buff but I'm thinking these date back to the twenties and thirties and must be part of a convention in town. Or are cars so well maintained that they still drive these models here in 2004?

Many of the faces walking by the cafe could easily be from Nova Scotia. White, plainly dressed ladies and young men with jeans and jackets. A number of men have walked by in rubber boots which is unusual, and even more unusual is the absence of ball caps. I don't see any men wearing the Pictou Country uniform of ball cap, hockey jacket and goatee with mustache. Also absent is any sign of professional men—no suits or ties. The clothing seems far more casual and dark colors predominate. One large, elderly man walks by with a patch on his back bearing the likeness of a bulldog and the words, "Mighty Mongrel Mob of Taumarunui". We don't see gang patches like that back home.

The brown faces are different from home too. From what I can tell, these faces are all Maori. None really resemble my Samoan taxi driver. They do look like versions of the old man at the cemetery in Taupiri and his small companion. Two of the teenage boys were Maori, both wearing pants at half-mast and sweaters with hoods pulled up even on this warm, though cloudy day. In fact, for a Friday, there are an awful lot of school-aged children about. I ask the gentleman about this when he checks on me at my table.

"It's the school holidays," he says, looking at me knowingly. "You must be visiting from overseas are you?"

"Yes, I am. I'm from Canada. What do you mean it's the school holidays? It's not summer or Christmas."

"I know, it's a tad odd isn't it? Schools are open for four terms now instead of three. They're just finishing a two week break. Can I get you anything else? Coffee?"

"No thanks, but could you tell me how to get to St. Patrick's school?"

"Sure, it's up in Rangaroa. Which way did you come into town?"

I point out my car to him and he continues, "Well, you turn around and go back the way you came but turn right at the gas station and go under the rail bridge. Then turn right again—you'll see a little brown sign pointing to the Catholic Church—then just down the road you'll see the incline on your left. Rangaroa is at the top of the hill. Turn left into the residential area and you'll see the school in the middle of everything up there. Look out for the blue and white buildings." He laughs lightly, "We call it 'Vatican Heights'. Are you looking to see someone up there?"

"Yes, I'm hoping to catch up with some of the staff if I can."

"Well, I doubt you'll see anyone there today. Teachers will all be on holiday too."

~

I consider booking a hotel before heading up but then decide to have a look anyway. At least I'll know where to go on Monday. I drive down the main street until I find a place to turn, then follow the gentleman's directions. The incline turns out to be a steep hill leading to what looks like a separate little residential area with no discernible exit. Turning into the area I see the blue and white painted church and drive toward it, recognizing the adjoining playground from the photos Frankie had faxed. I pull over, realizing that the house they lived in must be across the road. Directly across from the church is a house matching the photographs. It has changed in shape slightly and the tree in the front yard has been removed, but it's the same bungalow style with the small front picture window, along with the cobbled driveway and the covered car section further down.

I inhale deeply and feel a connection with Frankie that I have not felt in seven years. I have heard explanations for ghosts in haunted houses describing the phenomena as residual energy from those who have previously inhabited the space, as if it were a recording of their activity that plays back certain moments in time. I can see a blurred image of Kim on that tricycle, the red one that belonged to Jacob in Canada and that Mom and Dad sent over to Frankie and Kathy once they'd settled in. I can hear echoes of Jacob's chirpy voice nattering away to his parents as they try to carry on a discussion with the neighbor over the fence from their driveway. Frankie is in shorts, a rarity for him back in Canada, with his hair trimmed neatly and his attention focused exclusively on the conversation. Kathy is engaged, but side-on, keeping an eye on Kim in the driveway and motioning to Jacob to let him know that she is listening even as she needs to talk with the adults.

They had a life here. An immigrant life—no different to any of the strange new cultures infiltrating our own borders. Did they seem as strange to the people here?

I look across the playground and see the blue and white school on the other side, so I leave the Focus and make my way across the grass. There are no cars in sight, but I wander around the front area of the school, again thinking of Frankie—working here in his first full time job as a teacher. Jacob went to school here too.

But, as the gentleman intimated, there is no-one here, no answer to my knock on the door. I sit for a moment on the front step and think about my next move. Monday seems a long time to wait. What else can I do in the meantime? How can I find someone else in town who knew Frankie while he was here? I'll ring Dad. But first I'll find that hotel so I'm settled for tonight at least—and I can get in contact with him more easily from there.

Walking from the front of the school, I notice the other blue and white buildings in the area. Almost all of the small-town New Zealand houses I've seen have been single-story. The blue and white building to the left of the school is a larger bungalow. But across the road is another blue et blanc house which is huge, maybe three stories high. Next to it is a simpler structure, perhaps a hall. I walk out toward it and the front gate. A child's swing set rests in the front yard, but it's otherwise empty. Things are quiet in this neighborhood for a school holiday.

Outside the gate, I walk along the sidewalk toward the church. I suppose this church is where the funeral was held. It's an oddly shaped building, totally unlike the tall Gothic churches in Westville. We grew up attending the United Church, a brick goliath with a high tower for bells. This appears to be one story with three turrets at different corners. Near the side door stands a tall, red wooden cross carved with designs similar to the features of the Taupiri cemetery gatekeeper. Faces stare at me with protruding tongues. It reminds me of totem poles from British Columbia, but without the brilliant, painted colors. What an odd mix to see this Christian symbol so adorned. At the bottom is a female figure wearing what looks like a cloak made of feathers. Under her feet is a lizard. Between the faces are whirlpools. Some of the eyes in the faces have mother-of-pearl inserts that have lost their luster. Many of the eye sockets are empty.

I walk under a covered way and toward the front. I cringe at churches, but I try the door. It's locked and I'm surprised as I thought that Catholic Churches left their doors open. No matter. I'll come back tomorrow.

~

I check into Fern's motel, the first place I saw as I came into town. It's tucked down a side road—a small place with about a dozen units. The man who greets me is a smiling, over-the-top friendly fellow who seems intent on making me feel welcome and even loved, not in a smarmy way, but more in a "I want to share positive energy with you" way.

My room reminds me of my stay in Pukekohe. It's small and basic, but comfortable enough. The cloudy day has turned into a rainy one so I'm glad to be tucked inside. I consider having a beer from the fridge, but resist. I knew this temptation would happen. It's been seventeen months since I had a drink and some of my worst episodes used to happen on the road when following stories out of town. Here I am in another country, without my accustomed accountability to my job or my wife. I could just stay in for the night and sip a bit. The manager would probably even replenish the fridge for me or I could head down to Super Liquor. Thinking of Mom and my business here doesn't help. In fact, my anger at Frankie and my resentment toward this mission make me want to throw in the towel and be selfish just one night.

I've come too far.

And I have more papers I can read, so I flick on the television for more background sounds of New Zealand and settle in with a cup of instant coffee and Dad's portfolio.

There are more e-mails like Mom's birthday message, covering a mixture of dates over their early years here in Taumarunui; updates about Jacob starting school, a new house with a dog they couldn't handle—basically domestic tripe that doesn't lead me to any other contacts. Reading this, you wouldn't come to know him any better than if you bumped into him on the street and discussed the weather and sports results. Dad has included some hand-written letters, mostly notes that accompanied gifts. There are no more photos after the early faxes which I study again to compare with what I saw today in Rangaroa. Something stirs in my mind when I revisit these, but I'm not sure what it is—some hint of a helpful connection.

The escalating rain makes an impressive noise as it assaults the iron roof of my motel. Outside my sliding glass door a drain gurgles as if something is obstructing the flow of the water gathering on the ground. I flick on the television to help my mind rest and wander. *David Letterman* is on—at 4:30 in the afternoon. So funny. The king of late-night is the prince of afternoon TV in the South Pacific. The show is a few days old as his monologue is primarily focused on the "upcoming" debates between Kerry and Bush which have since happened. I leave it on this channel during the commercial break and make another coffee, before returning to the table.

As I scroll through more mundane letters, notes and e-mails, the weariness of travel overshadows me. I rest my head on my arms across the papers and close my eyes. I drift, listening to Letterman interview Drew Barrymore. She's talking about her movie, *50 First Dates*, and describing her character who suffers from short term memory loss. I picture Mom, sitting on one of the stools at home talking to Clio or Dad or Mavis and writing in her book. Since her recovery, Mom has had to use a little book to record important conversations. The telephone is especially difficult for her. When you sit with Mom and talk to her over the dinner table or across the lounge, she can see you as well as hear you and it seems to help her remember. But we do catch her out sometimes as she has learned to pretend she remembers things. She reads our faces to gauge the conversation. How many times have I seen her stop and say, "I've said that before haven't I?" and realize she has seen something in my face that cues her? She doesn't remember saying it.

Barrymore is talking about her character waking up each day with no memory of the events of the day before. Of course, it's not like that for Mom. It's so hit-and-miss. We don't know why she can remember some things and not others. She still remembers everybody's birthdays and what color dress Clio wore when she visited Great-Great-Grandma McLuhan back in 1983, but she can't remember what she ate for breakfast or where she put her purse. She has learned to put such important items in the same place, but how she learns to do that is a mystery.

Because of my own hindrances with remembering details, I've thought a lot about the nature of memory, but I cannot explain, nor can the doctors explain why Mom's brain works the way it does. She laughs about it now and we even tease her for it. If I phone her with a request or a task, she'll laugh and say, "I'd better go get your father." Dad, who once had a shocking memory for things, especially family matters, has now taken on the responsibility for memory in the house, and conversations with Mom tend to be limited to weather and property renovations.

And so my mind wanders between Mom and Drew Barrymore, between reality and fiction, between sleep and the television.

~

When I awake, it's dark in the room except for the glow of the television. An infomercial for a three-in-one clock/night-light/smoke detector is playing, so I assume it's after midnight. I stretch and stand, knocking some papers off the table. After going to the washroom, I pick up the mess and toss it on the bed. Then I change clothes and climb under the covers. I flick the television off and gather a few pages to read under the night-light, hoping I can read myself to sleep until the morning and get back on track with this jet-lag.

This time, a letter does finally stand out. Like the birthday message, it's handwritten and addressed to Mom only. It's dated 14 February 2000.

Dear Mom,

Here are some photos and a video from Christmas, plus some more pictures from summer. Sorry for the delay on the Christmas stuff. It took a little while to get a copy of the video made. Besides, we wanted to wait until we had photos developed from our trip to Napier last month. And of course we had to make sure we would all survive Y2K!

Our trip to Napier was cool. It's the first time we've been out of Taumarunui for that long and it was terrific even if it was only for a few days. Kathy did a great job organizing it and, as you can see by the pictures, we saw some interesting sights. Jacob and I had a lot of fun on the water slides at Splash Planet in Hastings.

School has started here again. I'm teaching Grade 5 students for a change. Jacob is in Year 2 (Grade 1). It's already a busy year. Each Wednesday afternoon I meet with our parish priest for catechism lessons. Remember when I did that for the United Church when I was eleven? I'm getting a lot out of our sessions. Father Van Rooyen is pretty traditional but he's putting a lot of time into me and answers my questions really well. He wants to know how I was baptized when I was a baby—was it a sprinkle of water on my forehead or was the water poured? I don't understand the difference, but he wants to know in order to decide whether I need to be baptized again or just skip to Confirmation. Can you let me know?

Either way, these lessons are all leading up to my Confirmation on Easter Saturday. I was keen to get baptized right away once I asked him to become a Catholic, but he wanted to go through the lessons and it's a tradition to baptize adults on Easter Saturday after Lent.

Anyway, I thought I'd ask and see if you remember. Hope you enjoy the pictures.

Love,

Frankie

This would have to be the most talk about religion I have ever been a party to in my family. We went to Sunday school as kids and Mom even taught some classes, but we never talked about it at home. Dad never went to church. I remember coming home from school one afternoon when I was about seventeen. My friend Jason had been telling others on the bus he didn't believe in God. His brother was giving him a hard time and Jason yelled out, "Connie doesn't believe either, eh Connie?" I was on the spot as I remembered my brief talk about this with Jason a few months earlier. We had been on our bikes heading back from a day at the river and talking about absolutely nothing when Jason said to me, "Do you believe in God, Connie?"

I said, "Nah," and he said, "Me neither." And that was that.

So on the bus when Jason called me out, I replied to my wider audience, "Nah," and he said, "Me neither," and that shut his brother up. Arriving home, I found my father home early from work. I said to him, "Do you believe in God, Dad?"

He said, "I don't believe in God, but I don't disbelieve either."

"Are you an atheist then?"

"Atheist is too strong a word for me. I'm an agnostic."

Never having heard the word before, I said, "I guess that's what I am too then." And that was the extent of my life's talk with my parents about religion. It was also the extent of all talk I'd had about religion with any of my family, including Frankie. To my knowledge, Frankie was agnostic too. He and Dad shared so much in common with their interests in literature, philosophy, sport and education, why wouldn't they share the same views about this topic? Yet, here he was, three years in New Zealand, and he's converting to Catholicism, the holy grail of religions.

The letter fascinates me and I read it again, hitting upon the connection I couldn't interpret earlier in the evening. The school might not be open until Monday, but the priest is surely around. I turn out the light, pleased that I have a plan for tomorrow.

CHRIST BEHIND ME, CHRIST BEFORE ME

I don't sleep long and I don't sleep well. Nor do I dream. Instead, I lie awake through the remainder of the night thinking about home and Jordan and Jade. These last few months have been extraordinarily stressful for all of us. While Jordan was helpful in sending me down here, she hasn't been all that helpful while Mom has been sick. She's never liked my mother, my sister or much of my family really. She says that we are too distant, too hard to get to know and always making excuses for each other in order to avoid confrontations.

I think about the last of our fights, which we seem to be having more and more of. I wanted to visit Mom and Dad again and she wanted me to stay home with her and Jade. She said, "You've been over there five nights out of the last six. Stay home. Jade is getting bored with just me here at night."

I told her that Jade would have to get over it, that if she was lucky, her grandmother would be dead soon and she wouldn't have to be bored any longer.

Jordan said, "That's not fair, you're being childish when you says things like that."

Childish. I told her that I may be acting childish because I'm concerned about my mother—the only mother I would ever have and that I wanted to spend as much time with her as possible. How dare she call me childish. I'm trying to be a good son.

She said, "You are a good son, but Jade needs you to be a good dad. I need you to be a good husband."

I told her that I was a good dad. How dare she tell me I'm not a good father.

And it went on like that until I left that night. I still know I've been doing the right thing. Jordan makes it sound like I'm selfish, but how can it be selfish to look after your mother in a time like this?

~

The morning brings sun and, after a shower and a coffee, I walk into town to look for some breakfast. It's about 7:00 in the morning so I'm hoping there will be a MacDonald's or something further on down, though I don't recall seeing any golden arches when I arrived. Maybe down another side street.

After a few tours of the main street and one street behind, I come to the conclusion that there is nowhere else to explore. There are hardly any cars around and the only pedestrians are a man cleaning up litter from the sidewalks and a woman washing some storefront windows. Nothing is open except for one bakery run by some Vietnamese-looking people. I buy myself a sandwich for later in the day and some pizza bread and an orange juice for now. Not much of a breakfast from a place open so early in the morning. But any better food might be wasted on this stomach of mine which still hasn't settled since the flight.

It may be too early to go knocking on a priest's door on a Saturday morning, but what do I know about priests' operating hours? I walk back up to Rangaroa via a tunnel that exits from the main street, and takes me under the railroad tracks toward the incline. I follow a walking track up the hill and emerge at the top, walking toward the church in the opposite direction from yesterday. Of all the blue and white buildings in this complex, two look like they could be a priest's house—the multi-story building across the road from the school, whose windows are completely darkened, and the single-story bungalow adjacent to the school grounds which is emitting light from all the front casements. I mount the steps to its front door and pause before ringing the bell.

From inside, I hear a voice intoning deeply, crying out in phrases like, "Jesus' name!" and "hedge of protection!"

Now I'm really not sure about this. But I've come a long way.

The bell causes the house to quiet for a moment but then I hear heavy footsteps approach. The door opens briskly.

"Hello," the deep voice says, warily, but not unfavorably. The man behind the voice is an imposing figure. He is fully dressed in the classic priest's outfit—black suit, white collar, cross swinging from his neck from the motion of his arms opening the door. He is tall and heavy set, taller than me and with jowls like Richard Nixon. His eyes are fixed on me, and above and between them, I see beads of perspiration gently giving way to gravity. He is young, probably in his early forties. I thought all priests were over sixty-five.

He holds a white cloth in his hand which he uses to wipe his cheeks, then his brow.

"Hello," I say somewhat meekly. Am I supposed to say, "Hello Father" or, "Hello your most esteemed worship of the holy cross"?

"I'm sorry to bother you this early in the morning—"

"That's no trouble, no trouble at all," he says. The voice is less gruff now. It has a heavy breathing quality to it as if he's just stepped off a treadmill. "Depending, of course, on what it is you're wanting." He flashes a smile that disappears abruptly rather than fading away.

"I've come a long distance to find someone who used to work at the school here and I'm wondering if you could help me."

"I may be able to do that. I've only been the priest here for a few weeks though, so I probably don't know the person you're looking for. Where have you come from exactly?"

"Canada."

"That is quite a distance. Would you like to come in?"

I hesitate, again not too sure about this whole priest thing. Will he try and talk about religion with me? Maybe offer me cookies for a seat on his lap? I shake it off and walk past him as he opens the door wide for me to enter.

"I'm about to make some tea. I assume you've had breakfast, but you're welcome to have a cup if you'd like." He says this as he moves past me and down the hall toward a kitchen at the back of the house.

"No thanks, I've had a coffee already this morning."

"Very good," he calls out. "I'll be right there if you'd like to wait in the front sitting room."

There are two rooms at this end of the house, one to each side of the hallway as you come in the front door. I look to the left and see a cluttered office with a computer in the center surrounded by books, loose papers and lots of large maps, some tacked haphazardly to the walls and many more strewn about the room, on the floor, on a table, even draped over the computer monitor obscuring the screen. The charts on the wall are covered in colored pins and highlighter. It's difficult to determine what geographical area it represents; it appears more topographical than political.

The room to my right is barren except for a small love-seat sized sofa and two cushioned chairs with rigid backs and arm rests. These sit on either side of a small electric heater designed to imitate a fire place. I walk into this room and wait for my host. A mirror hangs on the wall so I check my eyes for puffiness and wear and am pleased to see I don't look as tired as I feel.

"Please have a seat," the priest says behind me. I sit down and he settles in the chair across the fireplace-heater from me, placing his cup of tea on the floor beside his chair leg, along with a small plate of dry-looking cookies.

"I was thinking about your someone," he says. "You say she used to work at the school?"

"*He* used to work at the school, yes."

"I beg your pardon. Most of the teachers in this school's history have been nuns. You can see my mistake."

"Of course," I say.

"Yes," he continues, "the Sisters of St Joseph ran this school for decades from its inception. Sad to say, there hasn't been a nun teaching at St Patrick's in almost ten years. So that means your someone must have been hired as a lay person to work here, just like all the teachers over there now."

What the hell do I need this lesson for?

"So, even without asking you more about your someone, only by ascertaining that he is a male, I have deduced some information that may be helpful in tracking him down for you." He smiles at me smugly and bites vigorously into a cookie. Great, I've found Sherlock Holmes right here in Taumarunui, New Zealand. Watson's bound to knock on the door at any moment.

"It's my brother I'm looking for. His name is Frankie Murrihy. He worked here from 1997 until 2000. He knew a priest here named Father Van Rooyen."

"That's Father Van Rooyen, pronounced "rune" as in an ancient Celtic alphabetic symbol. He was a bit of a legend around here. He served in this parish for almost thirty years, a long time for a priest to be in one parish—too long really. Actually, he left here in 2000 and died overseas, in his homeland in Holland. That's the same year your brother left. We're narrowing things down even more here, eh?"

"Yeah, that's good," I say. "Have you heard of my brother?"

"What was his name again?"

"Frankie Murrihy."

To his credit, the priest pauses to think about this, but then says, "No, I have not heard of a teacher here by that name, but, as I say, I'm new here. What else can you tell me about him? Maybe I can deduce some more information for you."

"Thanks, but really I came here hoping that Father Van Rooyen could tell me where Frankie went from here. We haven't heard from him in over two years. Since he's gone, do you think you could put me in contact with someone from the school who worked with Frankie and may know where he went?"

"Perhaps. That's four years ago that he left here. Didn't he tell you where he went when he was still talking with you?"

"No, not really. He did tell us he was going into the priesthood, but we don't know where he went to do that."

"The priesthood? From a teacher to a priest? That's unusual. Well, the good news is that there are only so many places you can go in New Zealand to become a priest, so that narrows things down for us right there. More deduction my dear Watson!"

I can't believe he just said that. But I am excited as I'm sure he's right. New Zealand is a small country, so how many priests do they actually train? Surely it's not like there are universities all over the place for Catholic priests. I say as much to Father Holmes.

"That's correct. But I am surprised I haven't heard of him if he's four years down the road toward ordination." He must see the bewilderment in my face. "An ordination is the ceremony in which a man is administered the sacrament of Holy Orders and is officially anointed as a priest in the Catholic Church. This can only happen after seven years of education and training. I am heavily involved in the development of curriculum and protocols for this so that is why I am surprised I haven't heard of your brother." I nod to show I understand and to avoid any more elaborate lessons.

"Of course, we're presuming he stayed in New Zealand to study, but there are only two seminaries in the country—both in Auckland."

This is helpful, but I realize I may be hitting the road back north.

"So, you could still try and talk to someone from the school to find out where your brother went, or I can contact the seminaries for you and see what I can find out."

"That would be great, I'd really appreciate that," I say. "I wonder when you could do that?"

"Well, I will send them both an e-mail now. I do have to go and visit a parishioner this morning. Why don't I put you in touch with the school's principal? He may be able to help you. He is new to the parish as well but he'll know the staff better than I do." He stands and says, "I'll just get his number." He walks out of the room and into his office across the hall, returning to hand me a post-it note.

"Thank you again," I say, standing. "When do you think you'll hear back from the seminaries?"

"Why don't I give you a call? Where are you staying in town?"

"Fern's Motel. My name is Conrad Murrihy."

"Very good," he says as he walks toward the front entrance. I follow him and continue through the door which he's opened for me. "It has been very interesting meeting you Conrad. I hope you find him. I will say this however: I trust the reason you are looking for him is an important one—and I'm sure it must be if you've traveled all this way—because I have found that when a person makes efforts to lose contact with family, there is usually some significant reason for doing so. Of course, it is all for God to judge, but your brother may have responded to a call from God that requires him to sever bonds from the past. Jesus said, 'Anyone who comes to me without hating father, mother, wife, children, brothers, sisters, yes and his own life too, cannot be my disciple.' I've known a few priests who have taken His words quite literally and turned their backs on their families in order to pursue God's call on their lives more fervently."

I thank him again and say, "I don't know why Frankie has left us like he has, but there's no reason good enough for him to cut our family out of his life. Please call me when you hear back from the seminaries." We shake hands and I walk out to my car to the sound of his door closing behind me.

~

The mātāpuna—the source—is a place of purity and simple beauty, a place of innocence and vitality. The source of te wahine's tears must be the same—a child's cry, a girl's yearning, a daughter's lament.

Today, te wahine emerges from a whare. It is a large house with smoke rising from its roof. Io-wairoa does not permit us to see her eyes, but we know she has shed more tears this day. Her mauri is in turmoil, weakened, reduced by unseen events inside.

Our source has been tapped, diverted, and our mauri—our life force—now mixes with other rivers. As our water is reduced, so is our mana, our power, our dignity. We cannot feed our children, we cannot sustain their lives and our voice has gone quiet. How can they hear us call?

But prayer flows upriver, to the source. It is harder to undo an act, it is more difficult to create than it is to destroy. Yet the source is the key. Io-wairoa, hear our voice as we pray for our mokopuna, and as we pray for te wahine. Hear the cries of Your people, weep for us once again and fill us with Your Spirit.

~

It's still early for ringing a principal at home on a Saturday morning, so I drive out of town, exploring further south. It turns out there is more to Taumarunui than the two main streets. Off the highway I can see an extended residential area. The highway runs parallel to the train tracks and I see another river running in the opposite direction to me on my left. At a railway bridge I pass a sign reading "Whanganui River". I spend the next hour almost enjoying the never-ending hills and even seeing the snow covered mountains from a settlement called Owhango. This haunt of Frankie's feels very remote. More fields, more sheep, more rivers.

Back in my hotel, I ring the number the priest gave me. There's no reply but an answering machine inviting a message for "Charles, Beverly, Thomas, Tamar or Tristan." The principal's voice is chirpy and nasally, emanating from the head of one of those annoying families that needs to list all their kids' names in everything. I leave a message saying I'd been given his number by his priest (I'd forgotten to ask the priest his name) and that I would like to talk to him about my brother who used to work at the school.

With two phone calls to wait for, I settle into my room for the day. I nap but wake around lunch, still feeling groggy. I eat a packet of peanuts and drink a coke from the fridge. I flip through the motel-room guidebook for a place I can order a pizza but none of the places listed advertise take-out. I ring reception and my host confirms that you can't order food to be delivered in Taumarunui, but he suggests The Golden Kiwi as it is close to the motel. I don't want to risk missing a phone call so I decide to hunt and gather later.

It's late in the afternoon when the phone finally rings. From the receiver, the nasally voice of the principal says, "Hello, this is Charles Spencer, principal of St Patrick's school. You rang earlier?"

"Yes, I did, thanks for ringing back."

"I'm sorry I didn't get back to you sooner. I was chasing my kids around all morning at the netball courts and rugby field. You said your brother worked at St Patrick's?"

"Yes, I did, his name is Frankie Murrihy. Do you know him?"

"Wow," he says slowly, but quickly adds, "I never met Frankie. I've only been at St Patrick's for a year. But I do know of him. He's the man who lost his family in a car accident?"

"Yes, that's right." I feel excited. The degrees of separation have just been reduced.

"That was a terrible story. So, his children were your niece and nephew? I'm sorry for you—that must have been awful, especially being so far away from them." He sounds sincere in his Ned Flanders sort of way.

"It was terrible," I say, uncomfortably. I don't like talking about this with strangers. But, of course Frankie would be most remembered for the tragedy. I wonder what he might have been known for if the accident hadn't occurred. I ask him if he knows anything about Frankie's location after leaving St. Patrick's.

"No, sorry I don't. Jean tells me that he left to become a priest, but I really don't know anything more than that."

"Jean?"

"Yes, Jean Dimaguiba. She's our deputy principal. I think she might actually be the only staff member who is still working with us who worked with your brother. When did he leave again?"

"Near the end of 2000. I don't think he finished the year working after the funeral."

"OK, yeah. I mean, we're a small staff and a lot of teachers have come and gone since the sisters stopped teaching here. Taumarunui's like that. A lot of people come here to start a career, but move on after they gain some experience. Jean is the only one I've ever heard talk about him."

"OK. Is there any way I can get in touch with her?"

"Not by telephone, today at least. She's out of town until tomorrow. She'll be somewhere in the North Island with her camper-van and she doesn't have a cell phone. But she is coming back for Mass tomorrow. She's playing the music so she needs to be back for that. I would suggest you catch up with her at the church in the morning."

"Alright," I say. "What time is that?"

"Mass starts at 9:30. You're welcome to come of course. Are you Catholic?"

I stumble at the forwardness of the question. Mr. Spencer sounds like Ned Flanders and he is just as naively direct. "No, I'm not. What time does it finish? I could catch up with her then."

"Sure. Mass usually lasts about an hour. I'll be there so I can look out for you and introduce you to Jean. I'm sure she'll be amazed to see you."

"Thanks for that. I'll see you tomorrow then," I say, about to hang up the phone.

"Hey, don't worry about not being Catholic. You're welcome to come to Mass anyway."

"Thanks but no thanks."

"I'll see you tomorrow then."

~

After speaking with Spencer, I do go into town and get some food at the Golden Kiwi—a greasy spoon of a place, not a diner but a hole-in-the-wall that seems to be half fish market and half pizza parlor. The choices on the menu are limited to these and meat pies. I opt for the pizza.

I buy some breakfast supplies at the supermarket on the way back to the motel. Walking through the aisles is discombobulating with walls of foreign packaging and all their unfamiliar colors and brand-names. Again, it takes that much more of my concentration to discern items I want. I guess I hardly pay attention to what is around me when I shop back home. I know where everything is and what it looks like, so shopping is a quick stop and grab. Here I have to read every label carefully to get the chocolate milk or cereal I want. At least bananas look the same.

The pizza is a disappointment in comparison with Pictou County fare. It seems home-made and oven-cooked, unlike the gorgeous delicacies prepared back home in proper pizza ovens, plenty of meat covered in dripping, melted cheese. I miss the Acropole restaurant.

It's late and I still haven't heard from the priest. I spend the rest of the night reading more of Dad's documents and watching television. This time I watch several stations' news shows from the beginning of their broadcasts. Every station covers the exact same stories in the exact same order and I wonder if there really is all that much news to cover here. Typically, national stories about New Zealand are presented first—some religious joker who led a march a few months ago to protest civil unions, including an uncomfortable sight of men in black shirts pumping fists in the air and chanting, "Enough is enough!"; a speech made by a politician earlier in the year which was apparently racist; something to do with foreshore and seabed legislation which I don't understand but it seems to have to do with land and water rights being argued over by the government and the Maori.

The Prime Minister, Helen Clark, says, "The Act will ensure that our country's beaches and rocky coastline will remain the property of the Crown," while an unhappy, but composed Maori woman named Tariana Turia explains that her Maori party intends to establish customary title for Maori over foreshore and seabed. Maori party. Imagine that in Canada—a race-based party. Where would that end? The Irish Descendants' party? The French-speaking party? The Women-only party? The Catholic party? Forget voting for policies and principles, let's vote based on our gender or skin color. This place must have some deep fractures in it, as deep as the scars in the hills.

In international news, strife continues in Israel and the Gaza strip. I reflect that it seems such fighting over land and race is as familiar to New Zealanders as it is to other hot spots in the world. I never have understood it. Land is land and there's plenty of it in the world. Israel is a country—they've won. Why don't the Palestinians just go live somewhere else? There's plenty of land in the Middle East. So much pain and suffering and impeding of progress, and for what? Religion.

How can people argue for possession of land with arcane notions of a "promised land" granted to them by a deity?

I feel grateful that Canada has so much space to share. Nova Scotia has come a long way in sorting things out with the Mi'kmaq people. They have their own schools now and are expanding businesses on their reservations, especially near Truro. When I grew up, I hardly ever saw a Mi'kmaw. They used to come to our school to act out different myths, but outside of school I never saw any in the malls or in New Glasgow. Dad worked with Mi'kmaq students at his school, but this did little to enlighten me. It was only as a journalist that I came into contact with residents on Pictou Landing and grew to understand some of their issues and goals. I don't cover as many stories involving racism now. We've come a long way, and that's how it should be so that everyone can move on.

Between news stories and interesting commercials, I read. I'm pleased when I find a mention of Jean Dimaguiba in one of Frankie's e-mails. It's part of a longer message to Mom and Dad, mainly about the kids but also with a section on living in Taumarunui:

Taumarunui is a lot more multi-cultural than Nova Scotia. In our first six months here, I've met more people from different countries than I did in all my years growing up, even while going to university. Our school secretary is Indian, one of our teacher-aides is from South Africa and one of our teachers is married to a man from the Philippines. She's from Auckland but met him here in Taumarunui. Her name is Jean Dimaguiba. What a cool name , eh? Kathy has been welcomed into a group of Korean wives and we've met teachers at other schools who are from Australia, the US, Scotland, Thailand, even Canada!

I agree with Frankie about Nova Scotia. As I say, everyone looks like me back home. But in Canada it's changing, if television is anything to go by. More news broadcasters, sitcom characters and talk show hosts have names like Hanomansing. David Suzuki and Chief Dan George are no longer the exotic rarities they once were. There was one black face in our high school, a student younger than me, and one Arabic boy. Every person I work with has a Scottish or Irish name and half of those start with Mc or Mac. I'm all for celebrating your roots, but the world's changing—we're all part of the human race so it's time for us to stop letting old divisions hurt our evolution.

I organize the documents in chronological order which takes about an hour. The only patterns I notice are that the handwritten messages become less frequent as the e-mails begin to dominate; faxes disappear entirely after 1998. The e-mails also shorten over time. Skimming through the ones I haven't read, I review more news about Kathy, the kids, some mentions of his job but without much detail, Jacob starting school, the letter about Father van Rooyen. Then I remember that Frankie didn't just live in the original house on North Street and I study the letters again to see if he ever mentioned moving house. I can't find any, but I do find envelopes with return addresses in Taringamotu and Ngapuke. I could investigate these places tomorrow, but only if I have no leads from the church. I'm here to find Frankie, and I don't want to have to re-trace every step he took to do it.

FLOWING INTO GOD

After a better night's sleep, I finally feel quasi-normal. The only interruptions I had were loud trucks passing the motel. I eat a hearty breakfast and decide to go for a short walk down the river road just outside. If I can find it. Exiting my motel room, I meet a wall of yellow fog unlike anything I've ever experienced. It sticks to me and is more blinding than the night—not moving, but sitting all around me like something solid. But it yields to me as I step into it. From the motel parking lot, I walk down, what looks to be, a dead-end street with just a few houses before turning into a gravel patch that disappears around a bend. It could be a road or a driveway. I'm not interested enough to explore and unsure about New Zealand attitudes to strangers walking down their driveways just to see what's around the corner.

For a few minutes, I stand at the top of the bank and watch the river flow below the fog, moving to my left, heading into town and under the bridge I drove across when I arrived. According to my maps, this is the Ongarue River and it will hook up with the Whanganui somewhere in town. For some reason, the Whanganui wins this meeting because the Ongarue loses its name when they join, like a marriage. I picture the Whanganui as a male Maori warrior with a full facial tattoo scooping up the smaller Maori princess, Ongarue, in his arms and taking her into the woods to marry her at some old stone church designed by European settlers. The river is very calm, without a hint of resistance against its fate. It must be love.

Jordan uses a hyphenated name. I go along with it, but I don't understand it. She accuses me of not showing full commitment to our marriage, that I still spend more time with my parents than I do with her and Jade. She can't even commit to a simple thing like a name change. She argues the name is important as her parents had no sons—it would be like a death. But it's not a death, it's meant to be a union. This Ongarue River doesn't die when it meets the Whanganui—it adds its strength to it, and lives on in it. But it commits.

Three ducks appear on the bank just below and entertain me before I turn away, cruising out from the bank and letting the river sweep them along before paddling hard to return for some inscrutable reason. Birds fly amongst the lower branches of the trees. They look like sparrows from a distance but could be some species foreign to me. As I walk back, I can see a middle-aged woman with a fluorescent vest walking across the bridge into town at speed. She must have made an early start. The fog is beginning to give way to a brilliant dawn and I remember that it is Sunday and I am going to church.

~

We ask Io-wairoa, "Why do You show us these visions of te wahine? She is not Māori. She is not tangata whenua—not born of this land nor welcomed to it. Her mother did not bury her whenua, her after-birth, here. There is no wāhi tapu—no sacred site—here for her."

His only response is to show us another vision. Te wahine lies in her own bed, covered with wavy material which she tosses like our most fierce rapids. We see her face—her eyes are closed. She is beautifully upset.

Our heart cries out for her, a yearning to bring her healing, for that is our nature. To reach beyond our banks and our shores, to let words flow out of our mouth that would traverse the ocean breadths and cascade over her in that distant land. She is sacred as all women are sacred.

Io-wairoa, You use the foolish to confound the wise and You know our heart. Ka tangi hoki ko ahau. I also cry.

~

I decide to go to the service after all. I've nothing better to do but sit in a motel room or explore more roads and hills or maybe Frankie's other houses, but those don't interest me. Going to the church gives me a chance to meet with others who would have known him, not just his co-workers.

I drive up to Rangaroa feeling nervous. I've only ever been in a Catholic Church for funerals of relatives on my grandmother's side, and for my daughter's baptism. Each time, I've accompanied someone who's shown me what to do or where to go. I deliberately arrive late so I can sneak a seat at the back and watch without being noticed. It's not quite that easy as I'm not the only one late. A Maori family rushes down the street on my left, a mother followed by three teenage daughters and three younger boys. She's beckoning them to hurry up and they half-walk, half-jog behind her. We meet at the corner and she raises her eyebrows twice at me, flashing a smile with missing teeth. "Good morning," she says and stops to usher me in ahead of them. "After you."

"Thanks," I say, grinning back. I walk under the shelter and in through the opened doors. The congregation is finishing a hymn led by two women at the front of the church, one playing guitar and the other, the piano. My plan to sit at the back doesn't work as the rear pews are filled in all four seating areas. I step aside for the family behind me who all stop at the water basin by the door to cross themselves with holy water and then confidently, but covertly, make their way to the seats on the right where they slip into a pew surrounded by Maori parishioners. Many give her a smile, a little wave or that double eyebrow raise as she, then each of her children, bend down on one knee, crossing themselves again before taking their seats. Some older ladies ignore them and stare straight ahead at the priest who is now speaking at the front.

The interior of the church is as odd as the exterior. Everything is brown and wooden. There are great beams criss-crossing the ceiling which is very angular. Some supports must surely obstruct the view of congregants, especially if they are trying to read the words on the overhead projector. The altar area is covered with a dated orange carpet and is bathed in a weird glow as if sunlight is pouring through obscured stained glass windows.

I move along the back of the opposite section and sit in the first free pew I find. I remember Jordan telling me that, as a non-Catholic, no-one expects you to perform all the rituals in the church so I don't bother with the kneeling. Besides, I don't believe in doing things like that unless I understand and agree with them.

The Mass continues and I do try to pay attention as I used to in our church. Presumably, Frankie would have done this often and must have enjoyed it if he wanted to make a lifetime of it. We sit, we stand, we kneel, we listen, we stand again. The young priest's voice is bold and clear. He talks about the Mass being a performance for God and that people should perform it well. It sounds like a Catholic thing to say. More standing, more kneeling. At one point, we shake hands with the people around us. I'm surrounded by white people on this side of the church except for one Maori-looking lady behind me who speaks with a British accent when she says, "Peace be with you" to each of us. The music is awful and the parish seems disinterested or maybe they're still learning the songs, which are hymns but sound like folks songs meant to be sung around a campfire. At one point, after a bell is rung, a woman sings out from the back, "Haere mai! Haere mai Te Atua!" Everyone lines up to eat some bread and drink some wine. I remain in my seat and watch the individuals in this community. The musicians go up first and I try to determine which one is Jean Dimaguiba.

There are too many candidates whose face and attire might accompany the nasally voice of Spencer. I search for a family with two boys and a girl, but none match. If he's not here I'll have to approach the musicians myself.

The Mass ends and the priest exits the church followed by his two altar boys. Actually one of them is a girl, which surprises me—aren't altar boys supposed to be actual boys? The congregation sings the last song to the end and we are free to go. I wait as others kneel again, exiting their pews. The musicians chat and pack up their gear and just as I'm about to walk over to them I am greeted by a short man wearing glasses, a clean haircut, a striped sort sleeve dress shirt and tidy dress shorts. He holds out his hand and says, "You must be Conrad." It's Mr. Nasal.

I shake his hand and say, "Yes, Mr. Spencer is it? How did you know it was me?"

He laughs. "It's not hard to spot an out-of-towner here. I know everyone else in the building and you are obviously a non-Catholic. I'm pleased you decided to join us for Mass. Let me introduce you to Jean."

I follow him to the front of the church and the pianist looks at me, studying my face. "Hello," she says before Spencer can say anything. "Charles told me you were coming. So, you're Frankie's brother."

I nod and say, "That's right," and immediately her eyes water and she gives me a hug.

"I am so sorry for what happened to your family here in New Zealand. I met your parents when they came for the funeral. They were such lovely people. It was so sad. Have you been up to the cemetery yet?"

I hadn't even considered that. My niece and nephew are buried somewhere in this town and I hadn't thought to visit them.

"No, not yet," I say. "I wouldn't know where they are." I almost say that I'm in a hurry and that I'm only here to find out where my brother is, but stop myself, realizing how that would sound.

"Well, I can give you directions. Are you in town long?"

"Actually, no. I'm trying to find Frankie and was hoping you might be able to help me."

She sighs and looks at the guitar player then at Spencer. When she turns back to me, she has full tears flowing down her cheeks. She says, "I don't know where he is. We haven't heard from him since he left."

"We haven't heard from either, not in two years."

"You mean he hasn't even been in touch with his family?" I see anger flash across her face. "Why would he do that?"

"We don't know. I plan on asking him that when I find him. I did think he may have kept in touch with the school, but obviously not. Look, would you at least know where he went after he left St. Patrick's?"

"All I know is that he wanted to become a priest. I'm not sure how I even know that. He never told me himself, so I must have heard it from a friend or maybe Father Kirton."

"I heard the same from Tim Wilson," interjects the guitarist.

I look at her with a small smile of thanks, even though this does nothing to help me. "OK. Father Kirton? I thought Father van Rooyen was the priest when Frankie was here."

"He was, but he died right after he baptized Frankie. In fact, Frankie was the last person Father van Rooyen ever baptized. After that, he went overseas and never came back." She shakes her head.

"He served here for twenty-eight years and even wanted to be buried here. Then he goes back to Holland for a holiday and dies. Do you know, the nurses in his hospital said they had never felt such a feeling of peace as they did when they were in his hospital room? Anyway, Father Kirton took over here as a temporary priest. He conducted the funeral for Frankie's wife and children. Such beautiful children. I was Jacob's teacher when the accident happened. That was the worst event I've ever experienced in my career."

We all let silence stand between us for a few moments. Then I ask Jean if she can think of anything else that might help me.

"I wish I could," she says. "And I wish I could think of someone else who might, but other than our school cleaner and one of our teacher-aides, I'm the only staff member who knew Frankie. Father Kirton is in Invercargill now. You could try ringing him. Have you talked with Father Sampson?" she asks, nodding toward the door where the young priest has exited.

"I spoke with him yesterday. He said there are only two places to become a priest in New Zealand and that he was contacting them for me."

"That's right, our only seminaries are in Dunedin and Auckland," Jean says.

"Actually, the Dunedin seminary has moved to Auckland as well Jean," Spencer says. "They moved a number of years ago."

"Oh, I wonder why they did that. Imagine living in the South Island and having to move to Auckland to train. What a shame. These bishops make decisions that make no sense sometimes. Now, if women were in charge, the whole Church would look very different!" She looks at her friend and the two laugh together. Then she says to me, "You know, I think your brother will make a good priest if he's still training. He seemed to love learning about our faith and the Church when he was here. It was a great story for us, this Canadian teacher who converted to Catholicism after working in the school and parish. He was so keen to learn and participate. He played guitar with us sometimes," the guitarist nods as Jean continues, "and Father van Rooyen got him to lead a home-group before he was even baptized so he must have thought your brother was capable. Do you want to have a look at the school? There are some photographs of Frankie with his classes on our wall."

"No thanks," I say, feeling frustrated now. "I really want to find Frankie himself. Do you think Father Sampson is still around?"

"Yes—oh, he'll need to lock up." Jean turns again to her friend who picks up her guitar case. "We'd better get going." To me, she says, "He won't be able to talk long. He has to go to Kakahi to say Mass at noon. You'd better go see him."

We all turn and walk out of the back of the church and under the covered way. Father Sampson finishes a conversation with a small, grey-haired man leaning heavily on a cane and turns to greet me with a pudgy handshake as if expecting me to come through the door behind him at just that moment.

"I'm sorry you didn't hear from me yesterday. I was called away to deal with an ailing parishioner whose family needed support in moving him to our local nursing home. I've received word back from both seminaries," he says as he withdraws a neatly folded piece of paper from his coat pocket. "Here is the e-mail from the Marist Seminary in Freeman's Bay. I think you'll find part of what you're looking for in it."

I accept the paper and open it. Jean and Spencer watch me curiously as I read:

Greetings in Christ Gerard:

Yes, David Francis Murrihy was an Aspirant and Novitiate with us for a short time. He joined our seminary in November 2000 and was permitted to begin his Novitiate period after only a year with us as he appeared to be a remarkable aspirant due, we believe, to his conversion experience in Taumarunui and his recommendation from Father Adrian Kirton, despite the tragic circumstances under which he left his teaching job. He completed his Novitiate in Australia and returned to take his vows in Easter of 2002.

Gerard, we strongly advise that you direct your visitor our way as we have not heard from our brother Francis in some time and, considering the nature of your visitor's quest, he should come to Auckland to collect some of his brother's personal effects which I'm sure will be much valued by his family.

We will leave you to provide him with our contact details and we will receive him at whatever point in time is convenient for him from Monday morning on-wards.

Yours faithfully,

Father Leonard Fitzpatrick

I sigh. This is good news except for the request to drive back to Auckland. Surely, they could have at least told me where Frankie was the last they heard from him. I say as much to Father Sampson.

"It is strange, but I'm sure Father Leonard must have a good reason for not including more by e-mail. It could be he doesn't know much or it could be he's not happy sending such information electronically. He's quite an old codger is Father Leonard. But, as I say, he will have his reasons. Here." He hands me another folded paper. "This is the address for the seminary. I assume you have a map. I really must be going. God bless you on your journey."

We shake hands again and Jean walks with me to my car. She gives me a hug under the wooden totem cross. She looks up at it and says, "God is connected to his people like the strands of a plaited chord, like the beads of a rosary chain. I pray Our Lady will help you find your brother." I thank her again and drive back to my motel.

~

The journey to Auckland is uneventful. I saw no point in staying any longer in Taumarunui to visit old houses or even a grave-site. Finding Frankie quickly and bringing him back to Mom is all that matters.

The rain starts as soon as I leave town and steadily increases with the traffic as I drive north. The fresh spring leaves give way to the dominance of the grey air around us. At some point, perhaps the same juncture I noticed on my trip down, the hills finally open up and I breathe in a gasp of air, realizing just how claustrophobic the King Country had been. I pass through the same towns as before, stopping for some sushi at a small restaurant in Te Awamutu. My digestion has improved the further I get away from my flight. Driving past the signs for Auckland airport means I am entering new territory and a city I don't know how to navigate. However, after looking at the map in Te Awamutu, the seminary in Freemans Bay may be easy to find tomorrow, just off the main motorway.

By the time I get into the city and in sight of the Sky Tower, it's almost five o'clock. I exit at Greenlane and find another hotel, planning to visit the seminary first thing in the morning.

~

Another hotel, another hotel clerk, another night of television and reviewing letters. I've been in this country for four days now and it feels like nothing new ever happens. The same stories circulate. I've read all of Dad's documents. I've just had another breakfast of cereal and instant hotel coffee. At least the rain has stopped. Maybe it feels this way because I really don't give a fuck about what happens in this country. I miss my bed, my house, my roads, my truck, my parents. I didn't want to come here and I don't care if I see any more of this place. I want to meet with these bloody priests, find out where my brother is and get him on a plane. Maybe he'll even be with these guys and old Father Leonard is luring me up here for that surprise. Maybe I can be on a plane home tonight.

I check out of the hotel, rejoin the motorway and drive to Freemans Bay. Looking at the map, I see there isn't an actual bay nearby. I pass exits to places called Newmarket, Mount Eden and Grafton. The names are English in this city.

I take my exit and find Hopetoun Street immediately. It's in a busy suburban area, with a mixture of tall, modern buildings, separated by older ones and two-story homes that look like shrubs losing a battle for sunshine with oaks. Behind the buildings, I see there is a park with more of the typical greenery I've come to expect from New Zealand. I find the seminary and pull into a visitor's space. The sun is already warm on my back as I approach the front doors.

The bell is answered by a friendly-looking Indian man, slightly built and with a subtle twitch in his right arm. He speaks in an accent I can barely understand, but he does know who I'm looking for when I ask for Father Leonard. I think he asks me for my name so I give it to him and he invites me into a sitting area in the front of the building. I wait in a large echoing space with three doors exiting from the north, east and west of the room. Above each is a painting; one of a crucifixion scene, one of Mary, and one of a man I don't recognize, dressed in blue robes and holding up his forefinger and thumb. The Madonna picture is one of those whose eyes follow you wherever you stand in the room. They are lovely eyes but pictures like that creep me out. We had a large old photograph of my great-great-grandmother on a wall entering the kitchen. I feel like she's been watching me my whole life.

As I study the painting of the unknown man, a gruff, croaking voice speaks from the east door behind me.

"Do you know of Bishop Pompallier?"

I turn and sight a remarkable figure that I assume is Father Leonard Fitzpatrick. If anyone can be said to be "wizened", it is this man. He is hunched above an invisible cane wearing a grey, horizontally striped sweater over a white collared shirt. However, he is not wearing any pants. Instead, I can barely discern the bottom edge of a tiny pair of shorts beneath his sweater. His withered little legs lead down to a pair of blue flip-flops exposing the longest toenails I have ever seen on a man, or woman for that matter.

"Are you Father Leonard?"

"I am Father Leonard," he says and nods back at the painting, "and that is Bishop Pompallier. Do you know of him?"

Persistent bugger. "No I can't say that I do."

"Bishop Pompallier was the first Catholic bishop of New Zealand. He was one of the first Marists in the world and he came here in 1838. He signed the Treaty of Waitangi in 1840 and so was part of the birth of this country, bringing peace between the Europeans and the Maoris. From the very beginning of its time in Aotearoa, the Society of Mary has had the wellbeing of Maoris as an objective."

I don't say anything to that, because I really don't care.

He continues, "You don't look very much like your brother do you?"

"Not really," I say. I have never heard anyone say I look like Frankie.

"But you do sound like him. It's not just your accent, it's your tenor. Yes, you do sound very much like him."

"Do you know where he is?"

"I know where he was. Come inside. I have some things to pass on to you."

He removes a set of keys from beneath his sweater and opens the Mary door. I follow him through and then up a grand set of stairs, with railings of a dark, red hardwood. It's beautifully shaped and smooth. On the second floor, we walk down a hallway of old plush carpeting. The wallpaper is dated but clean. More paintings adorn the walls but these are more general in their subject-matter: some scenes of New Zealand landscape, including pastoral scenes or rivers or beaches. Father Leonard leads me into another sitting room, similar to the priest's in Taumarunui. Inside are the two chairs and a couch. On the floor in front of one of the chairs is a small plastic bin with a transparent cover.

The priest walks over to the other chair and motions for me to sit. "Please," he says.

I sit down and look at the box. "Is this Frankie's?"

"Yes, it is all that remains of him here. Francis, as we know him, took a vow of poverty before he left us so he did not own much. But really, he did not own much when he arrived. He was very clear about moving on from his old life when starting his new one here."

His old life. I've never believed in such an idea. We are each given a life to live and we move through it. I always hate it when people talk about starting a new life as if there could be no progression from the old to the new; as if the new life would have no traces or influence from the past.

"In that container, you will find journals written by your brother. They are very personal. So much so that I have not read them, nor has anyone here. I have only looked through them briefly to see what they are, but once I realized their nature, I did not want to intrude so far into his mind without his permission."

"Why did he leave them here then?"

The old man shrugs. "It is hard to say. Safekeeping perhaps. Perhaps he wanted to start yet another new life. Check the dates on the covers and you will see that they stop prior to his coming here, even prior to the loss of his wife and children. So, to my knowledge he did not write any more journals while he was here or, at least, if he did, he did not leave them with us."

I open the lid and look at the container's contents. There is a stack of maybe twelve books inside, some simple scribblers used by school students, others more adult-looking notebooks with artwork or scenic imagery. I open the first one, marked "1997—June to November" and recognize Frankie's scrawled handwriting. Or I should say printing. It's small and barely legible; words float in the spaces between the lines rather than sitting on the lines themselves.

Father Leonard says, "They are all in chronological order. There you have almost three years of your brother's life and thoughts. How long has it been since you last saw him?"

"Seven years."

"I'm sure it will be good for you two to catch up." With that, he stands as if to leave the room. "You are most welcome to stay here and read them. I can bring you a cup of tea and even offer you lunch later."

I stop him. "Wait Father Leonard. I'm not interested in reading these."

He sits back down, looking at me curiously, with his grim, withered face. "You're not?"

"No. I'll take them, but I don't care about Francis' past or his personal thoughts. I just want to find him. Why would I want these journals when I can just find him?"

He sighs and looks out the small side window which only faces a neighboring building. I don't wait for his response.

"Where is my brother?"

He looks at me and then down at his feet and says, "You know, your brother was a broken man when he arrived here. I have never known an aspirant so mixed: trying to keep his wounds closed, yet so open to the opportunity that God would heal him here. Others said it was a mistake to admit him, that he was too vulnerable, that he would need time to recover before making such a commitment."

I feel the same as I listen to his words. How dare they take advantage of a person who obviously wasn't ready for such a drastic change in lifestyle? Frankie was a son, a husband, a father, a brother and a teacher, not a religious fanatic, not a Catholic priest for Christ's sake.

"But, as I said in my e-mail, he came with a recommendation from Father Adrian, a man I've respected for many years. And we have a process to work through here. We allowed Francis to live here as a sort of refuge until January when we officially began a new year of study. That gave him some months to pray and to see what our way of life is like. No obligations. In fact, prior to taking the vows, we put no such obligations on any of our men—"

I interrupt him. "Where is my brother? I've told you I don't care about any of this. Where has he gone?"

"Please, let me finish, and then I will tell you what you want to know. But first I must tell you what you need to know."

Condescending prick.

"Had I thought, after his two months here, that Francis was in any way unsuited for this calling, this vocation, I would have instructed him to leave. I have never met a person more suited. As you would know, Francis was a new convert, and he was passionate. One could tell that he had committed much time to study and prayer on his own before he was baptized, and I do not mean just in his meetings with Father van Rooyen. His devotion to the Word and to our communal prayers and the Mass was second-to-none. When I discussed his continuing with us as an aspirant, he was eager.

"You see, each of our aspirants must spend as much as three years in prayer, seeking and confirming their call from Mary to serve as a witness to her son Jesus Christ in this world. Francis was determined that his new life, as he called it, would be to serve as a priest. In private consultation with me, he admitted that he lacked one thing: a clear calling from our Lady. However, I could see her korowai, her cloak, covering him and knew it would only be a matter of more time and prayer before he would hear her call.

"After a year of study and more time with us, the call became clearer to me, but it did not to Francis. Yet, his devotion to the sacraments and our Lord was unwavering, particularly in Confession. After one year, he was granted the opportunity to enter his Novitiate by living and serving with our brothers in Australia. I will not elaborate on our reports from this experience, other than to say that our brothers found his faith to be as remarkable as we had.

"When he returned, however, he seemed changed. He informed us that he would not continue his journey to priesthood, but would take the temporary vows of a brother in our order, end his time with us here in Auckland and serve in whatever part of New Zealand we wished to send him. As you can imagine, I had mixed feelings about this as Francis did not offer me much by way of explanation. But how could I refuse him? He was exemplary and he was telling us that he was ready to re-enter the world as a mirror of Christ."

The old priest breaks off into a fit of coughing, so bad that I have to ask him if he is alright and think that the only person who knows where Frankie is might drop dead at my feet here in this room.

"I'm fine, bless you," he wheezes. "You want to know where your brother is, but the best I can offer you is where he has been. He has been to the deepest, darkest valleys of the soul and he has ascended to the highest heights with the Holy Spirit. He has been secluded in this place and released to walk the deserts across the Tasman Sea. He then went to Wanganui."

I almost laugh at this, but then realize this has been his way of finally naming a city. I'm angry and feel like the butt of some joke, but I have the beginnings of real information.

"Wanganui? Isn't that near Taumarunui?"

"Not quite, though they are connected by the river. I don't know the area well, only having visited the city once. We had a request for support from the parish there at the end of 2002. They asked for a father and we sent them your brother."

DARK PLACES

I don't allow the old priest to restrain me any longer. Otherwise, I would risk more history lessons about a brother I released when he dismissed his family and got lost in this small, insignificant country I am now trapped in. I take the journals, toss them into the back seat of the Focus and get out of the city as fast as I can.

Before I left, the old man told me that Frankie had left for Wanganui immediately after his vows. He warned that he had not heard anything about Frankie for several months, maybe a year. He had heard rumors that Frankie had run into some trouble and was no longer working for the parish, but claimed not to know more than that. I asked him if he would call Wanganui for me, but he refused. I was angry, but not surprised. The old bastard seems intent on me driving every highway in the North Island.

All I know about Wanganui is that it is near Taumarunui so I launch onto the Southern motorway. I don't stop to check the maps until I see an exit for a gas station at Drury. Wanganui is located another couple of hundred kilometers past Taumarunui on the same highway, so it looks to be a straight forward trip of another six hours. It's noon, and there's a diner by the station so I have time to eat some lunch before continuing south.

The trip from Drury to Taumarunui is even more uneventful than my first two treks. The rain sets in again and persists deep into the King Country, so much so that I'm wondering where that top hat is when I need it. When I reach Taumarunui, I consider looking out for

Frankie's other two houses, but that is only curiosity mixed with the feeling that I've left a task undone. I remind myself that I don't care and continue through town as if I have no connection to it whatsoever. I repeat the drive out to Owhango and look for the mountains again, but of course they are obscured by the heavy rain and still darkening clouds.

After several more miles of twisting roads, the highway opens up to flatland at National Park village and I see the bases of the mountain ranges. They are impressive, even if I can't see the summits. The recent rain has not impacted the amount of snow on the largest of them and I wonder if snow could still be falling at such a height at this time of year. We have nothing like these in Nova Scotia. The tallest peak we have in Pictou County is Green Hill look-off. Our esteemed peak wouldn't even register in the last few hundred miles of scarred hillsides, let alone standing next to these giants. When I think of mountain ranges, I think of the Rockies or the Swiss Alps. This range projects from the middle of a huge plateau which stretches out and down the highway as far as I can see ahead of me. The village is gone as fast as it came and the mountains soon appear in my rear-view mirror.

The winding roads begin again and I pass through an even smaller township called Raetihi. I turn in for a coffee at an alternative-looking place called the Clown Cafe. Across the road, the buildings look like something out of *Northern Exposure*, run-down but renovated and restored. I'm served by a hulking, bearded man with dreadlocks who calls me "chief" after every exchange. He adds to the mess on his counter-top as he makes me a cappuccino, dumping in loose measurements of ingredients. You can't seem to buy a regular cup of coffee in New Zealand, only cappuccinos and espressos and the like. I avoid the omnipresent meat pies in the cabinet though these look expertly made with golden, swirly tops.

While the cafe is comfortable, the whole area surrounding the town is sparse and I expect to see tumbleweeds rolling by at any moment, if it wasn't for the damp. The rain here is colder and the wind has picked up. I reason that we must be at a decent elevation this close to the mountains and expect that it will be downhill from here to Wanganui. According to my map, the Whanganui River is following me even in places like this where passers-by would never sense its presence as it streams downhill from its source. Leaving

Raetihi, I spy an unusual white church or temple with red-roofed pillars on a hill overlooking the township. Religion has found its way to the most remote areas of this country.

It is all downhill to Wanganui, and it's the twistiest road I have driven in my life, far worse than the drives from New Glasgow to Sherbrooke which I always consider daunting. At one instance, you can see the mountains slowly falling away behind you and the next, you are in a gorge so deep you would never imagine a mountain view had been possible the moment prior. I navigate these turns cautiously, conscious of the rain and cold and with black ice on my mind. Other drivers are not so mindful. The speed limit is 100km/hour as this is a state highway, but in Nova Scotia, there is no way this road would be marked above 80km/hour. Cars pass me on bends that I'm sure will release vehicles from the other direction and lead us all to our doom down the edge of a ravine.

With such amazing and dangerous terrain, I'm not surprised to see no further major settlements. Who would live out here? This seems like such an in-between place. No mountains and ski fields, no ocean front or even riverside, just gorges and rocky ravines. At one point, traffic is held up by a group of Maori youths as one of their number cuts a tree from a cliff-side. They all wear black clothing with orange and white markings and flash drivers that double eyebrow raise as we finally are allowed to continue past. This road feels like an impenetrable gateway from one inhabitable place to another. At least, I assume that Wanganui will be an inhabitable place.

Finally, I sense I am getting somewhere. The roads straighten. Traffic increases from the opposite direction and more homes and farms appear along the highway. It is a bleak day. The rain has just not let up and I think of other places I've been that seem to always be hosting rain in my memory: Truro, Yarmouth, Antigonish. I'm sure it rains in these places as much as any other, so I must have visited them at a particular time when rain was heavy enough to ingrain itself in my psyche. Wanganui will be one of those places.

Through this mess, I see a classic little pointed-steeple church advancing toward me on my left. A sign tells me I am in Upokongaro, which doesn't sound like any Maori word I've encountered thus far. It sounds more Australian. Whatever it is about the name, and perhaps because of the weather conditions, I take an instant dislike for the place. Even in my Focus, and this far from the mountain plateau, this place feels cold to me and I'm happier when I've skirted through its edge. But I'm not sure what to make of its welcome for me to this area. It is here that the river reappears and I do consider what sights it has seen along its journey from Taumarunui. Across the river, another road runs parallel to us both and I wonder where it has come from and when it will join with mine.

Soon, residential areas appear on the other side and I gradually see more and more buildings, including some larger ones that remind me of the riverfront area in New Glasgow, and I start to grow fond of this river. State Highway 4 turns into Riverbank Road and then into Anzac Parade, all one road but with three different names. I never do see a sign proclaiming the city limit. It's almost eight o'clock before I reach the Dublin Street Bridge which takes me across the river and into this modest metropolis. The rain stops and the river below me thunders in celebration.

~

Today, te wahine walks among rows of foreign vegetation, fruit of distant trees, stacked neatly in coloured bunches under tepid light.

Our people once combed our banks, enjoying the shade and sustenance of our native bush amongst the tawa, kāmahi, rimu, rewarewa, rātā, punga and the mighty tōtara. They sheltered and played in our coves and caves, our cracks and our gorges, amongst knotted garlands of kiekie, moss, liverworts and parataniwha. All of this is us—the tributaries, the streams cascading out of papa cliffs, the shingle beaches, the whirlpools, our blossoming clematis, the fluttering tuis—all of this is the river, all of this is the people.

Te wahine does not live amongst soft green banks and supple green waters. She lives in a whare made of gravel surrounded by paths of gravel. All is grey and resistant.

We watch as she stops with a peach in her hand. We see her holding it, turning it over with her ringless fingers, then eating it where she stands, not moving from her spot until only the pit remains.

~

It took me well over two hours to finish the leg from Raetihi. Everything about me is exhausted and I sleep late into the afternoon.

Last night, I checked into the first motel I saw, telling reception I would be staying for at least two nights. I think she understood me though I barely understood a word she said. I don't know if she is Cambodian or Taiwanese or what, but it's shocking that a person could work that job with such poor English. No television last night, no reading. I just collapsed into bed.

Today, I feel lethargic and unmotivated. I've never traveled so much, even for the newspaper. New Zealand is a small country but it is still three times the size of Nova Scotia and I feel like I've been criss-crossing the goddamned place since I got here. I always thought I'd like to visit London and maybe Paris and take my time, photographing the history of the places, really appreciating the sights, sounds, smells, people and customs. I'm surprised at how little I care for any of that here. Maybe it's because of the awful experience of flying, maybe it's because it's a mission, not a pleasure trip, maybe it's because I miss home so much, miss my mother. I consider calling home, but the thought seems painful and distracting as well. I want to go home, but it's so far away. Maybe I'm close to finding this bastard. Maybe I'm close to getting out of here. But today, I feel like staying curled up in bed and watching baseball.

Outside is ashen. There's no heavy rain that I can see or hear from where I'm lying, but everything seems like it's painted with soot. Even my skin and clothes look pale and lackluster in the natural light from the window. I almost turn the television on just to see some color, even if it is artificial. I'm not hungry. In fact my system just feels messed up inside and the thought of food or even coffee irritates me. I turn over in bed and see my unopened suitcase on the floor and, beside it, the plastic bin with Frankie's journals.

Frankie used to write a bit, but I never knew him to write diaries of any sort. He was a good student in high school and probably university so I remember him writing papers of course. I also remember him writing one story which I never read. It was a stupid story but he included his friends' names in it and would read instalments of it aloud on the school-bus. Some of his friends seemed to get a kick out of it. I guess I thought it was funny, but weird too, for a fifteen year old boy.

I reach out without sitting up, flick open the container and extract the first book from the top of the small pile. It's the one dated 1997—June to November. I read the first entry from 19 June.

"When I want to read a book, I write one." – Benjamin Disraeli

<u>*Why a Journal? - Part II*</u>

"The more he wrote, the more he understood." That was the essence of Part I. Why did I not stick with a journal with that in mind? Too much focus on the move and family. New job. Bygones. Now I've chosen to keep journals to record my new thoughts based on all my recent reading and experiences. How quickly, however, did my reading take over again and my focus became new information/idea gathering. Granted, I have been spawning creative ideas of my own recently but have become a consumer again, not a producer. Exciting new ideas from Physics, Ecology, Philosophy and Religion have now become overwhelming. A tree no longer looks the same to me, nor the stars, strangers, movies, etc.

What will writing do? It will give me a sense of accomplishment. Doing, not just listening, viewing, looking. Complementary activities bound to be influenced by my internal pendulum. An ideas list, a collection of quotations, a resource, but most importantly a providence of a sense of common grounding with those I admire in literature, drama, cinema, science, life.

I've declared this a week for writing in the morning without reading. Time to balance the output with the input. I have resumed reading "The Bone People" at night and may occasionally re-visit the Bible or "Silent Power".

The stigmatic from San Giovanni Rotondo says, "In books you seek God. In prayer you find Him." I did sun salutations this morning and found breathing difficult with my bronchitis. I tried using "One" as my mantra which seemed a good focus until Kathy woke up. It may be the mind-clearing device I've been looking for. Not the only one I hope.

Brian Houston spoke about sin this morning and our need for a savior since we don't have the ability within us alone to overcome. Do we need a savior or connection with others/world/Tao to help us overcome our attachment to manifestations in our world? Of course, he says Jesus.

I have never heard this voice before and I have trouble connecting it with my brother. I flip through a couple of pages of Bible verses, all from "John", written in careful handwriting as if Frankie had been giving himself lessons. I find what looks like a poem.

Ode to Lawn-mowing

I love the smell of fresh-cut grass in the morning.
It smells like . . . Revelation.
Unheard are the voices and demands
Of wife and children
Unheeded are the pressures of work
And finances
Only by fully concentrating on his pattern,
His grass and hedges
Does he solve problems and discover
The eternal secrets of the universe

I laugh at this, recalling Frankie's attempts to sound deep while we were growing up. He used to meditate on the couch in the living room listening to Jimi Hendrix songs and proclaim things like, "The sounds he makes are from another place," and other shit like that.

I read through the rest of the first journal—a real mix of entries about the weather and what he did that day at school, along with the occasional poem or quote, usually a Bible verse. Overall, there's a sense of malaise coming through these, and sometimes he writes negatively about his family:

I want to cut out TV and spend more time reading these things and in prayer/meditation. My obstacle: Kathy. How can I shut out TV with her? It enables us to tolerate each other.

But it's not these entries that keep me in bed reading. I'm more interested in Frankie's multiple discourses about religious and scientific books he's reading or televangelists he's watching in the mornings. I never could understand my brother's religious conversion. So far, there's very little that would suggest he was keen on Catholicism, but he does seem excited about new ideas.

6 November 1997

OK, face it—you're at an ideological impasse—things going on and decisions in life are going to be difficult until you resolve this.

Last month I stated, unequivocally, that God is found in the connections—the meaning and search for it that we humans make and see in things and events. I followed this conclusion and it led me to powerful insights, feelings, positive relationships and general confidence in the goodness of our universe and literally all that it contains. I read the Bible, needed less sleep, exercised, communed with nature, meditated, looked on the bright side of life, inspired others. It also lead me to aura studies, paranormal and generally any new age ideas (not quite as bad as Astrology or Feng Shui).

This month I read Sagan's description of healthy skepticism and was sold on it. Without our rationale and insistence on rigorous, repeatable experiments, we can be led down many garden paths. This appealingly natural approach stimulates me. However, I have stopped reading the Bible, going to Mass, inspiring others.

The problem is not a belief in God. I still have no problems being skeptical and believing in God. God is good and we are Him. I still choose this as my universe and there is, in fact, ample evidence to support it.

The problem seems to be two-fold:

1. My stimulation over the last few months also came from being a significance junkie as if God's concerns lay with batting streaks and the welfare of my car motor.

2. (This is more likely) My all or nothing, dualistic nature is coming through again. Science is in, so I follow all things science. For example, finding the whale descriptions as interesting in "Moby Dick" as the language and brilliant plot—or reading David Attenborough.

It's not that I cannot conceptualize my belief system encompassing aspects of my scientific and religious worlds. It's the living it and staying true to both as they complement one another—like trying to get the left and right brain working together.

Returning to Dr. Schuller: "Decision-making is easy if there are no contradictions in your value system." A truism to be sure. What is my value system? How to live each day, making decisions as a significance junkie <u>and</u> a healthy skeptic?

I don't have an answer tonight. I have made a decision. With a new grounding supported by Sagan, it is a good time to return to the Bible, a source of wisdom, and some of its practitioners. I am sure to find answers now that I am clear on my question.

MĀORI JESUS

The staff at the Ballance Inn turns out to be as useless in giving directions around Wanganui as they were at telling me where I should park upon arrival. After a few minutes of frustration, I take their kindergarten map of the city and decide to go elsewhere for help locating the nearest Catholic Church.

I drive toward the city center looking for breakfast. Maybe I can find guidance from a waitress or someone. Looking at the map, there appears to be a park at the end of Campbell Street, so I drive further along Dublin and turn down Victoria which takes me into the heart of Wanganui. Fairly sure Frankie is somewhere in this city, I scan individuals on the sidewalk. When I last knew Frankie, he was a tall and neatly dressed man who wore modest clothes, usually blue jeans with dull grey or blue tops. He has an unusual gait—he looks like he's sitting as he walks, especially if he puts his hands in his pockets. It's really unique and I don't know how he does it. He sort of slouches back on his hips even as moves his legs forwards. If anything would draw my attention to him along the side of the road, it would be his walking posture.

But of course, this is a city, although it appears to be a small one, so the chances of seeing him this way are preposterous. However, I still hope it will be that easy now that I'm here. The sunshine today, and perhaps all the sleep I've had, give me a small sense of optimism. Besides, maybe as brothers we'll have a connection that the universe will use to draw us together. I scoff at the thought. We grew up beside each other more than with each other. We developed totally different interests and Frankie always kept me at arm's length. He made sure we never played on the same team in our neighborhood softball and road hockey games. He never let me near his precious comic book collection. Rather than big brother showing little brother the way, we acted more like two solitudes. I know Clio felt the same too although she'd never talk about it. But I find the idea of some kind of psychic brother connection funny in light of Frankie's journal writing.

The pedestrians who walk the tree-lined streets of Wanganui seem to be split between Maori and European. At the start of Victoria Street, where there are a lot of gas stations and car yards, the people generally dress drably; young men walk in groups with dark hooded sweaters even on a morning that is already heating up. I see a few more heavy leather Mongrel Mob jackets. Women slowly push strollers; there are no school-aged children around and I remember that the school break has ended. There appears to be a mayoral election going on as campaign signs dot intermittent corners and business fronts.

As I drive deeper into the city's heart I sense the river nearby. The streets narrow and more clothing and electronic stores appear. There in an increase in the amount of men and women wearing suits, mostly white skinned. I must be nearing the central business district.

To my right, just between and above some smaller buildings, I spy the tall brick spire of a church. Catholic cathedrals are often in the center of cities so I try my luck and navigate toward it. Two blocks down Guyton Avenue, I park across the street from St Paul's Presbyterian which reminds me an awful lot of our own St Paul's United Church in Westville—tall and completely made of brick; it's the church we grew up in, attended Sunday school in, where my grandmother still attends. While it's not the Catholic Church, I pull over with the intention of asking someone inside for directions; but I notice something better.

Directly across from St. Paul's stands an i-site, one of a series of information centers I've noticed in pretty much every town I've driven through. I see from the sign on the door I've arrived just as the i-site is opening. The building is located next to the Wanganui District Council building, a large modern structure which makes the i-site look tiny, even threatened.

Inside, there are magazines for sale in a small rack next to a larger display of tourist guides and maps. I pass a model of a ferry or riverboat with the name "PS Waimarie" painted on the side. Above the replica is a soiled black and white photo of a burly, heavily mustached man with a shocking lick to his hair fringe. The inscription below it reads, "Alexander Hatrick". Just past this display is a counter and behind the counter sit three Maori women.

I had heard their voices rippling as I came in through the main doors. The three voices sound like one person having a conversation with herself, and enjoying it, asking herself a question, giving a quick response and then laughing hysterically before making another comment on the topic. My approach does not calm the flow.

"So I says to him, yous fellas better slow down. Or else you'll all have sore pukus!"

Laughter, especially from the enormous lady on the right who rocks precariously on her stool. She is weaving wide grass-like strands into a large mat.

"Nah, you should let them drink all night Polly. Then you could have a quiet house to yourself the next day!" exclaims the lady on the left, the only one wearing a uniform.

"Well," starts the middle lady in a sober tone. She is stirring something in a mixing bowl. She stops to raise her wooden spoon as she says, "Them boys have been up to no good lately. You're in for trouble, I say." And for a moment, the echo of her lone voice rests in the space between them.

Then there is a burst of laughter in unison on either side of her.

"The same kind of trouble you and Hoani got up to I suppose, eh? The deed without a name?" It's the large lady. And the middle woman laughs too, re-uniting the three voices into one.

During the conversation, I notice the three ladies take turns glancing at me, so they know I'm here, but this doesn't deter them. Finally, the i-site employee rises from her stool and approaches the counter where I'm waiting.

"Tena koe love. What can I do for you?" she asks. Her friends resume their conversation behind her, lowering their voices only slightly.

"Hi there. I'm just wondering if you can tell me where the nearest Catholic Church is."

"Catholic Church," repeats the older, thinner lady. Did she just imitate my accent?

"Turituri!" my assistant hisses over her shoulder. "That would be St. Mary's sir. Do you know Whanganui at all?"

"Not really. I just arrived last night."

"Well, St. Mary's is not far from here. It's the largest Catholic Church in Whanganui." She says "Whanganui" starting with an "f" sound instead of "Wanganui" like all the signs say. I ask her about this.

"The signs say 'Wanganui' but the signs are wrong," she says with a sympathetic smile.

"We'll soon change that!" says one of the other ladies. I can't tell by the voice which one.

"It's time! It's time! We'll soon have a referendum!" says the thin lady.

They laugh together. "A referendum!" they say. More laughter.

The attendant continues to look at me. "Our people have always known the awa—our river—as Whanganui. This place has always been Whanganui. But unfortunately, some people have difficulty pronouncing our names so they pronounce things as they wish. And so they take the breath out of the land."

"*Some* people!" I hear repeated behind her.

"Yes, we are patient teachers here. So, welcome to Whanganui. Would you like a map of our city?"

"Yes, please. I've left mine in the car."

After she shows me the location of the church on her map, I thank her and she asks, "What brings you to Whanganui?"

"I'm trying to find someone." I am tempted to keep my business to myself, but then I consider that these ladies may know more than the locations of churches and diners. "I'm trying to find my brother—Francis Murrihy?"

The voices stop. The weaving and stirring stops, and I see a look flicker between the twins in the back. My helper continues smiling at me without any hint of a reaction like her friends.

"Francis Murray?" she asks.

"Murrihy."

"I don't recognize the name."

"Sorry ladies," I say, looking past her, "do you know the name Francis Murrihy?"

Both heads stare down at the fat lady's project. The thin woman raises her eyebrows and pushes her lips forward. "No we don't." The one speaks for three. She then says something to her friend in Maori and the other replies in the same tongue. No laughter. No beaming smiles or slapping thighs.

"Did you say he was your brother?" the woman at the counter asks.

"Yes, he's from Canada like me. He doesn't look like me but he's about my height and build. I suppose he would sound like me to your ears, you know, with the same accent."

"We get a lot of accents coming through here my dear. Many Canadians too. You do sound like them, eh?" She flashes that smile. "I hope you can find him. Whanau is so important. That's family. Is there anything else I can help you with?"

"No, thanks." Turning to leave, I expect to hear the laughter resume behind me. The i-site remains quiet.

~

30 September 1999

Today I prayed the entire Rosary for the first time. I can't say any great revelations were had, but spiritually I feel relaxed, connected, reflective. I just don't feel I'm being heard in the same way I do when I pray to God on the back step.

I've told Kathy I'm joining the Catholic Church. Her reaction wasn't encouraging and I'm confused. I know she has had some negative experiences growing up Catholic but she's always wanted me to believe in God. I have to be careful here. I don't want her to kill this thing inside me before it has a chance to grow stronger.

I plan on asking Jean more today.

Task: Brainstorm all the gifts you have from God which will help you to hear His vocation for you.

31 October 1999

Last evening, we had Leigh over for supper and had a tremendous discussion. In fact, he described it as like praying. In the end I told him of my decision to become Catholic. I appreciated his candor; so open to talk about the Holy Spirit in his life and very knowledgeable and rational. Even Kathy seemed to get a lot out of our conversation which is great, but Leigh's example has shown me that I need to carry on with this, with or without her approval. I've decided to record more questions, some of which we discussed and others that have been inspired by our talk. I write these to remember last night, to clarify thoughts, to intrigue myself and to glorify the Mystery of God's works. I now know I can make this positive step without needing to know all the answers first and with or without Kathy's support.

Q: Why is the Pope infallible? Do I have to believe this as a Catholic? If yes, how do I choose to accept or deny this and how will it affect my life?

Q: Do I believe in the Mary apparitions at Fatima, Lourdes, Medjugore? (The RCC says they are worthy of belief, not that Catholics must believe them).

Q: Ditto for stigmata

Q: What place does Mary have in my spiritual and religious life?

~

I decide breakfast can wait as the Catholic Church is located along Guyton Street as well, just a few blocks back. Finding the church is no problem once I retrace my route. If this is the largest Catholic Church in the city it should be known as a cathedral, but there is no sign posting such a title at the front of the building. Is Whanganui even big enough to be classed as a city? When I arrive, I re-check the map and see that St. Mary's is also at the top of Campbell Street, the same street as my motel. It turns out the dead-end I avoided this morning actually contains my target. The city seems smaller already.

The church is set on top of a small rise a few meters above street level. The building itself is grey and not overly large-looking from the outside. It reminds me of the church in Taumarunui in its strange angular features and I wonder if the same architect has been involved. But this church is more symmetrical-looking with triangle facades around each side. The peaks of these point to a lotus-shaped cone atop which sits a cross. There are a small number of cars parked along the street, but it is difficult to say if all their occupants are parked there for the church. It's a Wednesday morning, but I wouldn't have a clue if that was a busy day for Catholics or not.

Climbing the steps to the church grounds, I am greeted by the sound of a ride-on lawn-mower advancing on my right. I walk toward the front of the church building and see that the mower has changed direction with me and is aiming for the same position. Undeterred, I consider that this rider could be my first port-of-call.

He's a middle-aged Maori man. He wears sunglasses over a broken nose and an uneven mustache. As he swings alongside me, he turns the mower off and rolls up the sleeves of his three-quarter length t-shirt, reaching out for a handshake.

"Good morning boss," he says in a friendly voice that is not matched with any smile. His face is dower and grim.

"Good morning," I reply, shaking his hand. His grip is firm and feels like one enormous callous wrapped in skin.

"Oh, you're not from around here, are you? I can tell by the accent. Where are you from—America?"

"Not quite—Canada."

"Oh," he chuckles, again without a hint of a smile, "Sorry about that. I know you Canadians don't like it when we think you're from America. It's like us and the Aussies, eh? Are you looking for Father?"

"I suppose I am. Well, really I'm looking for anyone who can give me some information about someone."

"Well, Father can do that, that's for sure. Who are you looking for?"

"I'm looking for my brother, Frankie Murrihy."

There's hesitation in his face. "You're Francis Murrihy's brother?" Again, his voice is expressive, but his face remains stoic, if not downright stern. "You don't look like Brother Francis."

"So, you know Frankie—Francis? Is he here in Whanganui?"

"Well, no, actually, he's not. Yeah, I know your brother. You do sound like him, eh? He's from Canada isn't he? Have you come all the way from Canada just to look for him?"

"From Nova Scotia, yes."

"That's right, Nova Scotia. New Scotland, eh? I remember Francis telling me that. My ancestors are from Scotland—you wouldn't know it to look at me, eh? Yeah, I went over to Scotland once, to my grandfather's hometown. I was walking down the street and some fella comes up to me, shakes my hand and says, 'You're a McLay aren't ye?' He knew my look. Does Francis know you're coming?"

"No he doesn't. I haven't spoken to him in years. Look, it's really important that I find him. It's a family emergency."

"Oh sure, sure. Nothing's as important as family, eh? But I think it's best you spoke to Father. He's going to be back real soon. You can come inside the church if you like or into the hall. We can have a cup of tea, eh?"

I agree to this and we walk through the front door, but instead of entering the church itself, the man leads me through an impressive foyer, obviously designed as a social area, and into a small kitchen. The lawn-mower, who tells me his name is Pio, boils a kettle as we talk more about Frankie.

"I met your brother shortly after I started working for Father. That'd be almost two years ago now. He was working for Father too. We had a few things in common. We'd both lost our families. You know his wife and kids were killed in a car crash?" He pauses for a moment. "Oh sorry, of course you'd know that. It's just that you said you hadn't spoken to him in a while. Hey, those kids would have been your niece and nephew, eh? I'm real sorry for you." His voice sounds child-like.

I thank him and encourage him to tell me more about Frankie, accepting a mug from him.

"Yeah, I lost my family too. Only, they're still alive. I lost them to drugs, alcohol and my own two hands." He holds up his fists in front of himself and looks at them as he turns them at the wrist. "I don't get paid for working for Father. It's my penance. I lost my wife and kids, but now I'm two years sober. The judge let me have a shorter sentence as long as Father promised to look after me, and he does. And I look after him as best as I am able. I use these hands for good now - a proper handy-man."

He flexes his fingers then wraps them around his cup. "Brother Francis understood the guilt, you know? I mean, Father does too, every priest must do I suppose. But Francis carried it with him. He carried the guilt and he carried the forgiveness." Pio nods toward a crucifix above the kitchen door. "Here at St. Mary's, he was the tuakana and I was the teina. Do you know what that means?"

"No, sorry, I don't," I say.

"It means he was the older brother, just like Jesus, and I was the younger brother, just like the disciples or me or you. See, in Maori culture, the older brother is the mentor to the younger brothers. He has certain rights and responsibilities. He speaks first and the rest of us have to listen and learn. Just like it is with Jesus. Your brother was my tuakana here under Father. The Brother was my brother." He finishes with a shy chuckle. "And now I meet the brother of my brother! How's that?" This time he breaks into a laugh that insists on a smile.

I look closer at this man, the brother of my brother. He has taken his sunglasses off now that we are inside. His eyes carry a weight unlike any I've seen. I've covered stories about domestic violence and have looked into many faces of both the abused and the abuser. Usually, there is a vacancy, a disconnection as if the individual has gone deeper inside to avoid any more pain. Pio's eyes are cracked around the outside as you see in the faces of Nova Scotia fishermen after a lifetime in the sun. His eyebrows are heavy and his eyelashes are long and out of control. But it is the eyes themselves that carry a weight, not a vacancy, not a disconnection, but a weariness from holding onto heavy pain.

My father never laid a hand on my mother. Only once can I remember him showing any anger toward her, after spending too much money during a shopping trip. Even then, it was more an expression of frustration than anger. Instead, if my parents were upset about something, the house just became quieter. Silent treatments were the weapon of choice. And at times these carried their own heaviness amid their vacancies. I've never hit Jordan either. My weapons are retreats into video games, sports, alcohol, road trips; hers are good old-fashioned guilt-trips and nagging.

Pio is a burdened man. He tells me, "I've turned back to Jesus though brother, and back to my roots. I was raised Catholic and Father has shown me how forgiving Jesus can be and how wonderful His Church can be. I owe the Church my new life."

Time is ticking on here and there's no sign of this priest. I find Pio engaging however; his face would make for a candid photo. One of the reasons I started working for the newspaper was because I do find people's stories interesting if they are unique and genuine. Pio is up front about his life, about his faults and his new perspective.

I ask, "But you must do something for money Pio?"

"I mow lawns for other people too, mainly parishioners. I sometimes work as a cleaner and handy-man at a couple of clubs in town at the weekends. But Father looks after me. I live in the Presbytery with him and we share kai and things like that. Your brother stayed with him too when he was here."

"So he doesn't live here anymore?"

"No," and here Pio becomes downcast. "He's moved on. But you'd be better off asking Father more about that."

"Where is your father—I mean where is Father, Pio? Will he be here soon?"

"Yeah, he should be. He was only finishing something in town I think. I'll go and check on him, eh?" Pio stands and goes back through the small room toward the church. I do like this guy, but I need to get a move on again, especially if Frankie is no longer here. Dammit, I thought I'd find him here.

Pio returns and says, "Well, his car is back so he must be here somewhere. I checked inside the church, but he's not there. He may be back at the house. Come with me over there, eh?"

I follow Pio outside and across the grounds that he was mowing until we reach a medium sized, one level house bearing the same paint colors as the church. The front door is open. Pio removes his rubber boots and leaves them on the porch. I hear him calling from inside, "Are you there Father? It's Pio. You have a manuhiri." An elderly voice replies with something indistinct from within. A few minutes later, Pio emerges, trailing behind a tall, thickly built man with white hair and glasses. He's also wearing my grandfather's clothes complete with suspenders over his tan dress shirt, holding up a pair of neatly ironed brown dress pants.

"Hello," he says. "What can I do for you?" He has a rich New Zealand accent that sounds like it's been infected with another, as if he is a native but has spent a large amount of time abroad.

"Hello Father, my name is Conrad Murrihy. I'm looking for my brother Frankie. I believe he used to live here?"

"He means Brother Francis, Father," interjects Pio.

"Now Pio, I've told you Francis was not ordained as a Brother. You must stop calling him that." Peering at me over the rim of his glasses, the old man says, "Why don't we sit down out here and have a talk?" He gestures to a pair of white lawn chairs on his front step. "Pio, I wonder if you'd mind bringing us a drink? Would you like a cup of tea?"

"No thank you. Your man and I have already had one while we were waiting for you to come back from town."

The old man chuckles, "Back from town, eh?" and he glances back at Pio. Then he asks me, "Well how about a beer then? Do you drink beer?"

It's ten-thirty in the morning. "No thanks, I'm fine really. I wonder if you could tell me where my brother went when he left here, or even better, where he is now. Did he move to another parish?"

"Pio, would you mind bringing me a beer?" he asks his house-mate, and Pio disappears again. Even after he's left, it takes a moment for the priest to turn around and face me.

"No," he says in a slow, drawn-out voice, "Francis didn't move to another parish . . . not exactly. Now look, if you're his brother, that means you've come an awfully long way to get here. Are you by yourself?"

"Yes, and I want to get back to Canada as quickly as I can, with Francis. Our mother is ill. Actually, she's dying."

"Oh, dying. Well, I'm sorry to hear that." Pio arrives back on the scene with a glass of amber beer.

"Here you are Father Picard." He pulls a chair from a room inside the house and sits behind the priest, just inside the doorway.

"But let me ask you something son," Father Picard continues. "Why is it that you want to bring Francis back with you?"

I'm surprised by the question. "Well that should be obvious I should think. He should be back with his family. My mother wants to see him before she dies."

"Well of course he should be and of course she does. But you haven't answered my question. Why is it that *you* want to bring him back?"

I don't need this shit. First the old Maori man at the cemetery, then the doddery old priest in Auckland and now this priss.

"Why does that matter?" I ask, not feigning any patience.

He leans forward and stares directly into my eyes. "It matters because, if you think taking him back to Canada is going to be easy, you may want to give up now, unless it's something *you* really want to do and not something you're doing for someone else. I can point you in the only direction I know, but there are others who would tell you to leave now, family or no family."

He leans back in his chair still looking hard into my eyes. Behind him, Pio squirms in his chair and, despite sitting inside, dons his sunglasses again and looks past us both.

I'm not sure what to say. "I want to bring him back because my mother wants to see him."

"That's not the same thing. Why do you want her to see him?"

"I want her to be happy."

"Do you want to see him?"

"I couldn't care less if I never saw him again."

"Well, there's an honest answer, eh Pio? I'm sure Francis would be stung by those words, or at least he would have been when we knew him." He takes a long sip of his beer and wipes his mouth, silently, deliberately returning the glass to the plastic table between us. "There must be some bad blood between the two brothers, between our Cain and Abel here, eh? So which one are you? Are you Cain—the brother who failed to gain God's favor? Or are you Abel—the brother who pleased God despite himself and was punished out of jealousy?"

"Look," I say angrily, "I don't know what you're talking about and I don't care. I just want to find my brother. Where is he?"

"I don't know where he is," he says, releasing me from his stare. Pio looks at the back of his head curiously, grimly. "But I will tell you where he went."

LONGING

The sky is clear and ngā whetū shine bright above te wahine's bowed head.

When our ancestors traveled to Aotearoa from Hawaiiki by waka over the oceans, it was by the sky they navigated their way here. Matariki led them here and led them safely home until they stayed. It was by ngā whetū that they could venture out but then return home. The sky is the gateway here.

Te wahine wants to venture out but is worried she will not be able to return home. She prays for direction. Our people once prayed to us and as a way of speaking to Io-wairoa. Going downriver is easy and is the only way to reach the mouth, the place of experience and wisdom. But there is great risk too. It is a path of tears.

She raises her head to the sky and turns away before we can see if she has opened her eyes to His guidance.

~

Ratana.

Father Picard finally opened up and gave me a location with some details about Frankie's departure. He told me Frankie had worked with him in the parish for almost a year, mainly as an assistant, but also as chaplain for the local prison. He had some difficulty with him, as his original request was for a priest who would be actively involved in the Catholic schools in Whanganui and believed "this one" would work out because of his teaching background. But Frankie refused to work in the school, "wouldn't go near them." Father Picard contacted the Marists in Auckland who apprised him of Frankie's tragic background, but this was not an acceptable excuse for such disobedience. They had many fall-outs over this, Frankie steadfastly refusing to visit schools or take part in the sacramental programs for children. Instead, he worked in Wanganui Prison and co-ordinated various adult programs in the city.

Though he never claimed the title of "Brother", he did not dissuade confused or admiring parishioners from addressing him in that manner.

They also argued over prayer, which struck me as ironic. Apparently Frankie prayed too much. Father Picard had wanted a man of action, a man to get things done. Instead, Frankie stayed up all hours of the night and wouldn't begin his day's activities until late in the morning. He would sometimes miss Mass. At other times, the priest would find Frankie unconscious by the altar, presumably after a night vigil. According to Picard, Frankie did not show enough "restraint" and left under dishonorable circumstances. In other words, he was dismissed.

Father Picard had assumed that Frankie would return to Auckland and straighten things out with the Marists. However, he had heard from a prison contact that he had gone to Ratana, some sort of Maori religious sect south of Whanganui. Frankie had come into contact with some Ratana people at the prison. Other than that, he had heard nothing from him in over a year.

So, now I need to visit some cult buried in the middle of nowhere, New Zealand. I leave the Whanganui city limits, crossing another bridge over the river, headed south on State Highway 3. I have no idea what sort of reception I'll receive. Churches are one thing—strange to me, but mainstream enough that you can knock on the front door and expect the same exchange you'd receive at any business—but a cult?

I've only ever heard about one cult in Nova Scotia—the Fisherman's Basket—named after a diner in Stellarton where many of its members work. I attempted to write a story on the group but with little success. Anyone connected with the Basket denies knowledge of a cult, they simply say they are all related, which is partly true. The rumors in the county say the group started as a break-away sect of the Brethren assembly in lower Sackville. Somehow, they ended up living in Lourdes, between New Glasgow and Stellarton, and establishing the restaurant. The leaders are an elderly couple, dominated by the matriarchal Rose Shepherd. None of the other members are married and stories circulate about sexual promiscuity, even orgies. Some members have branched out to own their own businesses as carpenters or plumbers, but apparently offer all their profits to the queen bee. I tracked her down only once and observed her exiting a member's property. A disgusting figure of a woman, she rarely leaves her house. I could never wrap my head around the sex part. A friend of mine who frequents the Christian Fellowship Church in New Glasgow told me that the group regard her as a prophet and that would explain the power she holds over them; something about her interpretations of the Bible.

Bullshit.

~

5 February 2000

<u>Work</u>

I like my job. At times I almost love it. In the middle of class, when I'm "on" and handling 100 things at once and gaining the respect of staff I feel on top of the world. Then I take

one

step

       back

and look from the outside and see I'm not where I want to be at all and nobody seems to, would want to, understand that.

I just feel out of place, like someone's going to catch me and say, "You don't suit that job. Give it to someone who does."

God, I'm not being ungrateful.

Kathy, I'm not going to do anything stupid.

I just recognize and sometimes wish others would too, that I want to do other things with this life.

At 29 I'm starting to notice others wasting, even dying, and with Jesus with me I see that I'm not doing His will yet.

He is my standard bearer now and I will be measured next to him.

~

I assumed I'd have another hell of a ride ahead of me as I left the city, but the highway runs through an extended stretch of flatlands passing through places named Kaitoke and Whangaehu. Hills surround me again once I turn off the highway along Ratana Road, but there are no gorges or anything so extreme here. It doesn't take long at all before I drive into the settlement marked as Ratana Paa. It looks to be a very small village on my right, with a vast spread of flat farmland to my left. It's difficult to tell how well the land is maintained, but I get the impression that this is a place aiming for self-sufficiency. I wonder if the sect is based in this village or if the village is the sect.

Father Picard could not, or would not, give me a contact in Ratana, so I have no idea where to begin looking. However, a starting place materializes less than a minute after entering the village. On my right I see the back of, what looks like, another church. If Frankie came to Ratana, surely he would have had some association with this place.

I turn down Taihauauru Street, and then Taitokerau to park in front of the church. Or temple. While the back of the building is shaped like a classic, linear church with a steep roof, the front looks more like a mosque. It is a larger, more grandiose version of the church I saw in Raetihi. Two towers frame the building, each capped with rounded, green roofs supporting antennae-like additions. Each tower stretches just beyond the height of the main building. Halfway down, a smaller, perpendicular roof connects the two structures, itself supported by two Doric-like columns that look like they've been modeled after the Acropolis. The front doors are bordered above by a classic, round-topped triangular window which mirrors the other stained-glass windows of the building. From where I am looking, just getting out of the Ford, the temple is framed by the front gate to the property. The gate also has twin towers, each column filled with Maori names in the style of a war memorial. The metal gate itself supports two simple signs each bearing words in Maori. I wouldn't know if these said, "Welcome, come knock on the door" or "Trespassers will be shot", but I do recognize the words "Arepa" and "Omeka"—Alpha and Omega.

I consider taking a chance through the gate as I have no other options, but for a young Maori woman sitting on a curbside bench just past the gates. I move toward her and see she is not alone, but has a young boy with her who has just set his bicycle on the ground to crawl up next to his mother.

She looks sideways at me and then away, perhaps hoping I will walk by. I slow my approach so as not to intimidate her. I decide to try something new.

"Kia ora," I say, "I wonder if you could help me. Do you know if anyone is at the church today that I could talk to?"

The young lady doesn't look at me, but she says gruffly, "Temple is closed. Nobody there."

I'm stuck. I look around for anyone else who might be near. A group of small children ride their bikes along the adjacent street. Across the road is a huge green field, completely void of any human activity. It's just me and this grumpy girl.

"I'm sorry to bother you, but I've come a long way in search of someone who might be here in Ratana."

"Ratana."

"Sorry?"

"You're saying it wrong. It's Ratana," she says emphasizing the first syllable and rolling the 'r'."

Great. What is it about this country? Everyone has a lesson to teach.

"Who you looking for?" she asks.

"Well, I don't know if you'd know him, but it's my brother. He's about my height. He doesn't really look like me, but he speaks with the same accent as I do. He's from Canada."

"I bet he looks more like you than he does me," she says then smirks at her boy who has been leaning into her and playing with a small flower as we've been speaking.

I laugh awkwardly, not sure how to interpret her comment. Father Picard said that Ratana is a Maori sect. Would that mean that everyone living in this village is Maori? I imagine Frankie would stand out if that were the case. "I suppose you're right," I say. "Are you sure you haven't seen someone like that here?"

"We get lots of visitors here mister. The Prime Minister visits here every year for Te Mangai's birthday. We get heaps of people visiting here—politicians, prophets, lots of people. Some from Canada— though most of them is Indians. I don't know nothing about your brother."

I sigh and look again for help from around the area. What can I do? "Would you know of anybody who might be able to help me miss? It's really important to me."

"Nah," she says abruptly.

I consider offering her some money to see if that opens any helpful ideas in her head, but think against it. There's no telling what that would look like, a strange white man offering this woman money on the side of the road.

I thank her anyway and return to the car. There looks to be about a dozen streets in the village at the most. There must be someone I can find help from, maybe in a convenience store or something. I drive down the remainder of the street and turn right. For a brilliantly sunny Wednesday afternoon, you would think there would be a lot more neighborhood children running around the place. Where is everyone else? Play Station has a lot to answer for. I may have been right about the number of streets, but the houses are scarce. There are more open fields, some with sheep, but few buildings and no sign of life. I turn right on Seamer Street, knowing I'm completing a circle to the main road coming into the village. More houses, no people. I slow down to have a look at a cemetery. Many of the grave-sites are painted whites and reds and blues much like the temple. A flicker of light at the back of the cemetery makes me stop. It's a reflection from the sunlight that catches my eye and I realize it's the metal of a ride-on lawn-mower and, sure enough, its rider is bent down beside it clearing an obstruction from the blade. What are the chances?

I get out of the car and approach the gate. I remember my lesson in Taupiri and stop outside, electing instead to try and garner the lawn-mower's attention. It seems like a long wait, but he finally stands, so I call out to him, "Kia ora!" He turns and walks toward me between the headstones, silhouetted by the sun behind him so that it is only when he is a few meters in front of me that I make out his features. This is a very old man, which is a surprise to me as his gait and posture are so assured. His face is aged and his hair is white. He is Maori and wears the most amazing facial tattoo I've seen since the sign entering Taumarunui. He looks old enough to have lived two lifetimes.

"Tena koe," he says, "You look like someone who doesn't realize he's found what he's looking for."

Far out. "Hi there," I say. "Thanks for coming over. There don't seem to be very many people around here today."

"It is a quiet day, that's for sure," he replies casting his eyes around the neighborhood.

"I'm wondering if you can help me."

"Who are you looking for?" he asks.

"I'm looking for my brother. He was meant to have come here about a year ago."

The old man tilts his head back and regards me, looking over my hair, my forehead, down to my nose and chin. Then he fixes his gaze on my eyes and sighs. "Hmmm," he says in a low tone. "I know your brother. There aren't all that many who look and sound like you who come to live in Ratana. Come walk with me."

He opens the gate to the cemetery and I step in, feeling uncomfortable but invited at least. He refastens the clasp of the metal gate behind me and walks along the front row of graves. Some graves seem to sit above ground encased in large white sepulchers.

"Your brother came to live here for a time. I understand he knew someone in the pa who works at the prison—an idealistic young man by the name of Rawiri. Rawiri has since left Ratana for work in Palmerston North. Rawiri introduced your brother to the story of Ratana, Te Mangai, the mouthpiece of God. Do you know anything of our prophet?"

I tell him I don't. "Can you tell me where he went after he left here?"

The old man walks slowly toward the back of the cemetery, pausing at every second or third grave site to look at the headstones. Stopping, he says, "Here lay two brothers, twins. They died a long time ago, but I still remember them well. In fact, I went to school with them. I even kissed the same girl as Hamuera, the better looking of the two. Time has gone quickly and they have gone too. Where do you say they have gone?"

"I'm not sure what you mean," I say, cautious not to offend this man who may yet help me.

"When one leaves a place, they must go to a new place. When one lives a life, one must consider at times what that place is. What do you say about this?"

"Well, I don't really know what to say. Whatever I say would just be guesswork. I would most likely be wrong."

"Te Mangai teaches, 'Unite unto God and then you shall unite unto the land.'

He stops at another grave marked with more plastic flowers and a bright orange windmill and says," This is my mother's body. She left this place in 1918 during the flu epidemic. I miss her. Would you say she has gone to a new place or would you say something else to me?" He looks at me with sadness and expectancy.

What can I say? "I guess I would say she has gone to a new place."

He nods his head. "So has your brother."

POWER TO UNDO THE PAST

19 May 2000

Self-Confidence

"Humility deserves honor and respect, but a low opinion of yourself leads to sin." - Sirach 4:20-31

The more I study, the more I see that all sin issues from the sin of pride—where we put our belief in ourselves ahead of our trust in God. Thus we break Jesus' commandment to love God first. It comes back to our decisions being either selfish or selfless. To love (actively love) each other as Jesus loves us (unconditionally) is completely selfless. It is what Adam and Eve chose not to do and what Lucifer chose not to do before them. They wanted to be as God was without humility.

So my dilemma arises: How can I be humble before God and live my life with humility without being a doormat?

Again, we are forced to reconcile what appear to be two contradictory approaches. God tells us that it is a sin to be prideful and yet we must not have a low opinion of ourselves.

Making a distinction is necessary and God grants us wisdom to do so. The sin of pride is committed against God when we assume we have created, imagined, resolved without His influence, that is, by ourselves as little mini-gods. Our pride must be felt in our awareness and acceptance of His presence and involvement in our lives and especially in our decision to acknowledge Him and answer the door *when he comes knocking. As Mary said "yes" to the Spirit, so too do we have a choice in how we react to God's desire to be part of our lives.*

No, we should not lose sight of God as the Lord and Master in our affairs. However, we should hold our heads high, thrust our chests out, stand tall and show how proud we are whenever we say "yes" to God by helping others, bringing peace, teaching a child, etc. We are given opportunities to say "yes" every moment of every day. When someone praises me for doing a good deed, I don't need to boast, but I should feel proud that I am walking in God's grace, doing His will through my faith and love for Him and others.

These Pentecostals who refuse to accept a compliment (to the point of being rude) miss the point of pride. They fear any thought of it or at least fear displaying it. Feel proud! Know that you are on the right path and feel confident God will help you fear no evil in that valley of opportunity.

~

Sitting in my motel room, I've completed half of the beer I bought at a "Liquor King" on the way back from Ratana.

I'm in shock and have been since I left the old man at the cemetery. Frankie is dead.

The television is off. I don't give a fuck about New Zealand culture. I don't care about any other news. My brother is dead and still no-one will tell me where the fuck he is.

After his little Mr. Miyagi routine in the graveyard, the old man confirmed that Frankie had indeed gone to the same place as his mother. After spending two months in Ratana, he moved back to Whanganui, though not back to the Catholic Church. The old man didn't know what he did back here, but he did tell me that Frankie came back to Ratana about three months ago. He was sick—with a neurological condition—and he had returned to Ratana to be healed. I asked him what he meant by that and he told me that their prophet had been a tremendous faith healer and that there are some in the Church who continue in his gifting. However, Frankie's condition continued to worsen and a month later he left Ratana to die. The old man claimed he did not know where Frankie went from there.

Bastard.

I open another bottle of Heineken. It's not my favorite but at least I recognize it from home.

Home. What do I do about home? What do I do about Mom? Do I call and tell them this news? Do I just fly back and tell them I couldn't find him? What's the best thing for Mom? What's the best thing for me? I want to see Mom. I want to go home.

The beer tastes good. Would Jordan be disappointed? Worried I'll get back on this train? Or for once would she try and understand what I'm going through? If she could see me in this shitty motel on this tacky couch in the middle of the fucking Pacific ocean, my mother dying on the other side of the world and all because of an arsehole brother who's been too selfish to call home? Instead, he was more concerned about God and his mission in life and how good he felt. Well wouldn't God want him to care for his mother? Maybe if he'd come home he wouldn't have died, Kathy and the kids would still be alive, none of this shit would be happening.

Tonight, I finish off this case. Tomorrow, I sleep until I'm good and god-damned ready to get up. Then I go home.

~

I've never written a will. Jordan and I have never been mature enough to seriously sit down to write one. So if I go first, all my possessions will go to her and Jade I suppose.

A few years ago, I covered a story about a young Pictou County man who died at sea after being caught out between Caribou and Prince Edward Island in a freak storm, unheard of really in that sheltered stretch of ocean. In the coast guard report, no fault was laid on the preparations of the young man or his Newfoundland ship-mates. All were considered to be able seaman and had followed due protocols. Since then, I have reasoned that no amount of preparedness will prevent what will eventually come to us all. The rest is fall-out and will need to be managed by those left behind. I'm not hedonistic or callous, just pragmatic about the investment of my energy. Discussing such things with Jordan would produce nothing but diminishing returns.

What I have stated to her on several occasions is that I want to be cremated. I don't see any need for my body to take up more space than it has to. My family has started burying their ashes in a cemetery near Sylvester in neat little plots, clearly marked with respectable little plaques. It is enough. No sepulchers, no gaudy displays of resistance or false hopes.

However, on this morning, now that the shock and alcohol-induced anger and clarity have dissipated, I am confused as to what to do next. The rain does not help. It is pounding down now, battering the roof of my motel, clouding any vision out of my window and layering the steps outside my room with water that is already half an inch deep. I am confused about Frankie's body. And what's more, I'm confused about why it should matter to me anymore.

It's Mom again. I've woken up this morning knowing that I have to make that phone call, if not now then sometime between now and when I leave the country. It'll be Dad I speak to of course, and that will be bad enough, but knowing that this is the fruit of my mission for Mom is killing me.

But what are the alternatives? Stay? For what—to find a body? To bring closure to a dying woman who will still die regardless?

And at what cost? The old man at Ratana was not helpful. Where would I look next? Where would Frankie go "to die"? Auckland? Surely the Marists would have told me if he had come back to them. There was no hint from anyone that he had gone back to Taumarunui, perhaps to be buried with his family. Australia? Even if he had gone back there that trip would certainly add weeks to my stay here, more weeks away from Mom.

Ridiculous. What a ridiculous situation to be in and a cruel thing Frankie has done to us all. I abandon my breakfast, wash the dishes and pack my loose clothes back into my suitcase. I need to get on the road. I'll make the phone call from the airport where there will be no temptation to stay longer, no matter what Dad might say.

~

22 May 2000

<u>*My Anointing?*</u>

Lately, I have heard and read a lot about God's anointing of His people, giving us each a personal, individual mission to complete in His name. Along with this, He intends to give us all the gifts and help needed to accomplish this mission once we discover it and choose to accept it.

Each day I pray, "You anoint my head with oil." Up to this point I have associated this with Confirmation and the sacrament of the Holy Spirit. Now, I also recognize this as God's anointing for my mission in life. To discover God's mission for me, I must focus on the gifts He has given me from the beginning. Lord, reign in me.

~

The rain really is pissing down. I hate turning the windshield wipers on full-tilt but visibility is so poor. Driving out of this strange little city, over the muddying river via the Dublin Street Bridge has me in a foul mood. Traffic is light enough for me to cross over without issue and I'm able to get some respite at the gas station by the roundabout while I refuel the Focus.

Once the car is filled, I shelter inside the station with the attendant, a portly lady with short, red-dyed hair. I ask her, "Does it rain like this very often here?"

"Not like this," she says. "But October is our rainiest month. The lawns grow quickly this time of the year. Sometimes we get slips when the rain is this heavy."

"Slips?"

"Little mudslides and rockfalls. You may see some along the highway, especially through the gorges if you're heading north."

Great. "Are they big enough to block the road?"

"Not usually. Just be careful 'cause you'll have only one lane to drive in if you come across any. I reckon you might 'cause the rain's been heavy like this since I started early this morning."

I thank her for the warning and turn to go back out into the downpour. I stop at the doors wondering if what I'm seeing is an image created by the clouded glass and the shadows of the day.

Completely filling the road, moving from the right of the station, is a great mass of people, perhaps two hundred of them. At the head of the group, held by some unseen figures that have already passed by, is a large black, orange and white banner. The crowd is quiet and getting pummeled by the rain as they make their way across the roundabout and toward the bridge and city center.

They are generally dressed for the weather and it is clearly a protest of some sort. They carry placards which read, "How would you like it, Michael, if we took the H out of your name?" and "Can we have access to YOUR property?" I scan the faces as they process by. Almost all the faces are brown, Maori, of various ages, and a mix of men and women. One woman is holding the hand of a boy, a pre-schooler who is cuddling close to her under an umbrella long since broken against the rain. A few people behind her, I see a young man with no hat or umbrella but a full head of dreadlocks reaching down to the backs of his knees.

Peering closely to make sure, I identify the man walking beside him. It's Pio, the priest's grounds-keeper from the Catholic Church. He looks in my direction briefly and pauses long enough to make me think he spies me through the glass. What's more, his pause seems to cause the man behind him to look my way and my eyes meet his. It's Frankie!

I grapple with the door, pulling it when it's meant to be pushed. I rush out across the bay of the gas station, past the Focus and out onto the roundabout with the passing crowd. I've lost sight of him and desperately try and spot him or Pio or the man with the dreadlocks. I call out to him over the thunderous rainfall. Some of the protesters turn to look at me, many stare straight ahead, steadfastly advancing toward the bridge where the mass condenses into a thinner, impenetrable line. I push into the crowd trying to get to the entrance of the bridge before he does.

A huge Maori man shoves me. "What do you think you're doing bro?" He stares at me menacingly but I ignore him and continue my drive forward through the pack. I shoulder women aside and one man picks up his son and shouts something in Maori at me. I still can't see Frankie, but I spot the dreadlocks. He's about fifteen feet in front of me and nearing the bridge.

I try exiting to the left side of the group but am now hemmed in tight, and I notice the wave of antipathy directed toward me by these wet and determined faces. They are marching on with or without this intruder.

"Frankie! Frankie!" I shout at the top of my voice. "It's Conrad! Frankie!"

I'm knocked to the ground, pushed hard in the back, and the crowd steps around, over and on me. I sprawl on the wet cement until I feel a reprieve, as space opens and I hear a familiar voice.

"Brother! What are you doing man?"

It's Pio. He's leaning over me with his arms spread to ward off his fellow marchers. "Bro, what are you doing?" he asks, rainwater flowing down his nose and into my face.

"My brother," I splutter.

"Yeah that's right bro, I'm the brother of your brother."

"No, my brother. Frankie was right behind you. Where is he?"

"What, you mean behind me in the hikoi? Nah mate, Brother Francis isn't with us in this march. I told you, I haven't seen him since he left. You must be seeing things in the rain." He raises his head to look at the torrent out of one eye. "C'mon boss, let's get you inside, eh?"

He lifts me and I feel the strength in his arms. As he walks me toward the gas station, I look over his shoulder at the crowd which has now completely entered the bridge and allowed traffic to flow through the roundabout again. God this is awful, to hear his words and yet still believe what I saw. But I go with Pio.

~

Sitting in a back room of the gas station, I thank the attendant as she hands me a machine-made cappuccino. After restoring me to the indoors and assuring me again that Frankie was not with him, Pio has left to rejoin the march. The attendant has given me a towel to dry my head and kindly offered me a place to rest up before moving on.

After drinking the coffee, I finish drying myself as best I can and look forward to the car's heating system to do the rest. I walk out into the main area and see the attendant talking with another lady. She is about the same age with even shorter and redder hair.

"Bloody Maoris. You shoulda seen the way they treated this fella. I never seen anything like it. I mean, this guy was going mental, eh? He just took off into the rain and jumped right into the middle of them. I don't know what he was on about. But these bloody Maoris just shoved him on the ground and walked all over him, even with the ground being so wet and all."

The other woman snorts, "He had to learn the hard way, eh? Don't mess with Maoris when they want their land. They'll eat you alive."

The two women laugh and the attendant sees me walking toward them. "How's it goin'?"

"I'm OK, thanks." I nod to the new woman. "Thanks for the towel and the coffee. That'll really help. I don't have a place to go for a proper shower unless I book a motel again, so I appreciate it."

I turn toward the door, but she stops me by saying, "What did you think you were doing anyway?"

"Oh, I thought I saw someone I knew, that's all."

"Was it that fella who brought you in here?"

Just to keep it simple I answer, "Yes."

"Well it's a good thing you found him mister, or that he found you. We woulda been scraping you off the roundabout otherwise. You're crazy walking into a hikoi like that."

"Hikoi?"

"Yeah, it's a Maori march. These jokers are just imitating the one they did to Wellington a few months ago. It's because of the election."

Not really caring, but seeing her attitude toward the marchers, I say, "Well for imitators they seem pretty committed walking in that heavy rain like that."

"Crazy's more like it. They're just making a big show to impress whoever wins the election. We're gonna have a new mayor tomorrow night. They just want to remind them about Maori land rights. Not that it'll make a difference. Just like Moutoa, eh Sandy?" she says to the other woman.

"Aw yeah, what a pain in the ass that was. We couldn't walk through the park or do anything even near it. My parents were pissed off, eh?" She looks at me. "And get this, then they go and cut the head off the statue of that guy—what's his name—he used to be prime minister or something."

"Anyway," I say, "I'd better go. I've got a long way ahead and it's going to be slow driving in this rain. Thanks again."

"OK, seeya mister", the attendant says and the two friends continue their talk as I leave the station.

~

After the non-sighting of Frankie, I find it difficult to leave the city. Already the memory of it blurs, but I have to trust my eyes for a living, discerning or not. I know what I see and I see what I know. But I can't imagine why Pio would lie to me. Lying to a person on a mission like mine must be as sinful as it gets. I believe him. Frankie couldn't have been there. But it's like when you can't find your keys or your wallet in the house. You start looking in the places that make sense. You check the places you normally put them and you retrace your steps, trying to follow a logical path back to their location. When this doesn't work, you expand your search looking in other rooms, but while you do that, you periodically return to the places that make sense, even though you've checked them several times. Then you start to look in places that don't make sense—under cushions, behind cupboard doors, in the fridge. Logic has to be abandoned when it fails.

These are my thoughts as I drive up State Highway 4 and away from the last place I saw Frankie, whether he was there or not. The rain has not let up and I'm thinking about slips and trying to dry with the Ford's heater and air conditioner working overtime.

I hear Pio's voice and feel his nose rain fall on my face. I see the white sepulchers of the Ratana cemetery. I sense the river to my left, ever present this side of Upokongaro. Unbelievably, as I approach the village, the rain doubles its intensity. Even with the wipers operating at maximum, I simply can't see the road. In my rear-view mirror, I watch tail-lights of cars pulling over to the side of the highway. I do the same, across from the small wooden church, but keep the engine and air conditioner running.

I lean back against the headrest and close my eyes, feeling the fan on my clothes. My shoes are soaked so I kick them off by the pedals, lifting my socked feet toward the heat below the dashboard. I listen to the rain which sounds more like something rolling over the car than falling on it.

~

We remember Te Kooti and his stand-off at Te Porere pa near our headwaters. Some say Tūwharetoa allowed him to harbour in their lands so that he might be protected and his movement might continue. Others say that the site was not fit for such resistance and that Tūwharetoa orchestrated his failure.

We must be careful what we ask of Io-wairoa. Like the taniwha, like our kaitiaki, He is our guardian, but He is not safe. He will see His own will done and knows our hearts better than we know them ourselves.

Te Wahine prayed and today she is walking up the steps to another house, a house with a fine gate made of wood like totara, red and rich. She raises her ringless hand and knocks on the door. It opens and she is greeted by a man, a different man from the image. The two of them walk back down the bank and out of our vision.

We realize that this is Taranaki and te wahine is Pihanga.

~

Awaking, I've lost track of how much time I've spent on the side of the road. The rain has not relented and as I open my eyes, I turn my head to re-familiarize myself with my surroundings, or with what I can see of them. Across the highway, I make out the church and its sign, posted on a smaller, much simpler version of the Ratana temple entrance. In all this water, the roof appears to me as an upside down boat. I blink a few times to see that I'm reading correctly—the sign says "St. Mary's". Another one. Or am I back in Whanganui?

I look to the left, past a gate toward the river which has risen to cover a portion of a farmer's field. It rushes back toward the city and the ocean, taking its darker look with it. And I remember that it is here that the river meets the road.

Both sets of my grandparents lived next to rivers in Nova Scotia. My mother grew up near the West River—she used to jump into it from a rope slung from a tree branch. But the river of my childhood ran behind my father's parents' house, which was a short walk from my own. I have never known the name of that river; we just called it "the brook". While the brook must have had an extended relationship with the other parts of the area, to me the brook only existed between the bottom of a hill to the north of my grandparents and a road bridge to the south.

My brother and I, along with the other neighboring boys, fished for trout. We swam in the deepest parts we could find, though no part was over our heads and I never really learned to swim well. We ate and threw crab-apples. We went home with stains on our clothes from the tar and creosote of the bridge. We both had occasion to step on nails stuck in old boards lying around. When we were older, we hid cigarettes under trees along the higher banks. At times, we were the brook and the brook was us. And yet, we had no name for it other than the one we had given it. We knew its direction, its currents and its moods, but we didn't know its source or its destination.

Through the rain, I watch the Whanganui river rage south, moving toward me and away from me at the same time. The water I look at in one moment is gone the next and replaced by new water, yet all the water is one river with no distinct separation of parts. It surely has a source and a destination, yet in this moment, all that exists is the water and embankments in view, constantly the same, constantly changing. If I have any sense of eternity, I experience it in the mystery of a river. It is surely going someplace, even if I don't see where that is.

Frankie has gone somewhere. Mom will go somewhere. In Taumarunui, two rivers meet and move on to someplace together. I'm not sure where this leaves me and my brother, but I realize I have to stay here and try. I drive the car out onto the highway and turn back toward Whanganui despite the rain. Otherwise, I might change my mind.

THE NAVAL CHORD

28 June 2000

Today I found my calling.

A word of knowledge: "Francis! I have given you a great gift so that you can see what it would be like if I punished you for your sins. Turn to my righteousness with this word of knowledge so I do not have to test your character by experience. I have chosen you to be a model, a healer to your family and my flock. Walk in faith now, with integrity and truth toward your destiny. Move now before I move you!"

God has given me my calling, Jesus shows me the Way, and the Holy Spirit stays with me in courage.

I found it! I'm not letting go of it despite doubts, circumstances, tragedies.

~

The receptionist at the Ballance Inn seems happy to see me again, but who can tell what she actually thinks? I'm grateful to have a shower and put on dry clothes. The rain has let up slightly but it's late afternoon and I'm not in the mood to go out again just yet. Besides, I have two places to continue my search and one of them can be initiated in a motel room.

Where would Frankie have gone to die? Without any information, I need insight into his mindset and his connections. The original

Frankie I knew changed. He turned religious, he was depressed, he was non-communicative with his family. Today, I start by reviewing and finishing his journals. Tonight, or tomorrow, I'll track down Pio. Frankie would not have been well enough, and perhaps not inclined to travel far, certainly not to Australia or Canada, and hopefully not out of the North Island. I need clues—people and places I haven't paid attention to before.

I lean back on the bed with a coffee and his books spread around me, but in chronological order. There certainly is no pattern to his journaling. If there are any recurrent themes, they would be in his searches in religion and his periodic references to family, particularly Kathy. There are extended sections of planning notes for moving the family back to Canada—airfares, account balances, quotes from moving companies, estimates about sales of personal items. These appear repeatedly every few months as if it was a discussion that arose, then dissipated, only to re-configure. Jordan and I have those too. They seemed to have feet in both countries. There is also an increased focus on fixing himself—from organizational strategies to making reparations for increasingly smaller sins, like replacing cookies that he had stolen from staffroom supplies.

5 April 2000

<u>*God My Father*</u>

> *There are gaps inside me.*
> *These are a result of the imperfect love I have received from my parents and the rest of the world. I can recognize these failings without blaming or condemning them.*
> *They are a gift given to me by God wrapped in an imperfect yet beautifully human package.*
> *Up until now, I have regarded them as perfect and felt guilty if I ever found fault with them.*
> *In effect, I have idolized them.*
> *With "perfect parents", I felt no need for God as my Father.*
> *In fact, to acknowledge a need for the perfect parenting of God feels like a betrayal of my parents.*
> *I now understand this is not a betrayal.*
> *It is a realistic assessment of my parents' role in my life as models of God's love.*

It has been unrealistic to expect my parents' love to be as perfect and fulfilling as God's, whose love is all sufficient.

I can now forgive my parents for all their failings, mistakes and rejections.

I can also stop seeking their approval in all that I do and focus solely on God's approval, living as a God-pleaser, not as a people-pleaser.

I trust God to love me as a Father & Mother.

I trust Him to be nurturing and disciplining, my provider, protector, savior and inspiration.

I trust Him to bless my parents for all they have done and do.

Coming to New Zealand caused a separation from my parents. Here I have sought and found my true Father, my perfect creator who approves of me before-hand and has a great plan for me to restore and heal others.

Praise God. Thank you Jesus. Come Holy Spirit.

I feel angry as I read this—all this religion messing with Frankie's head and leading him further away from us. I toss this book aside and something falls out on the bed. It's a postcard. On one side is a picture of four children in silhouette all holding hands as they climb up a hill. In the bottom right-hand corner is the "Possibility Thinkers Creed" of Robert Schuller, a name I recognize as a television evangelist. On the reverse is a letter written in Frankie's handwriting, addressed to "Rev. Stephen White", St. Andrew's Presbyterian Church, Pictou. There is no date.

Just a quick update on Kathy, Jacob, Kim and myself. We're doing well here in N.Z. and are progressively achieving goals. As a couple, we have not yet found Heaven here but with less concern for in-laws in our daily lives, we are growing stronger together. I have chosen new directions in my personal life which have helped me dramatically at work and home. I think of our meetings often and thank you again for your wisdom and compassion. Please drop us a line, we'd be happy to hear from you.

Francis Murrihy.

I don't recognize the name of the minister, even from stories I've covered in the Pictou area, though I do know of St. Andrew's. "Our meeting"? Religious instruction? Marriage counseling? It was difficult to tell if Frankie and Kathy were having marital difficulties. Both seemed in favor of growing a distance between the rest of us.

It still hurts to think of their rejection of me and Jordan when they didn't come to our wedding. We never understood what we had done wrong. Mom and Dad said it wasn't us, that they just needed time together to forge a marriage without extended family.

A few weeks after they left for New Zealand, Mom broke down crying in my kitchen while relating a story about seeing Frankie in the supermarket a few months before. I had never seen my mother cry before and certainly not in the state she fell into that night. She told us that, while she was shopping, she saw Frankie down the other end of an aisle. He looked at her long enough to prove that he'd seen her, but he didn't acknowledge her at all. Instead, he pulled out of the aisle with his kids in his cart and headed in the opposite direction. For the rest of her excursion, she saw him deliberately avoid her several times as he made his way around the place with Kathy.

The cruelty of it pisses me off and I don't understand it. For all the fights, blow-ups and misdemeanors Jordan and I have inflicted on one another, we have never taken it out on our Jade or our in-laws. Family relationships are unconditional and non-negotiable. It's that simple.

Reading more of Frankie's next journal, and after wading through some type of self-help exercises, I find a little treasure that restores my faith a bit—a short note followed by two letters written to Jacob and Kim.

21 August 2000

Celebrate marriage—God's love shining into the world in the expression of a relationship between husband and wife.

Jacob,

You are my boy and I love you. You have been a shining gift to us since you were born and continue to be to all those who know you. I'm sorry if I don't spend enough time with you and I'm sorry we've taken you away from so much love that you had in Canada in your grandparents and family. You are a treasure from God, a perfect seed planted in our lives and, as you grow, you cause everything around you to blossom. Your spirit is loving and playful and you already show such wisdom and joy in God's world. You will surely grow to be a great man—loving God, your wife, your children, my grandchildren. I thank God every day that he has blessed me with you and has brought us closer to Him through you. I love you son and always will.

Kim,

You are my little girl and I love you. I never knew I could love someone as much as your brother until you were born. You were such a quiet baby—I would never have known that God had given you such a wonderfully bold, righteous soul. Your spirit and energy lift me every day. I'm sorry if I respond to you in anger too often. I'm sorry we've moved so far away from the love of family in Canada and for so long. You affect everyone's lives that you touch, giving smiles and songs, dances and pictures and beautiful stories. You are so good and God is working and playing through you, showing His love for the world as He gifts us all with the treasure that is you. You are a flower, a star, a music box dancer and my daughter and I will love you forever, I'll like you for always.

It's late, I'm tiring and I don't feel like I'm finding anything that's helping me. But I realize I'm getting near the end as this entry was written two months before the accident. For some reason, knowing this, I half expect there to be some foreshadowing of the tragedy in Frankie's writings, as if I am reading a story for which I already know the ending and the author is being fair enough to provide hints about the outcome. But of course, he didn't know what would happen. His journal continues to address Bible passages he was reading, interspersed with poems or prayers.

One entry, written just three weeks prior to the end, looks like a will and contains names of friends and family, most of whom I know well.

4 Oct 2000

To Kathy, I leave "Angel Eyes" because it meant something once, "With Arms Wide Open" because you like it and "I Will Leave a Light On", because I have so often felt like you'd left me for darker places.

To Maximus, I leave "China Grove" because it'll see you out of this world in style.

To Hamstring, I leave you "Shine on You Crazy Diamond", all parts and only to be listened to at 5am with headphones.

To Howard, I leave the entire "White Album" because we both know all the words.

To Lester, I leave "Bohemian Rhapsody" because I can still picture you head-banging in aisle 39.

To Jacob, I leave "Just the Two of Us": because Daddy loves you, Daddy loves you.

To Dingo, I leave "Stairway to Heaven" because we both know when to put the pick in our mouth.

To Peter, I leave the theme to "Mission Impossible", a show I'd never seen and a dance we'll never do again. Also: "You Shook Me All Night Long" and "Walk the Dinosaur".

To Manon, I leave "I'll Be There for You", though I never understood it.

To Moe, I leave "Whole Lotta Love". Thanks for the party and the Keith's and the Pep when I was down.

To Edmund, I leave "Bust a Move" because we did.

To Larry, I leave "Sultans of Swing" because a simple bass line is hard to find.

To Kim, I leave "Man, I Feel Like a Woman" because you will be so.

To Dad, I leave "The Minstrel of the Dawn" because of the stories and the humility.

To Mom, I leave "Jesus Christ Superstar" because I still don't know how to love you.

What a pity Frankie didn't wait to die before leaving all these things behind.

The rain stops and I sleep.

~

It's morning and it is quiet; so quiet, I can hear the river running even this far from the bridge, which doesn't seem possible considering how far away it is from my motel. No car noises, no wind, no Asian chatter in the hallways from the cleaning service. It must be early and I remember it's Saturday.

That would explain the crap I had to listen to across the street last night. Staying in the city, I expected it might be hard to sleep at times with unfamiliar city noises as back home, we live in a such a rural area. Once I was awakened by the voices, I watched some entertainment in the front yard of a small white house just over from my sliding glass doors at the back of the motel. It may have been the remnants of some party—four men, some dressed in red shirts or wearing red ball caps, speaking in deep, obnoxious and at times violent tones. They were only talking to one another, but constantly calling each other out as "fucking cunts" and threatening to give each other the bash. It was difficult to tell how serious it was going to get. After several minutes of this, the men would laugh and joke with each other, making consistent use of the same profanities. Then another period of threats and challenges to fights. As I say, entertaining but a lot of thuggish bullshit at the same time, and it was a wonder to me that no-one called the police to come around.

From my bed, I flick on the television set and skim through the channels looking for some news, maybe some weather for today and over the next few days. Although the sun is streaming through the sheers of my room, I only see children's cartoons and infomercials that may have been running all night. I settle on what appears to be a local channel reporting news about the mayoral election. Because of the hour, I presume it is a story originally broadcast last night.

It's Election Day—the issues separating the two candidates seem inconsequential really, but the current mayor has been in power for eighteen years, so people here are apparently sure the new man will win. There's no mention of the protest I saw yesterday and no mention of any issues I would imagine provoked Maori to run one. Perhaps the station attendant was right—imitative. I watch some highlights from a debate about the "foreshore and seabed act". A pasty man with thinning hair calls it a "race-based land grab" and says that, "Many who claim to be Maori have more European blood in them—there are no full-blooded Maoris left in New Zealand anyway." He is challenged by a scary looking Maori man with a tight t-shirt and slicked back hair who says that one drop of Maori blood is enough to make a person Maori. And so it goes. I wonder if the land issues in New Zealand are similar to ones we have in Canada? Have they ever had an Oka uprising? Have Maori ever had separatist ambitions like some in Quebec? Who knows, who cares.

I had hoped that reading Frankie's journals last night would have given me some ideas of where he went. I guess it was desperate— even if I had found something leading, I don't know this country well enough. He doesn't mention many other places that seem significant. He describes the trip they took to Napier on the east coast. He refers to a revelation he had while he was in Tauranga, but I think he was only there for a short family vacation. There are trips to Hamilton and Taupo mainly for shopping or courses he attended. He spent the night in Cambridge with a Catholic school teacher who was on the same course. He went canoeing on the Whanganui with the staff from St. Patrick's, skiing on Mount Ruapehu as a school trip. New Plymouth to see a concert. None of these places or excursions suggests a religious or spiritual connection that he may have re-sought as a dying man.

Spiritual. Now there's a word I don't use very often, or really understand. It's a word used by religious people, but also by those who claim to somehow not be religious—astrologers, Feng Shui practitioners, new age, crystal-praying gypsies or hippies you meet at markets selling their wares. Spirituality—religion without the ritual— for people who don't want to go to church but talk a lot about healing and second sight.

I once covered a story about a troupe of these gypsies traveling through Nova Scotia. They had set up one of their "mystic fayers" in New Glasgow without incident, but their intended stop in Antigonish was causing a stir. My editor sent me further afield than normal to report on the fuss, and contrast their reception in Pictou County with that in Antigonish. It was meant to be a piece to examine the cultural fabrics of small town Nova Scotia, always a popular angle in the Maritimes.

Antigonish has a long tradition in Catholicism—still evident in the presence of St Francis Xavier University, where Frankie studied while I attended St. Mary's in Halifax. The Bishop of Antigonish had issued a statement from the pulpit one Sunday morning, warning the faithful of the approaching gypsies and the false ideas they were spreading about spirituality, healing and religion in general. Another interesting component of the story was that the Bishop's views were being endorsed by an increasingly influential Pentecostal Church in the area, led by a man named Donald Merchant who was also referring to himself as a bishop. Merchant had established a reputation for criticizing the Catholic Church, a risky venture in Antigonish.

Gypsies, Catholics and Pentecostals. It did make for an interesting piece, but when I attended the fair in Antigonish, the anticipated fireworks failed to ignite. The event was attended by bored housewives, hippy-wannabe students, and any number of normal-looking Nova Scotians who may well have spent their Saturday at the fair and their Sunday in church. The gypsies sold their crystals, fortunes and new-age literature and left. Antigonish still stands and I'm sure the churches are still collecting their tithes. A lot of hoo-hah, signifying nothing.

That must be why my family has steered clear of religion. It was OK to go to Sunday school because that was tradition. But we had no desire for silly confrontations or spooky experiences and were quite happy with the world in front of us: our house, our friends, our lives.

What in the hell caused Frankie to get caught up in this shit? From the journals, he seemed unhappy in lots of ways, ways that he never showed in letters home. The pain he must have felt when Kathy and the kids died would have been unbelievable. We felt it too, all the way back home. But he was searching for something before then. The television evangelists always seem to prey on people who are unhappy—or stupid. Frankie wasn't stupid. Though he may have been naive, he was the smartest person I knew growing up other than Dad. So what was he searching for? Whatever it was, it's led him to this—death in a backward little island on the other side of the world, away from family and surrounded by moronic thugs, racist simpletons, unintelligible motel clerks and old men who keep secrets from you and then get pissed off when you break stupid rules you were never told about in the first place.

I get up and shower before heading into town to find something to eat. I don't know what time Pio will be around but I give him until 9:00 before I head over to the church. It's a beautiful morning with no indications of the deluge we experienced yesterday other than the roar of the river. The church grounds are quiet and there's no sign of Pio or the priest. I make my way over to the presbytery and ring the bell a couple of times. No answer. From the front porch, I survey the grounds looking for any evidence of life, but see no activity and hear nothing more but the occasional car driving by. What to do?

I sit in one of the plastic lawn chairs where I spoke with the priest a few days ago. Waiting seems to be the best option. Where would I go anyway? I don't have any other leads or contacts and I don't care to go sight-seeing. I'm no tourist here. I'm no longer looking for Frankie walking around the city, instead I'm looking for . . . what? Another grave-site? A headstone? Ashes scattered somewhere? What if he's been cremated and scattered? There will be nothing of him to take back to Mom. And if he's buried? I'm not about to exhume him and fly him back to Nova Scotia. I don't even have a camera to take a picture of a headstone for her and is that what she would want anyway? Is that the kind of closure she would want once she finds out he's gone?

A few hours pass. There's no sign of anyone connected to this place and it's lunchtime. My body's clock seems to have finally adjusted and I'm getting hungry at traditional times. I walk back to my car in front of the church, but before I leave I check a sign at the front for service times. The next Mass is this evening at 6:00. If I come back then, I can at least talk with Father Picard and find out where Pio is if he's not back here himself by then.

As I drive away from the church and toward the city center, I realize I'm entering the green area I avoided on my first day in Whanganui. It's a small park with few buildings. One prominent example is the Sarjeant Art Gallery, a white symmetrical building with an attractive round roof on the far end. Any other time, I would be curious enough to go in as I like art galleries. I drive past a war memorial and out of the park and left on Drews Avenue. As I approach the river, I see the beginnings of a row of industrial waterfront buildings similar to those in New Glasgow so I assume there's no food down that way and turn left on Rutland between some older brick buildings that remind me of the Westville post office back home. This city really seems to be a large town and very familiar for all its differences from Pictou County.

At the end of Rutland, I see another park and initially I think I've somehow circled back toward St. Mary's. But this green belt seems to be smaller. I'm curious to see the state of the river and follow its sound. Turning onto Taupo Quay, I see she is full to bursting along the banks, lively and dark, presumably rushing to meet the ocean further past the city center. I drive by the other side of the park and see its sign at the entrance. This is Moutoa Gardens and I remember the comments from the gas station attendant about the Maori occupation here. I look out for the headless statue but don't see it. The story reminds me of a photograph I took as part of an early job with *The Casket* in Antigonish. Some revelers had placed an empty beer bottle in the hand of the statue of St. Francis Xavier in front of the university so that he had a cross in one hand and an ale in the other. From what I knew of the activities that occurred on that campus, I thought the image was not only funny and ironic, but poignant. My editor agreed. The good people of Antigonish who rang to threaten and harangue me did not. Uptight, narrow-minded religious farts.

Just past the Gardens I find a restaurant and I eat one of the most delicious hamburgers I've ever had, once I've removed the beetroot from it. What an odd addition to a hamburger.

~

The story is told as the battle of the mountains. Mount Taranaki lived with the central mountains—Tongariro, Ngauruhoe and Ruapehu. He fought with Tongariro over the mountain maiden, Pihanga. Tongariro won and Ruapehu sent Taranaki away, following the river of tears to cool and cleanse his feet until he carved his own way to live in the west.

The story is told as the battle of the mountains, but Pihanga's story is never told, her mauri is never acknowledged. We remember—it was Taranaki that Pihanga wanted. But, no matter how strong a life force, who can argue with Ruapehu, Matua Te Mana? As it is said, "Whāia e koe ki te iti kahurangi, ki te tuohu koe me he maunga—seek the treasure you value most dearly, if you bow your head, let it be to a lofty mountain." We remember her tears as Taranaki left and took up his position in the west, looking forever eastward at his lost maiden, eternally betrothed to Tongariro.

What mountain did te wahine bow to? Now she is following the trail of tears. She is asserting her own mauri. But the mauri of a river changes when it reaches the sea.

Io-wairoa, where are you in all of this?

MURUA RĀ NGĀ HARA

25 July 2000

<u>Responding (The Response Isn't on the OHP)</u>

A man presses his face into the floor,
Pulling his hair at the nape.
Tears pool the aisle at the feet of the priest
Whose calm recitation harmonizes
with the repenting moans below.

A kneeler is banging down and up,
Interrupted only by the giggle and twitter
Of the toddler hidden by the pew,
Oblivious to her mother's wails
Of joy and dancing hands and feet.

The widow alternates between
Quiet sobbing and vicious retorts of
"Why? Why?" drowned out between gasps
and gnashing of her teeth
with fingernails lodged into the feet of the cross.

The school headmistress statues piously,
a mixture of true peace and example-setting,
whispering over her beads

gently rustling against the pew
behind the swaying couple.

Scattered throughout are the various stalwarts
who cross their brazen arms
and bow smirking heads.
One reads a missal,
searching for a prayer that will suit.

A woman in a wheelchair shouts for joy
while the footballer with a doctorate
mutters obscenities of injustice.
The grey-haired banker has been
speaking in tongues for thirteen minutes.

A song breaks out at the back,
a familiar hymn to those secondary school students
learned during their primary years.
They've forgotten some words and a bit of the tune
but laugh and cheekily carry on.

The organist picks up their melody
but breaks away into a ragtime variation.
The windows rattle arrhythmically
to the voices, the noises
and the Spirit.

~

Checking back at the presbytery there is still no sign of Pio or Father Picard so I spend the afternoon at the motel.

Mass starts at 6:00 this evening so I arrive at the church at 5:30, hoping to catch the priest in preparation. There is only one car parked outside the building, being vacated by a small elderly lady with short greying hair and a neat suit-and-skirt combination. She stops to look at me as I get out of the Focus and, not recognizing me, gives me a nod of her head, says hello and makes as if to go toward the church.

I say, "Hello," and this causes her to pause and look back as I walk over to her. "Hi there," I say. "Are you going into the church? I'm looking for Father Picard."

"Yes, I am, hello. Would you like me to see if he's there for you? I hope you won't need him for long, he needs to prepare for Mass."

"No, I just need to ask him a quick question, thanks."

We walk together, or should I say, I walk behind her as she briskly pushes ahead of me. She's carrying a stack of thin books and folders under her arm and walks with her head down. Her shoes are quiet as she wears flats with no heels. When we reach the front doors, I pause to wait for her outside. I assume she wouldn't feel comfortable inviting a strange man off the street into a building where she may be alone with him. However, she motions to me impatiently with her hand, saying, "Come in, come in," so I follow her through.

I walk behind the lady through the large foyer, past the small kitchen where Pio and I had tea and into the church proper where she disappears into a room around the left. The inside of the church is illuminated even with the lights turned off. It is much larger than the one in Taumarunui, though similarly laid out in four sections of pews all angled toward the altar. The large pyramidal windows I saw from the outside dominate the ceiling with multi-colored panes of stained glass. There are large Maori sculptures along the walls. From the inner room, I hear the lady's voice answered by the deeper, slower voice of Father Picard who emerges from around the same corner, dressed in white and green robes.

"Ah, it's you again," he says. "I didn't think I'd see you again. I take it you haven't found that brother of yours."

"No, I haven't. I went to Ratana but only found out that Frankie is dead."

I watch for the old man's reaction. I never did feel like he gave me the whole story about Frankie when I first visited him. Maybe it was the fact that he and Frankie didn't get along, or maybe it was Pio who seemed uneasy hanging around in the background of our conversation. That's really why I wanted to talk to Pio instead of Picard—Pio helped me with the protesters yesterday and seems to have a genuine affection for my brother. This man seems guarded and secretive.

But I don't earn any response other than a look of surprise in his eyes. The stronger reaction comes from the small officious lady. She emerges quickly from behind the priest and says, "Dead? Is that Brother Francis you're talking about? What has happened to him?"

The priest moves slightly, allowing her into the conversation, but he looks very uncomfortable. He says, "Yes, tell us what's happened." I can't help but think he already knows. The woman looks to him for some assurance or confirmation about what I've said, but then stares at me awaiting my explanation.

"I was told in Ratana that Francis was sick and that he left to die somewhere else."

"Who told you that?" asks the priest.

I never did ask the man at the cemetery for his name. "Someone who knew Francis when he lived there."

The priest bows his head and shrugs one shoulder before looking at me again. Was that a smirk? The woman behind him seems concerned by the priest's expression as well.

"When did he leave Ratana? Perhaps he has not died yet."

"Too long. I'm sure he's dead. But I want to find his body—or his ashes or something. My family will want closure."

"Of course," the priest says. "I'm not really sure what I can offer you though. As I told you, the last I heard of Francis, he had gone to Ratana."

Then it dawns on me—surely he would have heard of him again since Frankie returned to Whanganui for several months? I raise this point with him. "The man who spoke to me at Ratana said Francis only stayed with them for a short time—that he returned to Whanganui which is where he became sick. Surely you would have seen him around or heard about him being back?"

The priest scowls at me as if he were a school teacher being asked a question he has just given the answer to. "I've told you three times now that I never heard of Francis Murrihy after he left here. Now, if there's nothing else for me to do for you, I have a Mass to prepare." As he speaks, the church door opens behind me and a middle-aged woman with long fair hair walks in, crosses herself with the holy water by the door and makes her way to a pew on the opposite side from us.

"Father Picard, I am trying to figure out where Francis might have gone. Can you think of any special place he might have wanted to go before he died?"

"No, I can't. Your brother's world with us here was in this church and at the prison. He was very clear that he did not want to have anything to do with anything else." He softens his tone and his posture and says, "Now son, I wish you all the best. You're welcome to stay for Mass as all God's children are. Otherwise, God bless you and good day." He adjusts the scarf around his neck and turns back into the room behind him.

My church gatekeeper, who has not said another word while listening to our conversation, watches him go and then turns to me. Her mouth, which had been hanging ajar, snaps shut and she says in a curt manner, "I am terribly sorry to hear about Brother Francis. You're his family?"

I nod. "Did you know him?"

"I did, of course we all did here at St. Mary's. He seemed a good soul, well-liked by many, although difficult to get to know. Very prayerful. He didn't always attend Mass, which puzzled us, but when he did, he was very prayerful. He used to cry when he'd pray. Think of that, eh? He often stayed after the church was emptied. He sometimes wore a brown monk's habit, which was odd to us—I don't think Marists wear brown robes. But, he was especially loved by Pio and many of our Maori congregation. They called him 'Tuakana Tohunga" which was quite an honor really. It means 'brother priest' I think."

"Speaking of Pio, do you know where I can find him? I actually think he's the best one to help me figure this out."

"You won't find him here tonight; he's never here on a Saturday night. He comes to Mass every day of the week, but he works on Saturday nights at some bar in town."

"Do you know what the name of it is?"

"Ooh, I don't know any of them." She looks around the church as if to find someone who would. By now the church has about a dozen people in it, all kneeling behind pews at various points. "Father Picard would know, but I do think it's some place where they play jazz music or something. It's not a bad place, you know where there are fights and naked women or anything like that. Pio wouldn't work in a place like that anymore. If you look for a place where they play music like that, you'll probably find it. It will be downtown somewhere. Sorry I don't know more—and I'm so sorry about your brother."

I thank her and she quickly whips away into the church, with a job to do.

~

Far out. I've driven through the center of the city three times looking for any signs that would indicate a bar with jazz music. I've even stopped at a restaurant to look up place-names in a phone book and asked four gas station attendants where such a place might be. Nobody seems to know anything about jazz in Whanganui. One attendant was sure I must mean gas and suggested I try a place known for drinks mixed with sniffs of helium and oxygen for a buzz. A real cultured place this is turning out to be.

The more I think about that, the more I realize that any jazz club in this place must be a small one and not all that popular. Could it even be buried below street level? Not that I know any places like that in Pictou County, but you see places like that in movies. If that's the case, there's no way to find it driving around in a car.

I park in front of the Embassy Cinema on Victoria Street. It's after dark now and the city center is alive with pedestrians who exceed the number you would expect from the amount of cars in the area. Cafes are still open and movie-goers are trickling out. Again, despite its designation as a city and the amount of life here on a Saturday night, this street doesn't feel a lot different than a large town. It reminds me of going to a club in Stellarton when I was a teenager. Only a few places had anything really interesting going on but they were packed out.

Walking up Victoria, I am approached by a woman who hands me a leaflet, only saying, "Here, take this." I look at it as I walk - it's a simple image with one-half colored blue saying, "National-Kiwi" and the other side colored red reading, "Labour-Iwi." I discard it in the next garbage container. Listening to the conversations of passers-by, I discover that Laws has won his election. There's generally an excited air about this. I chuckle to myself. The winds of change are really blowing through this place.

Scanning the buildings in the area, I don't see any interesting extra doors, or rooms alight in the top stories of the taller buildings. No signs of jazz, just heavy bass sounds of rap music from a passing car filled with white boys with beanies and some poppy dance music coming from one bar with televisions inside playing cricket highlights.

Reaching the top of the block, I cross a roundabout on Ridgeway which has a memorial fountain in the center of it. On the corner is another street bar, the Rutland Arms, a Dickensian-styled place with plenty of customers on the sidewalk drinking around bistro tables. It must be a popular venue as there are also many patrons standing, and the line at the bar fills gaps inside. The music is loud and I recognize a familiar Celtic flavor in the hip-hop beats. I walk past and away from the music, still looking for any odd entrances. A few buildings further and the music at the Rutland stops. Between songs, I hear a different, more muffled tune playing, very bassy and possibly jazz-like. It's coming from behind me and across the street. As soon as I turn around, the music from the bar picks up again and the bass-line is lost to me. I cross the street and walk down in front of a large brick building. Directly above me, a dim purple light emanates from one of the windows on the top story. There is only one door on this side of the building but no sign of an establishment of any kind. I try the door, but it is locked and there is no-one around showing any interest in this corner. I walk back around to the Ridgeway Street side to find another unmarked door. This one opens at my push and the bass grows louder as I step inside.

At the top of the stairs, I enter a small room filled with the purple light I saw from street level. Its source is a disco-ball shaped light fixture in the center of the ceiling. The only other lights in the place are dim and white, one above a small bar in the far corner from the stairway entrance at which sit two men; the other is a small stage-floor spotlight directed at a strange looking Maori man standing on a modest platform in front of a trio of musicians. The man must be in his sixties and is wearing a blue suit from the seventies, complete with bell bottoms and wide lapels. As the trio plays a cool jazz tune on drums, piano and stand-up bass, he is reciting a poem of some sort in dramatic fashion:

I remember when I was a body builder, a rock musician, a priest.
I remember when I was a writer, a novelist, a keeper of the peace.
I remember when I was star cricketer, a financial player,

landlord entrepreneur.

I remember when I was a singer, a scholar, a doctor of literature.

I remember when I was a statistician, a Maths teacher, world champion drinker.

I remember when I was a computer geek, conductor and chess master.

The music stops emphatically and he finishes with, "When was I a son, a brother, a grandson, nephew, husband and father?"

It's truly awful stuff, but he is applauded vigorously by the two men at the bar and the rest of his audience, which I discover hidden around the corner to my right, in a larger section of the room all bathed in the same purple light and filled with about three dozen people gathered neatly around cheap square tables, each sporting a centerpiece made of multi-colored paper vases with little umbrellas available for drinks.

The people are predominantly European and dressed in all sorts of colorful attire. A few others are dressed like the performer who has just collected a drink from the bar and rejoined his supporters at their table. One woman is wearing a shockingly bright orange dress with frilly sleeves that have been deliberately ripped. She wears horn-rimmed glasses and I'm uncertain if the large full-bosomed figure behind her wearing a floral-patterned outfit is a man or a woman. Many others are difficult to distinguish in the lilac light especially in the back corners where a deep throated man has just finished applauding the last performer, calling "encore" in clichéd fashion.

One of the men at the bar has stepped onto the stage. He addresses the audience, saying, "Brother Harris, that was some righteous stuff there man. So many dreams, so many distractions, so much loss. Deep man. Well done wool-sack. Thank you. Who do we have next everyone?"

The deep throated voice calls out, "Pio's got one Miles!"

"Pio! Come forward my little soul brother. Our band is ready if our ears are willing."

Pio emerges out of the dark corner and I am glad to see him. He does not look like he's been cleaning bathrooms. He's dressed in a very dapper pin-striped suit straight out of 1930s' Chicago—all he's missing is a tommy-gun and a long-tailed cigarette. He strides to the stage with a completely different gait and expression than when I met him on the church lawn. His teeth glow in the purple light between wide Cheshire lips. His shoulders are back and confident.

He grabs the microphone from its holster and winks at someone seated at one of the front tables, either the grey-haired, solidly built woman with sweat pants and a t-shirt which reads, "I have the pussy so I make the rules" or the man beside her dressed in a long-sleeved blue satin top with sequins on his collar. The music starts with a walking bass line backed by single chords on the piano and soft steady brush strokes on the drum. The whole scene is too groovy for words.

The grim, awkwardly chatty Pio I have come to know now croons his spoken-word poetry into the microphone. The audience seems spellbound.

"Horses of women," he begins,

working all hours, three o'clock, day or night,
Any manner of jobs, from lawn-mowing to pool maintenance.
Huge women, with big hips and bigger gum boots,
yellow teeth in a ready smile,
shy waves to us cousins, neighbors, whanau.
Strong women, mending goal posts, washing graffiti,
speaking gently to the local artists skateboarding on the court.
Beautiful women, sisters with children, mothers and aunties
under one car and van, married to this place of simple poetry.

The place erupts when he finishes, the two odd figures at the front table leading the charge with a standing ovation, calling out "Ka pai wool-sack!" and "Well done bare-bone!" Pio's smile is rapturous and he bounces off the stage toward his friends. As he starts across the concrete floor, he spots me standing in my corner near the stairs. The smile vanishes for a moment and he flashes a look somewhere between recognition and terror, but then his friends, who have come forward from their seats, are upon him and he returns his attention to their adulation, beaming in the purple glow. After the hugs subside, he comes over to see me.

"My brother," he says. "What are you doing here?" His voice is friendly and slightly out of breath, but his grim demeanor has returned.

"I'm still looking for Frankie. I think you're the only one who can help me—or will help me," I say over top of the music which has started again for the next performer.

Pio looks back at the stage, then takes me by the arm. "We'll talk soon, eh? Come sit with us and watch my friends."

I go with him because I can see there is no way he is going to surrender these moments. I suffer through three more spectacles. To their credit, the band is impressive in their variety of backing orchestrations. But the poets themselves are grating in their melodramatic presentations about broken toys, unrequited loves and, this one by the butch woman, lack of job satisfaction. After she wraps up the set and her friends acclaim her, Pio introduces me to his table-mates. The woman is called Thalia, at least on these nights, and the man in the satin shirt is named Raoul, despite his red hair and freckled face. While the poets have wrapped up, the band continues to play quietly in the background and conversation is easier.

In the initial chit-chat, I'm told that this bar runs these spoken-word sessions once each month. There is no name for the group or event, it is not advertised other than by invitation and word-of-mouth. The purpose is sharing, creativity and expression of the oddest parts of one self, confident in the applause of others. Pio does not mention how he knows me.

"It's very liberating," Raoul drawls. I'm certain the accent is put on for the night as well.

"How did you find me?" Pio asks. "Did Father Picard tell you?"

"No he didn't. I was given a hint from a parishioner before Mass tonight."

"I didn't think so. Father Picard is not a fan of this. He worries it will take me off his path of holiness for me. But I need these nights, and these friends, just to hold onto some parts of me that God wants to tame."

"Hey, you make it sound like we're doing something wrong here," Thalia says, and then grabs him in a headlock, tousling his hair. "I told you, there's nothing wrong with this, there's everything right about it. That old priest is filling your head with a load of rubbish man."

Pio straightens up and smiles contritely at her, then sheepishly at me. "I didn't mean it like that. I know God is OK with this. It's

Father who frowns at it. It's all good." Then he asks me, "Are you alright after yesterday?"

"Yes," I reply.

"Ooohh, what happened yesterday?" coos Raoul.

Pio relates the story about hearing me call out in the middle of the hikoi and how he helped me out of the rain. "I'm sorry I didn't stay longer. The hikoi was very important to me. Whanau—family—you know?" He looks at me for a sign that I understand and I nod.

"Speaking of family Pio, I still need your help." Pio nods back, looking sullen. His friends lean in as if I'm about to share some terrible secret.

"I went to Ratana looking for Francis—"

"Francis? You know Francis?" Raoul interrupts, his eyes widening and his accent unmistakably New Zealand.

"My friends," Pio says, "this is our beloved Francis' brother."

"Well, fuck me," says Thalia, leaning forward and studying my face. Then she and Raoul look at Pio, waiting for whatever comes next.

"Did you know Francis as well?" I ask.

"Prune is a bloody legend here!" says Thalia. "He was awesome, eh Raoul?"

"We just loved Francis. Everybody here did."

"Well, almost everybody."

"It's just awful what happened to him."

"Yes," I say, "I found out he was very sick and—"

Again, Raoul interrupts. "Sick? Oh dear, I never knew he was sick. Is he alright?"

I look at Pio trying to work out what he knows about all this. He has been quietly watching our conversation as if hoping it would steer into another topic. "No, he's not alright," I say, fixing my eyes on Pio's. "He's dead."

Pio doesn't even pretend to flinch while his friends alternately gasp, reach out to touch my hands, and put their heads in their own hands. Raoul gasps, "Sweet wag," and they look at Pio for a reaction but he shows no sign of surprise.

"What do you mean, he's dead?" asks Raoul. What's happened to him? Pio, what's happened to Francis?"

"Pio," I say quietly but directly. "They told me in Ratana that Frankie had left them to die. Do you know where he went?"

Pio stands from his chair and pushes it in, looking ashen even in his brown skin under the purple light. He turns his back to us and I stand as well, ready to grab hold of him if he runs. He doesn't move, however, but just stands there with his back turned to us. His friends don't move either. They seem unaffected by his actions as if they've seen this behavior before. Pio raises his head and looks toward the stage at the jazz band that has started to play again. He then turns back toward us and says to me, "I cannot tell you where he went, but I promise you he is better off left as he is."

I stare back at him and say, "That's not good enough. I need more. My family needs more."

Pio stares back just as intently and I see warning in his eyes. "I have not heard from Francis since he left. You know your brother is precious to me. I would not want him or his family to suffer in life or in death." He looks at Raoul and says, "Please come with me to the toilets. I feel unwell." His friend stands and moves beside him.

"I'm not going anywhere Pio. You need to tell me more."

He nods and Raoul says to me, "I will talk to him."

"Make sure you bring him back here."

The two walk off together behind the stage and I consider the shape of the building and wonder if they will leave from some other exit. Have I lost my one contact?

Thalia sees my concern. She says, "They won't leave. There's only one way out and that's back down the stairs. Raoul will talk to him. Pio can be very fearful but he wants to help people. I promise you, he'll be torn up inside, especially if it concerns Prune. He must be afraid of something. Tell me, what was wrong with your brother?"

I tell her what the old man in Ratana told me. She looks genuinely surprised.

"The last time I saw Prune was here. In fact, the only time I ever saw him was here. Actually," here she pauses for a moment, considering whether she should share her next thought, "I saw your brother here two last-times."

"What do you mean?"

"Well, the first last-time I saw him was on a night just like this. We'd all gathered for our bit of fun. I think it was in July—it was definitely in the winter because I remember we had a gas heater lit. Prune shared his last poem with us. We didn't know it was going to

be his last poem, but as I said that was his first last-night with us."
Thalia looks at me to see that I'm following her.

"I remember how powerful his poem was because he seemed so
weak that night. Maybe he was sick then, eh? I don't think anyone
here knew he was sick. Maybe Pio did. Anyway, he was dressed like a
Maori warrior that night—not the whole get-up—he still had trousers
on. Pio had painted a full-faced moko on him and he was dressed in a
korowai—that's a feathered cloak—and was holding a taiaha. That's a
sort of staff used for fighting. But Prune wasn't holding it like a
warrior; he was holding it like a cane, a tokotoko. That's what I
thought made him look so weak, but I also thought he was doing that
on purpose, you know, like part of his performance. His poem was
all about the land and how Maori were the spiritual gatekeepers or
some shit. I don't really go along with all that tangata whenua crap.
I'm a New Zealander, I was born here, so I should have just as much
rights as them, eh? Anyway, that was the last time I ever talked to
him."

"Do   you   remember   him   saying   anything   about   going
somewhere?"

Thalia pauses to think but then shakes her head. "Nah, I don't."

"So, you mentioned another time you saw him?"

Thalia sighs and then laughs, shaking her head. "Well, yeah I do,
but you're gonna think I'm nuts."

I smile and say, "Too late for that," and she laughs.

"Yeah, I am pretty nuts. OK, so we were here again, probably two
months ago, so that would have been August. It would have been
just about the same crowd as the one here tonight. I finished my
poem about euthanasia and when I came down from the stage, I
looked out into our little audience here and everybody was
applauding and whistling, just like you saw tonight, you know?" I nod
and she continues, "When I see Prune standing behind Pio and he's
clapping away just like the rest of them. He's all purple from the
lights and he's wearing that same korowai, but without the moko. I
thought maybe he'd come in somehow while I was reciting, but I was
sure he hadn't. As I came down across to here, Raoul and Pio rushed
over to me to give me my hug and when we separated I saw that
Prune was gone. He was just gone!"

I sigh and lean back in my chair. This is a weird story, but it
doesn't help me in any way. I look past Thalia to see if Pio has re-

emerged but only see another poet taking the stage. It's going to get difficult to talk in here. I say as much to Thalia.

"Yeah, well let's go then, eh? I'll see if I can get Pio and Raoul and maybe we'll finish our little chat somewhere else." We both stand and walk toward the washrooms area when Pio and Raoul emerge and meet us at the top of the stairs. Thalia explains our plan. Pio looks as if he's been crying. We all descend the stairs and walk out onto the sidewalk of Victoria Street where Raoul suggests that we go back to his place, which is close, but I'm not keen to separate into vehicles. Thalia suggests we head down to the river.

Our walk is slow and quiet. I content myself to wait until we re-settle before asking any more questions. I don't want my delicate witness to recant any promises to tell me more if Raoul has managed to get him sorted. I feel like an arresting officer escorting my ward through the city streets to lock him up downtown. We finally make it to the end of Victoria and the trio leads me down to Moutoa Quay which runs along the river and under the bridge.

Thalia says, "That Laws fella promised us he'd build a proper river-edge walkway here. I guess we'll see if he delivers, eh?"

We find a bench which Thalia and I sit on while Pio and Raoul sit cross-legged on the grass. It is quiet here too for a Saturday night. Cars are crossing the bridge in regular intervals and the occasional couple walk behind us along the quay but we are otherwise left alone to talk.

I don't ask my questions again, as Raoul is looking at Pio in expectation. He's obviously convinced his friend to share something.

Pio speaks without raising his head. "Please forgive me my friends and forgive me brother of my brother. I have told many lies to you." Raoul looks at Thalia in surprise. Whatever he was expecting Pio to share, he wasn't expecting it to start like this.

"Our dear friend Francis was more than a poet friend of mine. As you know, we enjoy our spoken-word nights because of our expression of who we are but also because of the anonymity we can keep about other parts of our life. When Francis joined us, I pretended I didn't know who he was, that I was meeting him for the first time just as you were."

"Ha-ha! That's cool Pio," Thalia says. "Raoul and I used to think you guys fell in love with each other pretty quickly. Don't worry about it mate. Where'd you guys know each other from?"

Pio looks up at his friend and smiles. He sighs, "Through the Church. He lived with me and Father for a while. He is a Catholic brother, also known as Brother Francis."

"What the fuck Pio?" says Thalia.

"Are you for real?" says Raoul.

"There's no way he was a religious Pio. He used to bash the Catholic Church, and give you a hard time whenever you would go on about that old priest of yours."

"He never bashed the Church," Pio glares at Thalia. "He just criticized it. He was like you guys—he thought the Church was too religious, too bound up in rituals and not free enough to really love people. That's why he came out with us. That's why he and Father never got along, that and—"

"And what Pio? Keep going," says Raoul. "It's good that you tell us . . . if you want."

Pio looks at me. "Father Picard lied to you about why your brother left. He didn't leave just because they argued about Francis working in schools and not going to Mass enough."

Thalia sniffs, and crosses her arms. "Not going to Mass enough," she mutters. "Fucking Catholics."

Pio ignores her and says, "Father kicked him out for doing stuff he wasn't allowed to do."

Raoul and Thalia draw in a single breath. My skin wrinkles and I recall stories I've heard about Catholic priests doing things they shouldn't be doing. We grew up hearing of the horrors at Mount Cashel, in Newfoundland. I quickly run through my memories of Frankie searching for any signs he could have had that in him.

Pio seems to know what we're thinking and says quickly, "No, nothing like that. Francis wasn't like that—he wasn't! Francis was kind and sincere—and he was especially loved by the prisoners he visited. Those men had so much guilt—rape, p-labs, home invasions—Francis would tell me some of their stories to try and make me feel better about my own sins. They wanted to unburden themselves, so he would listen to them and then his heart would lead him to grant them absolution."

He stops, apparently expecting this statement to have some intended effect. Thalia speaks for the rest of us.

"And . . . ?"

Pio looks at her, then back at me. "Well, this is a grave sin in the Church. Only a priest may hear confessions and grant absolution. Francis was being terribly disobedient and Father Picard was so angry when he found out—it was very bad."

Thalia throws her hands in the air and lets them land back on her wide lap. "Far out man, why do you stay with that old fart?" She points at him with a firm, chubby finger. "I'm telling you, get outta there while you still have any brains left at all. That Church is evil man. Look what they teach everyone about abortion and sin and . . . and gays! How can you stay in that when you have friends like us, eh?"

"No, no, no, no, no Thalia, please, I've explained this to you before. My friendship with you is not affected by my love for the Church. I disagree with the Church about some things just as a wife disagrees with her husband, but still loves him passionately. I love you Thalia," he turns to his grass-fellow, "and I love you Raoul. And you both need to know that Francis loved you too, even as a brother in the Church. Besides, he left the Church after father kicked him out and threatened to have him ex-communicated."

I jump in here. "How do you know Pio? I thought you didn't see him after he left."

Pio lowers his head again and says, "I lied to you brother. As I'm sure Thalia has already told you, Francis returned to us and our group. I knew he would return—he loved us and he would never stop his ministry of hearing confessions. He had known God's healing spirit too well and too often for himself and for those he helped. I knew he would choose that calling from God over any membership in the Church. But . . . I am telling the truth when I say I have not heard from him since he left the second time . . . I have only seen him."

"You've seen him? Where? Where did he go after Ratana?"

Pio looks at Thalia who gives him a nod before sitting back again with her arms folded. "Go on," she says. "I already told him my story so you can tell him yours."

Pio smiles at her and says, "I have seen your brother on at least three occasions since he disappeared. Once, while mowing the grounds, I saw him crossing from the car park toward the front doors of the church. I went into the church and he was not inside. The second time I saw him was over there." He points across the river on the other side of the bridge. "He was walking away from me up-river. By the time I ran up the bank and under the bridge, he had vanished around the bend. The third time, he visited me in my room."

Pio closes his eyes as if to see his memory better. "I was drunk and I was hurt. You don't know about this one either Raoul and Thalia." At this, his friends both move closer to him, Thalia joining the pair on the grass. "I had stupidly tried to find my ex-wife. I thought I could go to her and tell her how sorry I was about the years of abuse I had inflicted upon her and my children." He's sobbing slightly now. "I found her at home and she was having a party. Some of my old mates were there and they weren't happy to see me, but one of them, Bernard, took me outside and shared some of his drinks with me. I hadn't had a drink since moving in with Father. We drank and laughed. I tried to tell him about my plan to apologize and how sorry I was, but he wasn't listening. He just kept pouring drinks and talking about old times, sporting matches, other girls we had . . . known.

After too many drinks, I tried to go back inside and find Mere, but I couldn't find her downstairs. I thought I'd see if my boys were home, so I went upstairs. I found them playing in their room and Mere was in the next room with her door wide open and making noises . . . no noises that sons should hear their mother make with a man.

I went into that room," he says holding up his two fists and staring at each of them, "and we smashed that fella offa her and then we smashed her one more time." Pio is crying now, his face contorted and angry. "But her man rescued her from me. He beat the shit outta me and I had to crawl down those stairs and leave my two boys with them.

"I walked all the way back to the presbytery and managed to get back to my room without waking Father. I cried and then I prayed. I prayed that God would take away my sins and help my two sweet boys, and that's when Francis came to me."

Pio looks at me harshly, wipes away his tears with the back of his pin-striped sleeve, straightens up in an effort to regain his composure and says, "Your brother . . . our brother . . . healed me that night. He heard me confess my sins and I shared everything, things I had never thought to share with any priest. It was like taking off a mask I had worn all my life. He listened to my sins pour out of me and he didn't say a word. I knew from looking at his lovely face when I needed to say more and when what I had said was enough. Then he gave me absolution by raising his arms above me and blessing me and, as he did so, I felt God's grace wash through me—I have never known such cleanliness. It was like a liquid that flowed through my heart, my veins, my lungs, my pores. I have never breathed better, never seen clearer. I bowed before him and when I lifted my head and opened my eyes, he was gone."

Pio pauses to look at each one of us who are sitting in stunned silence. Then he says to me, "I don't know where our brother is resting, but God has given us a wonderful gift through him. Do not disturb it."

FACES AND NAMES

Tihei mauri mate! Behold there is death!

We know something of broken covenants, of broken treaties and promises. Our whenua is seeped with the blood of struggle and disunity. But it is also blood that binds us.

We remember the rārangi matua, the order of things which binds the celestial and temporal realms.

We remember Tamakehu and Ruaka and their children.

Tupoho, whose children people the lower river.

Tamaupoko, whose children people the middle river.

Hinengakau, whose children people the upper river.

Three ancestors, three hapū. One People.

Our poropiti—our prophets—speak for unity, a plaited chord which binds the three strands into one. Io-wairoa understands threeness and oneness for He is living water.

But now another strand has been woven in—new people, new interests—and that strand is here to stay, and the mauri changes. As each strand dies to itself, the chord grows stronger, just as our tributaries die, yet live as they join us, and we grow stronger together. Just as we die at our mouth yet live on in the seas.

Today te wahine visited Taranaki again. She ate with him, laughed with him, and walked with him through a forest of brilliantly coloured trees whose leaves fell over them like rain.

~

I try to persuade Pio to tell me more, that I really need just an idea of where he might have gone, that my family need closure of some sort and that surely wouldn't affect whatever it was he believed had happened. I even try using God to plead my case, assuring him that his God would want to return a son to his dying mother. But Pio won't talk anymore and his friends implore me to leave him alone. They both walk on either side of Pio, escorting him as he shuffles his way back toward town, creating a hedge around him and preventing me from getting closer.

I keep my distance, following them back as far as my car where I stop as if to leave them to it. I watch them go back up toward the intersection past the memorial. Once they turn the corner, I move after them, weaving my way through a crowd exiting a late show at the theater. Around the corner, then back, I search for any signs of them returning to the jazz bar, but see none. They don't seem to be mixed in with the Rutland Arms crowd who are still enjoying the barrage of house music. I've lost them and know I have one option.

I drive back to the church hoping they have taken Pio home. Finding it is even easier at night, as I navigate toward the glowing cross on the city's horizon. When I arrive, there is just one vehicle stationed outside, so I drive further down the road near the entrance to the park and wait for the driver to return. I'm not waiting long when I see the recognizable figures of Raoul and Thalia making their way back to their car. I consider going after Pio, but realize I would have to go through the priest again. Besides, Pio has made his stance clear.

Instead, there are a few points I want to ask Thalia about, or even Raoul so I drive after them. Surely these guys don't believe Pio's stories or at least give such credence to them that they will keep me from finding where Frankie is buried.

Now, pulling over a few car lengths behind their vehicle, I watch Thalia letting Raoul out. He drifts into a small one-story house just down from the Dublin Street Bridge. Perfect. I know where he lives if I need to retrace my steps. I follow Thalia as she makes her way across the bridge, through the roundabout, past the gas station and into a suburb signed as Wanganui East. The streets are much quieter on this side of the river as we drive into more residential areas. We travel through several side streets until Thalia pulls into a driveway. Damn. I was hoping she would park on the side of the road, but now she's driven down, deep behind the house at the front of the property. Uncomfortably, I pull in behind her. There are lights on in the house and another car parked in a bay in the backyard, so she isn't alone. This could get awkward.

She's waiting for me as I drive in, looking below her hand to see past the glare of my headlights. I dim the lights and she rolls her eyes in recognition. "Far out man," she says in a loud voice which must carry through half the neighborhood. I open the car door and stand behind it with an arm outstretched. "Thalia, please, can I talk with you for just a few moments more?"

She looks at me blankly, then shrugs her shoulders and says, "Oh sure, alright. Hang on." She walks in back of the house and I hear her say something inside to someone with that deep, loud voice of hers. Then I hear a screen-door clatter shut and watch her walk further into the backyard behind the garage whose doors remain shut. "C'mon then," she says, "we'll go out here. My dad's going to bed."

I close the car door and follow her into the dark. As I round the corner of the garage, I see she has gone inside through a side door and this is affording a patch of light for me to see my way back. Inside is a sparsely furnished, one bedroom apartment. Thalia ushers me in. "C'mon," she says, "it's getting cold out there."

She tosses her keys on a television set in the corner and steps over stacks of old record albums on the floor to sit on the edge of her bed. She points to a chair just inside the doorway and I sit down.

"Geez man, you don't quit do you? Did you follow me all the way from downtown?"

"Not exactly. Just from the church."

"Huh," she says and looks at me out of one eye, then chuckles and shakes her head. "Well okay then, what do you want?"

"I want to know what you meant when you said that it was terrible what happened to Frankie."

"What do you mean? You told me he was dead! That's what was terrible!"

"No, before I told you that, you told me that something else had happened to him."

Thalia looks down at the floor for a few moments, then looks up with eyes wide open and says, "Nah, that wasn't me man, that was Raoul who said that!"

Yes, it might have been Raoul. "OK, but can you tell me what he was talking about?"

Thalia lets a whoosh of air escape and rocks on her bed. When she stops, she looks at me sideways and says, "Look, you've come a long way right? And you're his brother, so I'm going to be straight up with you. Just don't get upset at me or nothing."

I say nothing and wait.

"You know what our nickname for your Frankie was? Prune." She laughs, "When we first met him, we didn't know his name—well me and Raoul didn't. It turns out Pio did. Anyway, he shows up and joins our little society and calls himself "The Lawn-mower Philosopher'. Can you believe that? What an awful name for a poet. He told us it was because he used to get his ideas when he was mowing the lawn. Well, we noticed that a lot of his poetry had to do with cutting back on bad habits, you know, in order to live a better life. So we called him Prune. Do you get it? Like pruning shears?"

I nod to let her know I get it and am hoping that she gets to her point.

She sees the desire in my face. "Look, I'm sorry for your loss and I know you want to bring some closure home to your family, but . . . I think the best closure you're gonna get is to go home and tell your family about Prune's awful end and leave it at that."

I can't believe my ears. "Thalia, if you know something, you have to tell me. Don't close ranks on me like Pio. That's not your call to make."

"I'm not like Pio. I'm not even sure I know what he's on about. It's just that sometimes it's better not to know some things." Thalia leans forward, clasping her hands together, rotates her thumbs around each other and sighs. "But, OK, I tried to tell you. Everything I know, I know from Pio and a little from Prune himself. I was really surprised the papers never picked up on the story about him and I'm even more surprised after finding out he was some Catholic priesty thing.

"I realize now that he must have been living with Pio and the priest when we first met him, but for a couple of months your brother stopped coming on Saturday nights. Then about a year ago, he showed up again. Prune mentioned how he had moved house and that he was staying with a woman named Marietta. I thought that was cool and all, no worries, eh? But, apparently she had two kids and she accused him of . . . touching one of them . . . or something, I don't know all the details. This is just what Pio told me, Prune never talked to us about it." Thalia looks at me as if to say, 'You wanted to know.'

I'm stunned. This was not Frankie. Even this far away and this far removed, I know Frankie did not have such evil in him. He had his own kids but, growing up he never showed any interest in other people's children, let alone an unhealthy interest in them. He would never pick up new babies at family gatherings; he would never spend time with younger cousins, always preferring to hang out with the adults. My mind swirls at this. "How far did these accusations go?"

"To the police," Thalia answers. "He was investigated and everything and Pio said that he was kept in jail for a night, but never arrested. Instead, the police spent a long time putting a case together trying to decide whether they could press charges, making sure they could prove it in court I suppose. They interviewed Pio. He told us all about that, but they never talked to me or Raoul or anybody. I still wonder if Prune even told them about us. Like Pio said, we like our anonymity."

I consider what that must have been like for Frankie. It would have been terrifying. There was a hockey coach in one of our small towns who was accused of grooming one of his students a few years back. The only reason I heard about it was because I often visited the courts when I had no other stories to follow. I happened to be there when he was being arraigned. It was a difficult story to track because the police were coy about everything, even though I was allowed to make the story public. The courts had granted name suppression, but there is only one minor hockey team in this particular town and not too many coaches, so any story published about it was going to reveal his identity to the community. I decided to try and find out more before taking it to my editor. We don't like to publish stories like that if we think it will do more harm than good for the community.

From what I learned about the coach, and the shame he was going through even before the trial, I decided not to write the story. It wasn't my job to decide whether he was guilty or innocent so I waited for the courts to decide. He was found not guilty, but still moved out of the area after. It's a hard reputation to escape once the finger has been pointed. I know Frankie hadn't spoken with us for over a year when this happened, but I would imagine this would add to his reasons to not contact us. He would have hated us knowing this and

I see now what Thalia meant. Not only do I go home with news of a dead son, but do I also share even this hint that he may have done something so awful? Mom doesn't need this.

"Thanks for telling me this Thalia." Her shoulders relax and she leans back on her bed against the wall. "So, you're saying that Frankie was being investigated right up until you saw him last?"

Thalia nods. "Yeah, I think so, and then you told us that he was sick. I'm not surprised. If I was under that kind of stress, I'd be sick too."

"Do you know anything more about this woman, Marietta?"

"No, not really. He didn't talk about her much."

"OK, thanks." I stand up from my chair and another thought reoccurs that was nagging at me before I came here. "Thalia, there was something else I wanted to ask you about. When you say you saw Frankie last at the club, do you think it was a ghost? I mean, just like in Pio's story? Because his story sounds like that too." And I remember my own story, seeing him in the crowd of protesters.

Thalia shakes her head, "Nah. I mean, I believe in ghosts alright, but he looked too real to me. I don't know how to explain it."

I nod and turn toward the door, still perplexed and not sure where to take my question anyway, when Thalia says, "Besides, think about it—"

I look back at her and she says, "According to your story, Prune was still alive in Ratana when he appeared to me and Pio."

~

14 April 2000

<u>*"Bathtized"*</u>

The water level is just right—templar. He's edged his head to touch the bottom. For a moment, he hesitates, wary of the water that might leak in if he opens his eyes. He wonders why he wants to open them at all. He does anyway, even just to test the water. He smirks as he looks up, then to the left, then to the right. He can see the surface either way and his eyes stay dry.

Satisfied at this pleasure, he seals his lids and listens. No television, no wife, no voices in his new sound-scape, just a heartbeat, a dripping tap and his own breathing. He feels the tenuous epicenter—a carnal existence separated by a line made of water and air. The air enters from above, into his lungs under the surface and then returns to the world above. Life enters the tomb and exits. He wonders at how close he is to baptism and imagines how he could drown himself even now. What would he need to turn his face down so that only his hair would enjoy life's gas? When water first entered his lungs, would he be able to force his head down or relent to instinct, spluttering and revived?

He knows he would never do it of course, yet he does wonder, who could do such a thing?

He opens his eyes and shivers at the chilling water. He looks to his left and then to his right and smirks again at the closeness of it all before rising, reborn out of the depths of reflection and imagination.

Lord, a man is made of flesh and blood and he changes, yet isn't he the same man? Why won't you let me forget?

~

When I was about fifteen years old, I did one of the stupidest things, but the only criminal thing, I've ever done. I stole a magazine from a gas station in Saltsprings. If you asked me today, nearly twenty years later why I did it, I still couldn't give you a sensible answer. The one criminal thing I've ever done, and I was caught. Even now, sharing the story is one of the most embarrassing things I can do: the humiliation as I was brought back into the store by the security guard in front of my friends who were waiting in the car; my father meeting me at the police station; the knowing I would have a criminal record until I was eighteen.

What is it that drives us to do wrong? I have interviewed many old ladies and storekeepers who have given me the classic line, "He seemed like such a nice young man" after police had been around to cart one of their neighbors or customers away for all sorts of misdemeanors and worse. I am no philosopher. I don't spend time thinking about those big questions like, "Why do good people do bad things?" or "Where does evil come from?" or "Is man inherently good?" But, from experience, I have learned that the evil that men do is often surprising, emerging from packaging that would deceive the most discerning of psychologists, detectives and skeptics. I suppose we all have our sins, but only some of them are against the law.

Frankie was immersed in sin; if not his own, then certainly in that of lots of other people. How can priests and psychiatrists or movie censors spend inordinate amounts of time encountering our most depraved expressions of the human heart, and not be affected themselves? No matter how much I knew the original Frankie as a boy and as a teenager, how much did I really know him as an adult? I certainly didn't know him as a New Zealander or a Catholic monk. It is so messed up to imagine my brother doing what he's been accused of. Thalia said this woman has two children. Did Frankie develop an inappropriately close relationship with them, born out of the loss of his own kids? I never did think he could have healed properly from that loss, especially without family support.

But maybe the charges were unfounded. Maybe they were cleared up before he disappeared. Not that I could ever tell Mom anyway, but maybe I can get closure on this matter at least. So, this morning, I'm visiting the police to find out more. Besides, after Thalia I've once again run out of leads and perhaps the police kept track of Frankie's whereabouts and may even know where he ended up.

It's Monday morning. After a late night with Thalia on Saturday night, I slept in yesterday. I rang home to find out how Mom was doing. Dad told me that she had had a couple of bad days and they did call for the doctor, but an adjustment to her medication seems to have helped and she has been awake and talking more. I miss her.

I only told Dad that I had not found Frankie, but that it would seem he was still in the area. I'm just not ready to go there yet. It took me awhile to consider what to do next and when I phoned the police in Whanganui, I was told that the local office would not be open until this morning. I spent the day in the motel, re-reading the journals which was a useless enterprise. Last night I watched the news to see that the election of the new mayor in Whanganui was a national headline. Apparently this Laws character is also some sort of radio and television personality. This morning I learned that Christopher Reeve has died. I guess it comes to us all, even Superman.

Yesterday, I also popped out to locate the police station so I would have no problem finding it today. I knew it was nearby as I had seen it last week in my drive by Moutoa Gardens. I hope this goes smoothly. Mom surely can't hold out much longer.

~

The receptionist at the station tells me the chief investigator in Frankie's case is able to see me right away. After only a few minutes, Detective Chris Daniels emerges through the security door to greet me. Daniels is a short balding man, though not old. He is dressed in a dowdy suit and tie, as if he has just landed the job and found the closest thing for the position in his closet. He wears glasses and speaks in a whining voice with a thick New Zealand accent. These things can be hard to put a finger on, but I take an instant disliking to him.

He says hello and asks, "What can I do for you Mr. . . . ?"

"Murrihy, Conrad Murrihy," I answer, fully expecting a reaction of some sort.

He plays it pretty cool, not showing any assumptions. "Very good Mr. Murrihy. What can I do for you?"

"I understand you're familiar with my brother, Francis Murrihy."

Now he is free to show his recognition. "Yes, yes I am, absolutely. Look, why don't we talk in my office inside?"

"Sure, that'll be good," I say and follow him through the security door, down a short corridor and into a small room containing just a desk and a couple of chairs. The window has a simple, tidy venetian blind covering it. The walls are sparsely decorated with a faded painting of the water tower from across the river and new-looking promotional posters produced by the New Zealand police. I doubt very much this is his office. It seems more like a generic meeting room for all sorts of customers; similar to a few I've visited covering stories in New Glasgow and Stellarton. And not unlike the one I visited during my burglary incident as a teenager.

Daniels wheels his chair out from behind the desk so that he is facing me and sharing the same space; an attempt to appear less officious I suppose, or to dominate our position. He asks, "So, what brings you to Wanganui Mr. Murrihy?"

"I'm looking for my brother. I don't suppose you know where he is?"

"I wish I did," he says with a serious look on his face. "You say I'm familiar with your brother, are you familiar with what your brother has done?"

This is not good. "I have just learned this weekend what he has been accused of doing. I was hoping to find that there has been some misunderstanding."

Daniels shakes his head. "No, there has been no misunderstanding. I don't know exactly what you have heard, but I can tell you that we spent months looking into the accusations against your brother and are determined to put him on trial." He leans forward and stares hard at me, making sure I know he's watching how I respond to his next statement. "Now, if you have any information about where he might be, I do suggest you share it with us."

I place my elbows on my knees, sigh, and flick my hands out to the sides helplessly. "I really don't." I'm so exasperated by all this. "Look, can you please tell me what's going on here? I have come all the way from Canada to find my brother. My mother is dying. Then I find out he's being charged with . . . something awful. Look, I can't imagine Frankie doing anything like he's been accused of. There has to be some mistake. What happened?"

Daniels seems to relent a little, leaning back in his chair again.

"There are many aspects of the case I can't tell you, but I can say that he is charged with assault of a minor. You'll understand why I won't give you details about the child or the family—"

"The family he lived with," I interject, then realize from the look on the detective's face I should keep my mouth shut about this.

"I understand you will find this difficult and emotional, and you want to find your brother, but you are under no circumstances to try and make contact with them. Do you understand that Mr. Murrihy?"

"Yeah," I say. "Of course, yes, no I won't try and do anything like that."

"Very good. Well, perhaps we can help each other here. You may have some information that could prove useful to us in tracking him down. When was the last time you heard from him?"

After these last couple of weeks, it feels strange to be the one answering the questions. I tell the detective about the years of silence from Frankie.

"That is unusual. Nothing at all? Not a phone call, not a post-card, not an e-mail for someone's birthday?"

"Nothing."

"OK, so what have you been able to find out while you've been here?"

Something, perhaps some primitive fraternal loyalty, causes me to hesitate. I don't want to help this man find him, but then I remember that there is no suspect to capture, only a burial place to locate. I tell him about the old man in Ratana.

Daniels draws a book from his shirt pocket and writes a note. Then he asks, "When did the old man say he left Ratana?"

"About a month ago."

"And you say he supposedly went somewhere to die?"

"That's right."

The detective jots more notes, then puts his book down on the desk beside him. He strokes his chin, takes his glasses off, pinches his nose several times, then replaces the glasses so that they are lower on his nose and he looks at me over the top of the rims. "My turn to share then. We know that your brother came to Wanganui about two years ago. We've interviewed Father Picard whom he lived with and worked for. We know they had a falling out of some sort and that Francis left town for a while, presumably to live in Ratana with a prison worker. We've not been able to find that worker as he has since left the prison and is not where he told people he was going."

"Palmerston North?" I ask.

Daniels looks impressed. "Yes, that's right. Francis didn't stay in Ratana long, but moved back into Wanganui. You already seem to know that he moved in with the family who has made the allegations against him."

"Yes, just on that detective—"

Daniels gives me a warning look, but lets me continue.

"I don't want to know about the family, but I do wonder how he would know anyone else to live with in Wanganui. Was she another contact through the prison?"

He considers for a moment, then says, "It was through church circles, I guess you could say. But I'll not say anything more on that. You should know that your brother was also reported as regularly visiting children's stores—clothing, toys, those sorts of places— suspicious behavior for a single priest. I'll finish by saying that he stayed in Wanganui while we conducted our investigation and was very co-operative, until he disappeared, avoiding arrest." He studies my face for a moment and then says, "Cooperative and cold, I have to tell you Mr. Murrihy. Normally when allegations such as these are made, the accused is extraordinarily upset—and that goes for the legitimately guilty as well as the legitimately innocent. When I brought your brother in here and informed him of the allegations— in detail—he responded to it all calmly and even peacefully, which is not a word I use often. Yes, peacefully and coldly."

"Frankie was always the calm one. But, I can't explain why he would respond like that. I hardly know him now really." My understatement levels me. Fuck. Two weeks ago, I had all feeling for my brother buried. This should be about Mom now. God-damn it!

Daniels continues, almost sympathetically. "At the same time, during the investigation, we saw your brother's health deteriorate. At first, I thought it was the stress manifesting itself. I've seen that before. But, just a week or so before we were set to press charges we found out he was genuinely ill." He looks at me square on. "But that has no bearing on his case. We waited a long time before pressing charges. Do you know why?"

I shake my head.

"Your brother is a Catholic priest and this is a small community. A story like this would rock our town. We really did make sure there was a legitimate case against him before pressing charges. Then he disappeared. You say he went back to Ratana. At least that much is news to us and we can investigate there. You say he then went somewhere to die. Do you have any ideas where that might be?"

"I don't—that's all I've had to go on and I have no answers. I don't know him well enough and I don't know this place well enough."

Daniels nods and leans back again. "Well", he says, "that might be all we can do for one another today. I will give you one more bit of something, however. You say that Francis left Ratana a month ago to die. The old man assured you he was at death's door, did he?"

"That's right. I mean, I don't know anything about his illness, but the old man said that he was definitely on his death bed."

"That is interesting," says the detective, "because your brother was sighted here in Wanganui three days ago. You're not looking for a body Mr. Murrihy. You're looking for a fugitive."

ADOPTION

13 October 2000

<u>*Reaching*</u>

And still I keep reaching
Out to you, into you, back for you,
Up to you, down to you,
As I reach out to Him
And as He reaches for me

Once you reached for me
And I held you close
I reached for you
And we wouldn't let go
I held out my arms
And you stepped on the water
We laughed and walked together
And when you fell, I reached for you

Even when the storm engulfed us,
We weathered it all together
We thought we could sail
The currents, no matter how strong.
You leaned on me and I swore
I'd brace you and keep us afloat

But I fell, and we fell,
Drowning together, we drifted away

Then I reached for you,
Out to you, into you, back for you,
Up to you, down to you,
As I reach out to Him
And as He reaches for me

But you drew back from me,
For fear of your falling
And you built walls to keep me out
I don't blame you
My arms hurt from the stretching
My hands clenched and still empty
I've built walls of my own
Round my lonely heart's echoes

Still I keep reaching
Out to you, into you, back for you,
Up to you, down to you,
As I reach out to Him
And as He reaches for me

Won't you reach for me?
Out to me, into me, back for me,
Up to me, down to me,
As you reach out to him
And as He reaches for you?
Won't you reach for me
As I reach out to you?
Won't you reach for me?

~

Before I left the police station, Detective Daniels coerced me into promising to contact him if I even found a possible lead to Frankie's location. What choice would I have? Being charged myself is not going to help anybody. And Daniels promised he would contact me or my father if he found him first.

Frankie is alive. That's good news of course, but it complicates matters. Had I found his burial site, I could have at least reported his death back to Mom and Dad and omitted any stories about the charges against him. But now, even if the police or I find him, I won't be able to take him back to Canada with me. So what's the point in finding him at all? So I can tell her that I saw him but that he can't come back? And why can't he come back?

Still, with such a recent sighting of Frankie in the city, I must be very close to tracking him down. Why would he be back in Whanganui if he knew it might mean his arrest? With a sin complex like he seems to have developed, maybe he's ready to turn himself in or get himself caught. But why now? What's changed?

Or was he here for another reason? Pio told me that Frankie was basically on a mission, helping people with confessions. Was he here for that? He seemed willing to sacrifice his status in the Church for it. And if he's sick, is he traveling alone or does he have someone helping him? If he does, who could that be? Pio? If Frankie was in town three days ago, it was the same day I was caught in the rain and in the protest. Could it actually have been him in that crowd? Pio could be lying—he's made it clear he doesn't want me to find Frankie.

Unsure what to do, I finish my lunch and my coffee at this cafe on Guyton Street and return to the Focus. I really don't know what to do next. I feel like driving all around Whanganui, just looking for him. He seems to pop up for everyone else around here, maybe he'll pull one of his appearing acts for me down some side street or something. Fucking Hell.

Marietta is the woman who's accused Frankie. Would she be of any help finding him? Probably not. She'd be working with the police, who'd be pretty pissed off with me if I chased after her. Father Picard? Maybe he'd like Frankie to be found and caught. But disowning him seems to be his strategy—better to dissociate the Church from this mess. Pio? I could try and shake the shit out of him for some answers, threaten the cops on him. The prison? Now there's a place I haven't checked. It sounds like Frankie spent a lot of time there over these past two years. And between the church and the co-worker who put him up in Ratana, his lodgings have been connected to his work there. It may even turn out that Marietta had a connection to the prison. I don't see how Daniels could have a problem with me if I went to the prison and happened to run into her while I was there.

Done. I recall seeing a road-sign for the prison on the way to Ratana, so once again I head south of town, crossing the bridge at the end of Victoria Street.

It is a beautiful day in New Zealand, the most brilliant I have seen since arriving. The temperature and humidity have amped up and I'm grateful for the Ford's air conditioning. The turn-off to Wanganui prison is much closer than I remember, nowhere near the distance to Ratana. I exit State Highway 4 onto Pauri Road, following the directions on the smallest of road signs indicating the prison.

Immediately, the road changes, narrowing between a corridor of trees, large flax bushes and rustic, thin fence lines bordering farmlands. Even on this clear, dry day I reduce my speed, still unused to the twisting narrow roads. There are many turns marked with signs warning even the experienced drivers against high speeds along here. Not that there are many drivers, I only pass one small truck along the way. Of course, prisons aren't usually built in the most popular residential areas.

I encounter a fork in the road, with a blue sign saying, "Wanganui Prison, Area 3". The left branch turns into a one-lane gravel road while the right seems to carry on as normal. I continue on the main road but wonder if I've missed the prison entrance. Further down the road, I see two more blue signs in front of a complex of buildings and I arrive at the main entrance in Kaitoke.

In all my modest years of journalism, I have never had cause to enter a prison. There are no prisons in Pictou County and there are none nearby until you get to Truro and that is only for women. Any crime stories I cover usually end at the courthouse with an interview with the newly exonerated or with family of the newly incarcerated. Prison interviews are for the in-depth investigative journalists.

I park my car in the visitor's area, beside a white Holden Commodore sedan, which is being re-occupied by a lovely looking young woman and an older lady with the same fine bone structure in her face. A mother and daughter perhaps. Stepping out of the Focus, I overhear their conversation. It seems tense, but their tones are low and controlled.

The mother asks her daughter, "Are you sure it's still worth it Michelle? It's another three years of this, you know."

The daughter, as lovely as she looks, rolls her eyes petulantly. "Stop asking me that, for fuck's sake. God, you have to say the same thing all the time don't you? I've told you my answer to that so many times. Fuck off." Her words are harsh, but she shows little emotion or anger in her voice.

I walk away, unable to hear the mother's response, as they close their car door. I've heard similar conversations between parents and children, no matter what age levels, usually in court cases or domestics. I certainly hope my daughter and I don't end up in whatever situation has brought them to this prison today, but I'm sure we'll share the eye rolls and the exasperation.

As I walk toward the main entrance to the prison, I pass two men sitting on some chairs under a tree. That sun is blazing now. They both wear different styled uniforms. One man, with long hair tied up in a ponytail and wearing what appears to be a guard's uniform, ignores me completely, perhaps deliberately, as he stares in the direction of the women in the parking lot behind me. He's smoking a cigarette. The other man, with a trim haircut and beaming smile, is wearing coveralls weighed down with a large ring of keys and assorted tools. Across his left breast, an ironed logo reads, "Wanganui Locks and Bolts". He's speaking to the guard, saying, "OK, explain this to me friend, what's the deal with Maori cemeteries? Our cemeteries are special too but we don't go stopping people from walking on them or going through them to get to the beach." He catches my eye as I walk by and calls out, "G'day mate" in a brash American accent. I nod and say hello and he continues to watch me as I enter the front doors, even as he resumes his conversation with the smoking guard.

The front foyer of the prison is painted in dull peach tones. More blue signs ornament the walls like the ones on the roadsides, detailing initiatives of the Department of Corrections. Other signs outline procedures for visitors. Across the entrance area, I ring a buzzer on an unmanned desk and wait for reception. After a few minutes, I ring again and immediately there appears a very short, but muscle-bound man wearing a guard's uniform. He enters through a back door behind the desk, looks at me, then looks around inside the receptionist's area with a confused expression on his face.

"Is there no-one here?" he asks me, wide-eyed.

"No, I haven't seen anyone yet. I've just rung the buzzer for the second time."

"Yeah, I heard that. Usually Sharon is here. She can't be far away. OK, anyway," he says and then shambles across closer to me, but not so close that he would disappear behind the desk, "are you here to see an inmate?"

"No," I say, "well, not necessarily. I'm looking for anyone really, that might know a person who used to do some work here. He used to visit prisoners from the Catholic Church in Whanganui?"

The guard squints at me out of his left eye. "Oh yeah, was his name Father Pritchard or something like that?"

"No, his name is Francis."

He shakes his head. "Sounds familiar, but—"

"Do you think you could ask around to see if anyone here remembers him?"

"Well, I am pretty busy, but I could ask one of our directors here. She looks after visiting chaplains and things like that."

"That'd be great, thanks."

"Have a seat, eh? I'll be back real soon," he says and then disappears back through the door behind the desk.

I survey my waiting area. There are no seats or benches, so I don't know where he thinks I'm supposed to sit. I go back outside to see if there is a bench nearby. The only one is near the two men and it's too far away from the entrance for me to watch for the director to emerge. I survey the two men again who seem engrossed in a more serious conversation now. The locksmith is animating his actions and voice tones saying something about, "the dead burying the dead," while the guard is nodding his head, alternating between watching the speaker and looking around the grounds.

I hear a noise through the open door behind me and I turn to see a huge woman walking toward me. She must be at least six and a half feet tall. She is big-boned too with long dark hair. "Were you looking for me?" she asks in an unfamiliar accent.

"Are you the director who looks after visiting chaplains?"

"Yes, that's right. Aaron said you were asking about a priest who used to come here?"

"Not exactly. It was my brother Francis. He worked for the Catholic priest in the city."

She nods her head and looks at me more knowingly. "Do you mean Brother Francis? Are you his brother? You've come from Canada then?"

"That's right. I'm trying to find him but he's proving to be elusive."

"Yes, so I hear. I take it the police haven't found him yet either."

I shake my head. "I've just come from them. We have a deal to try and help each other." I throw this in, hoping it might buy me some credibility and make her more open to sharing information with me. It works, as she invites me inside to talk with her. Her office is much like that at the police station. Bare walls with Corrections posters. Desk. Two chairs.

She opens our conversation. "Well, Aaron was right. I would know the most about Francis here. What might I know that would help you?"

"I'm not exactly sure. I just keep moving from one lead to another and hope something will reveal itself. I've been told by some that Frankie—Francis—went off sick somewhere. Others have said they have seen him when he should have been somewhere else. I guess I'm hoping to ask you about his time here and see if that helps me put some pieces together—that something will make sense about where he might have gone to die—or to hide."

"Well, Francis was an unusual visitor here, that's for sure," the Amazon says. "You know he really had two different periods here? The first time he came here, it was as a representative of the Catholic Church—St. Mary's".

I nod my head and she continues, "He came with all the recommendations from Father Picard. We've known Father Picard here for almost a decade, but it had been awhile since the Catholics had sent a prison chaplain. I understand he was pretty pleased to be able to do so after so long. Your brother's role was to make himself available to any inmate requesting his services, Catholic or non-Catholic."

"Did he meet with many inmates?"

"Oh yes, though not many at first. There was another chaplain here who was well established. He's still here—an Anglican. At first, Francis didn't have many takers other than a few die-hard Catholics, but word spread about him and more and more asked to meet with him."

"Why was that, do you think?"

"Well, the prisoners liked him, I guess. Reverend Lancaster is known for being a good listener and very compassionate, but Francis seemed to draw something else out of people." She rolls her eyes and says, "Especially from the inmates in Te Moenga, the sex offenders unit. How bloody ironic is that?" She sees the reaction in my face and says, "Sorry—but it's pretty awful if it's true what they say about your brother. Anyway, the inmates talked of feeling much better after meeting with him. He had built up kind of a following until he left for Ratana. Do you know about that?"

"Yes, that was when he had his dispute with Father Picard."

She nods. "Yes, and that did make it tricky when he came back. Credentials are important here as you can imagine, and Francis had lost his. Plus his methods were somewhat unsound. It might have been best if we hadn't done so, but we let him back in."

"Why was that?"

"Well, if you've been to the police, you'll know why."

"No, I know about the charges, but why did you let him back in?"

She sighs and says, "Well, there were a few reasons. At first we refused because there has to be some accountability for the chaplains here. They need to be able to report back to someone or we at least need to be able to report back to some superiors if something goes wrong. But Rawiri lobbied for your brother and convinced me and our board to let him back in."

"Rawiri?" I repeat, remembering the old man at the cemetery.

"Yes, Rawiri used to work here. He was one of the key members involved in establishing and running the Maori Focus Unit. We couldn't understand it, but Rawiri did two things to us, both foolhardy in retrospect. Once he found out we'd declined your brother further access, he organized a petition signed by the inmates saying they wanted him back. He argued that he did this because of the strength of feeling the inmates had for him and the connection he had with them. The other thing he did was elicit support from some high-ups in Ratana. I never understood it. To my knowledge, Francis had only lived in Ratana for a couple of months and yet they were supporting his involvement with prisoners and willing to offer the credentials previously supplied by the Catholic Church." She looks hard at me, as if trying to discern something without asking, but then she does say, "Your brother didn't strike me as a particularly charismatic fellow. I don't know how he did what he did with the inmates or with the big-wigs in Ratana, but he sure fooled some people." She looks at me even more accusingly and asks, "Do you know how he did it?"

I shake my head and stare back dumbly. "I really don't; honestly, this doesn't sound like the Frankie I knew at all. That's why I need so much help here." To revive the flow, I ask, "So, he worked here for a few more months?"

She sits back in her chair which creeks loudly under her bulk. "That's right, and this time it was more intense. Something was different from the first time. Because of Rawiri, Francis got heavily involved with the inmates in the Maori Focus unit. He was visiting here every day, coming in with Marietta."

I stop my breath for a moment, afraid I'll sabotage something, aware of Detective Daniels' warning.

She continues, "Over those two months or so, we had a lot of strange behavior from those inmates. More and more were wanting to meet with Brother Francis and many were highly emotional about it. There was a lot of Jesus talk and a lot of men who were claiming to be truly changed, that sort of thing. We get that in prisons a lot, but there was a widespread enthusiasm going on here." She laughs lightly and says, "Reverend Lancaster wasn't very happy about it. He warned us about false theology and told us that it was a lot of hype, that the men were in danger of thinking they were healed when what they needed was careful, professional counseling; counseling they would refuse if they thought they were cured. I have to say, he was right about that, although I wondered if he just felt his patch was being threatened."

"So, it went on like that until Frankie left?" I ask.

"Pretty much, yes," she answers. "And you know what? Maybe it wouldn't have ended that way if we had controlled it all better."

"What do you mean?"

She studies me carefully, weighing up some decision, some calculation about me and what she is considering sharing. Then she says, "If you tell anyone this, I will deny ever having said it."

"Ma'am," I say, "I'm not interested in anything but finding my brother and getting back home."

I must measure up because she continues. "There is a chance your brother is innocent."

Again, my breath stops. "What do you mean?" I ask.

"During the height of the excitement around here, your brother and Marietta took an inmate off-site several times." She sees my surprise and says, "That in itself is not unusual. Most of our prisoners here are not maximum security. Many are near the end of their sentences and have shown evidence of reform. Chaplains are occasionally granted custody of an inmate to take them to a church service in the city. Marietta and Francis were doing just that a few weeks before he left us. The records show that they took him to a Pentecostal fellowship, named after an eagle or dove or hen or something, these places are always changing their names. The thing is," she says regarding me with that same calculating look, "the inmate they took out was a sex offender—one of those who were so passionate about their healing from God."

She stops talking and waits for my response. But I don't know how to respond. Again, this is all too much for me to fathom. For Christ's sake, I just want to find this bastard brother of mine, innocent, shamed, dead, whatever! I want to go home and see my mother, not stay here and prove Frankie's innocence. I don't have the time for this, I don't have the strength for this, I don't have enough love for him to do this.

All I can say is, "Did you tell the police this? Why are you telling me?"

She shrugs her shoulders. "To assuage my own conscience perhaps. As I said, I will deny it if you tell anyone. I will fight any hints that this prison is culpable in some way. Besides, no matter what it looks like, the accusation from the boy and his mother is against your brother, not the inmate. I only tell you this because you say Francis is dying and I say that is enough of a burden for you to bear. He was weakening when I last knew him here and was obviously very sick. I believe he will die before he is caught. Once you find him, dead or alive, go home and rest knowing that he did some good and may very well not have done the bad he's been accused of."

~

17 August 2000

<u>*Exile?*</u>

Alone, surrounded by wind and water
Stripped of all followers
To whom I've listened for so long
No use for ears or tongue

When, in the Spirit of the Lord's day,
I heard behind me a loud voice say,
"I am the Beginning and the End,
Write what you see and show My servants."

Then I turned to see the voice that spoke
It was the Son of Man in a golden cloak
His head white as wool, His eyes like a flame,
His feet like brass, from His mouth a sword came.

I fell at His feet, but He laid His hand on me
And said, "Do not be afraid for I am He,
The one who lives though He once was dead
And who has the keys to the House of Dread."

He said, "Write what you have seen
And the things which have been
And the things which take place after this
To reveal to My servants all that is."

~

There don't seem to be any more avenues open with this lady after our strange conversation. I ask her if it is possible to speak with anyone else, maybe some inmates who knew Frankie well, but she tells me that inmates can only be visited when they request a certain visitor and that even then, the process takes several days. She assures me that no other employees at the prison would know his details more than she did. I go so far as to ask about Marietta and she looks at me with as stern a look as she's given me all day and informs me that Marietta no longer visits the prison and that it is time for me to go. She leads me back out to the front entrance and says goodbye and I am, once again, enlightened without new direction.

In what must be the longest smoke break in unrecorded history, the locksmith and the guard are still engaged in conversation by the park bench. I feel very uncomfortable watching them as I walk by, as the locksmith is now seated on the bench with the guard who appears to be crying. His head is in his hands and his torso is shifting up and down in gentle sobbing motions. The locksmith is resting his hand on the crying man's shoulder and is speaking, not to him, as much as over him, with his eyes closed.

I look back at the entrance door just in time to catch the Amazon turning her eyes from the pair, shaking her head and retreating into the interior of the building. Walking closer to them, I overhear the locksmith speaking but I cannot make out a single word he is saying—it sounds like no language I know. At first, I think it is Maori or some sort of Arabic, but I'm certain it's neither. Just as I am about to carry on, the locksmith opens his eyes, even as he babbles away, and looks intently at me. He pats the guard on the shoulder, who seems to have calmed down, and stands to his feet.

"Hello friend!" he calls in that drawling accent. "We were just praying over here. Would you like to join us?" He sounds sarcastic and I wonder: was I staring?

"No, I'm good thanks."

"What you heard just now was a heavenly language my friend. Tongues—spoken by God's angels themselves and given to men as a gift of His Holy Spirit."

I'm mildly frozen. I really don't have time for this shit. I look at the guard, who has now raised his head and is smiling at me as he wipes the tears from his face. He says, "Dude, you gotta hear what this man has to say. It'll blow your mind. These brothers are nga mangai man, mouthpieces for God Himself."

I launch toward him, ignoring the locksmith and his cheesy smile. "What brothers are you talking about?" I ask him.

The guard points at the locksmith and says, "Guys like this man. I haven't heard a word like that since Tuakana Perohuka was here. Different message but same Spirit man—a true word."

The locksmith laughs, "Tooakana Parastroika? That sounds like tongues right there!"

"No man, *Tuakana Perohuka*—it's like the pruning brother, you know—as in pruning shears?"

I practically grab the guard. "Do you mean Brother Francis? Is that who you're talking about?"

The guard laughs and puts his hand on my arm but then says conspiratorially, "Yeah man, that's him. Do you know him?"

"He's my brother—I need to take him back home. Our mother is dying—but I can't find him!"

"Well," says the guard, who then leans into me and says quietly, "I can help you there."

VOIDS AND BEGINNINGS

The guard, whose name is Cobbler, would not tell me where Frankie is, but is meeting me this morning with the promise that he will take me to him. Too good to be true? I really don't know. Can I trust him? I really don't know. But it is the only lead I have left—and besides, even in our short encounter yesterday, I'd trust him more than his praying companion. I offered to give the guard the name of my motel, but he refused to let me tell him. Instead, he designated this place for our rendezvous, and why would I be surprised at it? It's Upokongaro. Cobbler told me to meet him at St. Mary's Church and this day I've had some time to inspect the grounds since he's late by at least an hour. I'm grateful that there is no rain this time, though Whanganui has been hit with the same yellow fog from Taumarunui. It was a slow drive out here this morning and my patience is wearing thin when he finally arrives.

I can't believe my eyes when I see him drive in. He's behind the wheel of a small pick-up style truck, hauling a smaller speed-boat on a trailer. What's worse, he has the locksmith with him—I can see his teeth glinting through the front windshield. I don't have time for this shit.

"Kia ora bro!" the locksmith says as he swaggers out of the truck's cab. He's left his coveralls behind and is wearing loose blue jeans and a plaid shirt with sleeves rolled to the elbows. He looks like a hairless lumberjack. I ignore him again and walk over to Cobbler on the driver's side.

"Don't tell me you're planning on taking me somewhere in that thing. I'm not a tourist. Just tell me where I need to go."

The guard sits back in the truck's seat adjusting his hair-tie, and speaks to me from inside. "Hey now man, I get you, I get you. But it's not so simple bro. Your brother is upriver, yeah? And you can't get there by road, at least not today. They're fixing up a slip from the rain this week."

I ease off, allowing him to step out and walk back toward the boat. He looks relaxed in his shorts, sleeveless top and flip-flops. Leery of the vessel and of the unexpected travel partner, I ask, "Why aren't you two working today?"

"Time off for good behavior," Cobbler says and the locksmith laughs. "I work four days on and four days off," Cobbler clarifies. "Twelve hour shifts."

The locksmith chips in, "And I am self-employed! I've left my apprentice to answer any call-outs and I'll be back on the job tomorrow." He gives me a wink.

Cobbler puts his hand on the boat's front rim and says, "If you want to see him today, this is the way to do it. Besides, you'll never forget a journey on our awa."

~

Cobbler convinces me that, "it's all good," and I join him and the locksmith in the truck, leaving my car at the church where he assures me it will be safe for the day. We drive a short distance back on the highway, turning down a road to the riverside where there is a decrepit looking jetty and a small slipway. The whole thing looks like it's been through some wars.

"We had a bad flood here last February," Cobbler says as he and the locksmith untie the chords securing the boat to the trailer. "Our new mayor is talking about rebuilding this jetty for the Waimarie. We've been told not to launch from here anymore, but she'll be right mate, no worries. My tupuna have been navigating this river for forty generations."

"We're in good hands friend," the locksmith chimes.

Before we board, Cobbler says, "First, we must say a karakia to honor the kaitiaki, the guardians of the river and ask them for safe travel." He bows his head and recites a string of words in Maori, finishing with "Amene." Then he says, "Ooh, did you here that bird whistle just then? That's the pipiwharauroa. When it drops its whistle like that, it means it's going to rain. We'd better get going. Welcome to the Queen's highway, my friends—the Rhine of the South, the River of Memory!"

In just a few minutes we're loaded into the small metal craft and are pushing our way up river, the motor purring away fairly quietly. We're not moving quickly and Cobbler tells me the trip should take a few hours. "Shouldn't we have life jackets?" I ask him even as we reach deeper waters.

"She'll be right mate!" he says from the back of the boat where he is operating the motor. "My ancestors never worried about life jackets. The river will look after us."

Your ancestors could swim, I think, resignedly, but then ask, "Where are we going?"

"Hiruharama."

"The City of God!" interjects the locksmith. "The joy of the whole earth, the perfection of beauty, Zion!"

I look to Cobbler for an explanation and he nods his head and laughs.

"We're going to Jerusalem."

~

Pure water comes from Para-whenuamea, yet what makes water pure?

The fresh water, the water of rivers and lakes, comes from Rangi-nui. The water of the oceans comes from Tangaroa. Which is pure? Who would tell Tangaroa that the salt of his water makes it impure? Who would tell Rangi-nui that his water is made impure by flowing over the stones and earth of his love, Papa-tū-ā-nuku?

Yet we know some things are tapu, some things are sacred.

Today, we watched te wahine visit Taranaki at his whare once again. This time, he welcomed her in through his gate and closed it from our view. Then our vision was obscured by a thickening fog. Behind it, the sun descended and all went dark.

~

This river is muddy but beautiful. Just as I noticed it appearing alongside the highway at Upokongaro on the way to Whanganui, now I feel the disappearance of the highway and with it, our connection with civilization. For the first leg of our journey, the river is flanked by smaller roads on each side, but there is no traffic to speak of, and eventually these vanish as well. Other than the motor, all is quiet. The river banks change to great limestone cliffs and shaggy walls of vegetation; rolling waves of plants, drooping trees, some standing tall and filling the sky with their giant leaves, others caressing the river's edges with their branches, creating shelter for ducks and minor snags for Cobbler to negotiate in narrow sections. There's a tangy smell of forest-laden air. Cobbler points out some empty holes in the cliff-sides and says, "My ancestors made those when they used to pole upriver in their waka—their canoes. Now they are homes to kingfishers and river ducks. We know there's a flood coming if they're empty." Around another bend, I point out one longer mark that looks more like a scratch than a hole and he tells us it was made years ago by a "very hairy monster," and I wait for him to laugh at his joke but he only looks at it grimly and carries on.

If Cobbler keeps his promise, I will see Frankie today. I would be relatively happy to sit in this boat and wait for that while taking in the river views and sounds, but the locksmith wants to talk. He quizzes Cobbler on Maori names for aspects of the river; he marvels about the beauty of God's creation in Aotearoa, New Zealand, "Godzone" he calls it; he offers to steer the boat which Cobbler, thankfully, refuses. Otherwise, Cobbler seems to enjoy every word that comes out of the locksmith's mouth and I am grateful that he is at least leaving me alone, until he finally addresses me.

"What an amazing thing that we ran into you yesterday, eh mate?" he says, leaning back with one arm resting on the side of the boat.

I play along. "Yeah, it was. I don't know what I'd be doing if Cobbler wasn't helping me out like this." That much is true.

"God is good brother. Do you believe that?" he asks.

"I'm sure He is," I say, hoping the conversation will turn to something else, but realizing he's got an agenda and a trapped audience here in this boat.

"Are you a good person Conrad?"

What a leading question. I recognize the type from certain lawyers I've observed in minor courtroom dramas back home. If I say yes, there will be a reason why I am not. If I say no there will be a reason why I am. Either way, he's going to steer me along his river of reasoning.

"I don't really think about it much," I say, hoping to deflect him.

He looks at me sideways and chuckles arrogantly as if he's pleased I've given him a challenge. "That's an interesting answer mate," he says. Do you know what most people say?"

I give him what he wants. "They probably say they are good. Most people want to believe they're good."

He leans forward, looking delighted as if we've made some profound connection with each other. "That's exactly right," he says. "And do you know what I ask them next?" He pauses, waiting for me to carry on the conversation which is really a Q&A monologue with two voices. I tell him I don't know. Cobbler looks on as if fascinated by his friend, intrigued by what he is doing with me.

"I ask them, how do they know they are good? What exactly does it mean to be good—how do we measure it? Do you have an answer for that question?"

"Not really," I say, certain he'll tell me anyway.

"Have you ever stolen anything?" he asks.

"Yes."

"Have you ever told a lie?"

"Sure."

"Have you ever sworn using words like 'God-damn' or 'Jesus Christ'?"

"Yes."

The locksmith looks very pleased with himself, sitting back again to rest along the side of the boat. "Well, from what you have just told me, you are a lying, blaspheming thief." He smirks at me, obviously expecting a pre-determined reaction. I refuse to give it to him.

"Isn't everybody? What's your point?"

He sits up again and snaps his fingers at me, pointing his index my way. "That's my point—everybody is the same. We are all lying, blaspheming thieves. Do you know what the Bible says about that?"

"I wouldn't have a clue."

"It says that 'all have sinned and fallen short of the glory of the Lord'. That means that we are all sinners in the eyes of a perfect, sinless, good God. That's you, me and Cobbler, brother!"

I need to draw a line. "Is this what you were talking about with Cobbler yesterday?"

"As a matter of fact it was."

"Well, if you think this conversation will end with me crying and you hugging me, you've got another thing coming."

The locksmith just laughs and winks at Cobbler behind him. He looks at me curiously and we sit in silence for a few moments, watching scattered bits of debris float by—driftwood and pumice rocks. I listen to the motor running and look at the occasional house further up from the river banks. It seems there might be another road running alongside the river, perhaps the one Cobbler told me about, the one I wish I was driving on by myself right now. But for now, the locksmith's not finished with me.

From behind me, he says, "Hey Conrad, if God is so good, and we are not so good, what do you think he's going to do with us when we pass from this world?"

"I don't know, send us to Hell I suppose," I say, trying hard not to hide my sarcasm.

This only excites him again. "Yes! You see, God is not only good, he is holy and he cannot abide any sinfulness in his presence. And we are all sinners. It's a real problem isn't it?"

I turn to face him. "For some it is, depending on what you believe. I don't worry about it—I may have done some bad things, but I don't think about them as sins and I don't believe in a God who wants to punish me for them."

The locksmith persists. "Yeah, but friend, he has no choice but to punish sins, unless those sins can be removed. And he's made a way for that to happen because, even though he's a holy God and a just God who must punish sin, he loves us and wants us to be with him."

"I suppose this is where Jesus comes in then eh?" I've seen enough televangelists to recognize the "God's made a way" pitch.

"You got it brother!" he says and then looks at me cheesily. "But do you really get it?"

I don't answer but shake my head and turn to watch the front of the boat cutting the edge of some rapids which are causing us to bump along roughly. I'm feeling annoyed, but he seems to take this as a sign that I'm reflecting on what he has just said.

"The only way you'll really get it is if you allow the Holy Spirit to reveal it to you." I feel his hand on my shoulder. "Do you want me to pray with you about this friend?"

I shake his hand free. "Fuck off," I say a little more harshly than I intend. He's just so annoying with his creepy smile and his theatrics.

"That's cool Conrad," he coos, and I hear him settle back against the boat again. A number of minutes pass as we move through the water and I see signs of settlement along the riverside. Some teenage boys are swimming in a deeper section round a bend and Cobbler waves to them, saying something in Maori. The boys call back, giving him the finger and other presumably obscene gestures which makes Cobbler growl and utter his own playfully threatening noises. We continue our journey without stopping.

"That's my marae—Pungarehu!" Cobbler says to us, after casting a final look over his shoulder at the boys as we round another bend. The river is filled with twists and turns in this section. "Those were my nephews. I was telling them off for not being at school. They could at least be doing some fishing and make themselves useful."

I'm grateful for a new conversation topic that doesn't involve the locksmith. "The river seems to have some good swimming holes," I offer.

"Not as good as in the old days. Our awa has been abused and reduced," he says. "This here water used to be green as and it tasted like kowhai trees. Did you see how far back from the river the buildings are? That's 'cause the river used to be three times its size now, before they built the dams and stole our waterway at its source," he points to the north-east, "way over there on Mount Tongariro. Now Taupo has our water and their homes are filled with the power she generates. It's a long story, but it's one we haven't forgotten here—us and the eels!" he says and chuckles to himself, shaking his head. "I used to take bags of eels out of this river, mate, bags of eels. Now there's no more grayling or huia, it's not good."

The locksmith can't resist getting involved in whatever conversation is happening. He asks, "I suppose the white man has done a lot of damage here Cobbler?"

"Yeah, bro, that's for sure. We've had our awa's gravel stolen so that riverboats like the Waimarie could take fancy tourists up to Pipiriki and Taumarunui. We've had our pa tuna—our eel weirs—destroyed. Our soils are not nourished by flood waters. A lot of our kainga—our villages on the western banks have been deserted since the road was built. Everyone depends on the road now.

"The river provides everything a body needs and we love her for it. She's a doctor, a priest, a larder, a highway, a moat, a shelter, a tupuna . . . a mother. That's the thing man, you pakeha look at the river like it's a resource or a commodity, but how can you buy and sell your mother? Like the proverb says, 'Ko au te awa, ko te awa ko au—I am the river and the river is me.' Yeah, we Maori got it sussed eh? You'll see, someday the whole world will understand and say, 'Hey, Te Atihaunui a Paparangi know what they are talking about.'"

He leans over the bow and lets the water run through his fingers. "We're still fighting. Genesis Energy is trying to get resource consent for the dam for thirty-five years! But we're appealing. We'll restore our awa—bring healing to her, to the land; bring back our people, our tangata whenua." Cobbler speaks dreamily, as if to someone not here or not in this moment.

Then he gives his head a shake and smiles at us both. "Still," he says, "Pakeha have not just brought damage and mayhem, eh? You guys have brought our Lord Jesus Christ." He looks fondly at the locksmith. "And you've brought some good medicines and blonde women and KFC!" He launches into a fit of giggles at this and we can't help but join him in a laugh.

"Of course," he continues, "Maori medicines are still pretty good, eh? In fact, I reckon the choice medicines are the ones that combine the best of both worlds." He looks at me with a wry smile and says, "You'll see."

~

When Frankie and I grew older, we graduated from our brook. Our neighborhood friends, always the more adventurous, introduced Frankie to a new swimming hole that could only be reached by bicycle for us boys who had yet to get our licenses. Frankie went first, of course. He was the older of us which meant that he could get Mom and Dad's permission, but he also needed to do these things first with our friends to show they were his friends first. He always kept me just to the outside of the group, never wanting me on his team, always submitting to letting me play our neighborhood games of baseball and road hockey only if the teams needed someone to even up the numbers.

So he would come home with stories about the new swimming hole. He told me about how much deeper the water was than in the brook, which scared me but intrigued me at the same time. He told me about the leeches and how Derek, the oldest boy in the group, knew to take a shaker of salt with him to detach these alarming creatures. He told me about the giant dog-berry trees that grew on both banks near the swimming hole which enabled two teams to arm themselves and conduct war games across the watery trench. He told me about the huge tree which had long since fallen half-way across the river creating the swimming hole as, after years of erosion, the river had carved out a lower bed, navigating its way around the fallen log.

So, I graduated from the brook through stories until it was my turn to venture forth. It was Frankie's idea to go together, just the two of us; I don't know where the others were, but I'm sure if they were around, he never would have asked me. I suited his purpose at that moment—Frankie wanted to go to the swimming hole and he needed someone to go with.

It was a great day after several of heavy rain. Frankie rode his five-speed bicycle with the one front brake and I rode my CCM, my pride and joy because it was built heavily and looked like a motorcycle. However, the bike's bulk turned out to be a treacherous aspect of our day. In his enthusiasm, Frankie insisted we follow the same route through the river as he and our friends had on their previous visits, despite the swollen waters. We were not long in the river when we both discovered the power of the fast-flowing current. We pushed our bikes through until they were completely submerged and we were up to our armpits in brown peril.

Frankie fell into one of his panics, yelling at me frantically and analyzing the situation at the same time. "The river is flooded! It's not normally like this! Pull harder Conrad!" Comical really. I don't know how we managed to rescue those bikes and ourselves. It's funny to think that I was certain the bikes might be lost, but never once, even in that deluge, did I consider that one of us might get hurt. It's only in retrospect now that I see the true danger and picture my name in a front page story about drowning boys. Heaven forbid that my daughter should ever put herself in a situation like that. But then, I trusted Frankie, I guess. He was like Dad in that way. It's only as an adult now that I recognize some of the scary situations and pressures

Dad faced when we were growing up. But we kids trusted him, and I trusted Frankie.

~

According to Cobbler, the Whanganui is looking nice and full today, after those heavy rains, but of course is still nowhere near what it used to be. To me, it feels like we're going back in time, into a lost world, following a path left by an uncoiling snake, or perhaps an eel. We've been sitting quietly for several minutes now and I've also taken to letting my hand drift in the cool brown waters as he slowly pilots the craft through calm sections, occasionally uplifted by some decent rapids. Cobbler was right, he knows what he's doing and I feel safe with him, though I am anxious about our arrival and his intentions.

"How much farther is it to Jerusalem?" I ask.

Cobbler nods in the direction past the front of the boat. "Just around there is Atene." I follow his line of vision to an unusual-looking hill coming into view as we make our way toward the bend. As we approach, I see it's a forest-covered mound, a protrusion surrounded by cleared land as if everything around it had been settled and civilized while leaving the hill primordial and pristine. It reminds me of the cemetery at Taupiri. The river road is clearly seen here and has been following our river trek closely for some time now, though no cars have passed by us from either direction. I ask Cobbler about the mound.

"That is Puketapu, our sacred hill. Many tupuna live there—our ancestors."

"What do you mean, *live* there?"

Cobbler smiles and says, "We believe our ancestors stay with us, they guard over us. We honor them where they are buried and acknowledge the unbroken line that exists in us in our blood and in our spirit." He then says something in Maori toward the hill and I notice the locksmith shift uncomfortably in his seat. He looks like he's literally biting his tongue, but remains quiet as Cobbler steers our craft around another bend where the dense jungle returns to surround us on the high walls of our winding way and we continue crawling toward Frankie.

The river is quick but quiet and the rain is picking up, obscuring the reflections of me and my companions on the surface. The sound of raindrops landing all around us is rhythmic and oddly comforting despite the growing discomfort of getting wet in the boat with no rain gear and only a vague idea of how long we will be exposed to the elements. I don't like being out of control in this way, trusting these men to guide me, but also leaving myself this vulnerable, this unprepared for whatever might come next. Yet, the rainwater eases my feelings of isolation.

Along the river, there are occasional settlements. The road is obviously nearby even when you can't see it and some hills look cleared for farmland. But the river, even in its supposed diminished state, is daunting, certainly wider and stronger-flowing than any river I've encountered in Nova Scotia. It seems younger and older at the same time—as if it is filled with an enthusiasm for the future but also carrying hurts from the past.

The locksmith hunches forward to warm himself in the rain. It is not cold but there is no shelter out here in our little boat. Cobbler raises his chin to greet the droplets. He even takes his sunglasses off and I catch him closing his eyes as he steers us through small rapids and near peninsulas of land jutting out from oxbow bends.

Soon, we come across two such peninsulas, one on either side of the river. The landing on our right has a clear path leading from it to some unknown settlement further up the bank and behind a crop of trees. Cobbler steers toward this until he pilots us to a full stop on its shore. He gets out and says, "I'll be right back—just got to go see someone at the pa for a sec. You can grab some shelter from the rain under those trees if you like." Then he scampers up the track and disappears from sight.

The locksmith and I disembark and it feels good to stretch my legs and walk on solid ground. We duck under some large-leafed trees and I am surprised at how sheltered we are. The locksmith shivers and says, "The rain gets inside you, eh?"

"It's not too bad actually." I'm surprised that I really don't mind it that much. "I just want to get there."

"Jerusalem, eh? That's a pretty cool name for a Maori village way down here in the South Pacific, don't you think? I bet you never thought you'd visit Jerusalem."

"I never really thought about it much. I only know about the real Jerusalem from the news—all the fighting between Israelis and the Palestinians, unable to share land but willing to kill small children for it. I know some people are keen on visiting it for religious reasons. I had an aunt who visited 'The Holy Land' with her church friends."

"I've been there you know—it's terrific. I've set foot in the river where Jesus was baptized, I've seen where he was crucified outside of the limits of the old city, been to the wailing wall where the Jewish people still pray for a restoration of their temple. Someday, they will get it back to what God intended. Just got to get rid of that mosque that's built on the site." He laughs and says, "Not an easy job, but God will show them the way."

"I don't see how that could happen without a major war."

The locksmith shrugs. "Could be—God will have a plan. I don't know how it might work, but He keeps his promises and He has promised that land to the Jewish people." He smiles and says, "That's why they call it the Promised Land! Think about it too—Israel was established as a country in 1948 after centuries of dispersion of the Israelites around the world. If you look at a map, you'll see they are surrounded by hostile Arab nations that would all love to see them destroyed, wiped off the face of the earth—Iran, Iraq, Syria, even Egypt. But God has kept them protected. He's got a plan."

"A plan involving nuclear armaments provided by the U.S.? Sounds like a plan alright."

"Like I said, I don't know all the ins and outs, but God keeps his promises. He made a covenant with Abraham, promised him as many ancestors as there are stars in the sky and he promised him that his people would live in the place we call Israel. It's gotta happen my friend."

I shake my head and look out at the passing river. The rain has let up slightly and is just making its mark in tiny droplets barely visible on the water's surface. Sometimes, it seems the drops make pencil-like drawings and one can imagine seeing sketches of all sorts of creatures appearing and disappearing. A light wind has picked up, the first I've really noticed on our journey, we must be so protected by these hills which continue to loom all around us. It's claustrophobic. The locksmith is still talking.

"What do you think about what Cobbler said about his ancestors still being here?"

"He can believe what he likes."

"But that attitude represents one of the great problems in our world—it's a trick of the devil to convince people that we should just let each other believe what we like. If I had cancer and I believed the only cure was to eat nothing but mushrooms, should doctors just let me believe what I like or should they try and convince me to accept their treatments? I am a missionary my friend, and I have been sent by God to the Maori people to show them the Way of Jesus Christ, who will lead them to Him and set them free from old superstitions. But what do you think about it? Do you think the soul of his dead great-grand-pappy is still wandering these hills, trapping eels in the river, following us around?"

As he says this, I look up at a sound coming from Cobbler's path to see the oldest looking man I have ever set eyes on walking toward us. He is a Maori man, stepping slowly, but ably down the path with the aid of a cane. His face is completely covered with a tattoo which is warped by the wrinkles on his face and disappears under a cap on his head. Other than the markings, it is the face of a man consigned by time to its most fundamental elements.

"Possibly," I answer the locksmith and nod toward the old man approaching from behind him.

The locksmith turns and says, "Woe," then looks at me and winks. "That was pretty cool."

Following the old man, Cobbler waves to someone hidden behind him on the bank. He catches up to his companion and says something we can't hear while putting his hand on his shoulder. The old man snarls, "Haere atu koe!" and swats his hand so Cobbler leaves him to reunite with us.

The rain is falling heavily once again and even Cobbler is squinting at us through the haze of water. "Sorry guys, I'd invite you up to the pa to dry off but my grandfather won't wait any longer. He's been wanting to get up to Jerusalem for a few days and insists on going with us now."

He turns to our new geriatric boat-mate. "Are you alright there Koro?"

"I told you, leave me alone," the old man growls in a rich tone that sounds like three voices layered into one.

Cobbler looks at us as if to say, "See what I mean?" and then holds out his hand to indicate we should embark.

The locksmith and I steady the outboard while Cobbler helps his grandfather into the craft and settle onto the back bench. Then we board, this time both of us sharing the front seat, but facing each other with one leg on each side. The old man says something else in Maori to Cobbler who retreats back under our tree where he plucks off a branch. He returns and tosses it into the boat and then pushes us out onto the filling river before nobly hopping in from waist deep water to take his spot with the motor and we are away.

Other than the addition of our new crew-member, the journey carries on as it had done, only far more miserably in the driving rain. It is difficult to see the hills and road through the wall of water which creates a mist and haze that may well be as thick as the fog. The locksmith and I swap grim looks but do not speak. The old man is yet to acknowledge our presence, instead staring ahead of us, seemingly oblivious of the rain covering him.

The river straightens out during this part of our journey, with fewer sharp bends, but still hemmed in by the imposing hills in all directions. It's a wonder any sunlight is getting through to this place at all. The river is not completely barren, it has obviously been settled for some time as we see various buildings along the bank, some that may indicate larger villages or residences connected with the river road beyond. We see no signs of life however, other than some ducks at various points. Even they are finding shelter, huddling together under the over-hanging branches.

It really is too much and I call out to Cobbler over the pounding torrent, "Do you think we can pull over somewhere until this rain stops?"

Cobbler looks at the back of his grandfather's head, which doesn't seem to register my voice. He says, "The only place would be London," as he points toward a farm-house type of building coming up on our right, "but I don't think the queen would want us dripping on her fine carpets!"

"Ranana!" It's the old man growling again. He's turned to look at his grandson, who is chuckling away to himself.

"I know Koro, Ranana." Then he says to us, "Ranana is the name given to the pa by Richard Taylor, an Anglican minister who lived here in the 1800 and somethings. Ranana is meant to sound like London." I can barely hear him above the din. "Our last stop was at Koriniti—Corinth. Atene is Athens. Jerusalem is Hiruharama."

"Well, can we stop in Ranana?"

"Nah, man. I know you're soaked, but Hiruharama is not much further now. Just around some corners! We can dry off there, eh?"

With that, Cobbler guns the outboard motor again, calling out, "She'll be right!" and we carry on round another bend.

In Nova Scotia, we have our share of precipitation; great snowfalls and enough rain in March and April to melt snow and cause some level of flooding, especially around rivers. But our rainfalls never reach the torrential levels I experience on the Whanganui. The only thing I have to compare it to is a heavy rainstorm my family drove through on a trip to Florida, somewhere between Virginia and Georgia. The five of us were packed in an '82 Tercel and slowly making our way through some steep Appalachian hills when the rains came. I remember sitting in the back, sandwiched between Frankie and Clio and trying to see through the front windshield, as if by my watching, my father would have clearer vision as he drove. My mother suggested we pull over somewhere, but my father continued, either out of obstinacy or out of a fear of pulling to the shoulder on a major highway when oncoming vehicles would not be able to see us.

It seemed like a situation in which, to stop was to risk getting smashed into by someone else you didn't know and whose driving skills you couldn't trust, in effect completely handing over your fate to strangers; or to keep going, even blinded, taking some control of the situation in order to somehow decide your own fate.

Back at Upokongaro, I had handed my fate to Cobbler and this river. Even if I tried to wrest it back, it would be a long dog-paddle, or maybe a long hitch-hike back to Whanganui. Either way, I would be as wet as I am now. I resign myself to the damp and urge the outboard motor on-ward to Jerusalem.

~

After Ranana, even through the rain-induced haze, we can see the river road follow us closely along the bank to our right. We pass through relatively calm waters, interrupted by only the rainfall and small islands in the middle of the current. The trees are still thick and the hills continue to stare down at us from their distant heights. During one relatively sedate patch of river, I see a chunk of pumice floating alongside us and it takes me a second look to realize it is not passing by us, but following us upriver.

"That's weird," I say and as I speak, the pumice releases its hold and drifts downstream behind us.

"What happened?" asks the locksmith.

"Oh nothing, just my eyes playing tricks on me."

Cobbler calls out, "What was it? What did you see?" and even the old man seems interested.

"I saw some pumice . . . It looked like it was floating upriver."

"Are you sure?" asks Cobbler.

"It must be a glitch in the system . . . It happens when they change something!" the locksmith calls out, laughing.

But Cobbler only looks at his grandfather who raises his eyebrows at him.

Cobbler slows the boat alongside a larger island and calls out to us, "This place is Moutoa; it is wahi tapu—sacred land! Lots of our people died here in 1864 in a kind of civil war between the Hauhaus and the Whanganui people. I don't know though, those Hauhaus might have had the right idea."

At this, the old man breaks his silence with another growl at Cobbler. "Bible burners!"

Cobbler winces but doesn't protest. He only gestures toward the banks and adds, "Our ancestors are buried all along this river."

The old man calls out some words in Maori toward the island and seems to drink in the rainwater through his upturned face, as if he is rejuvenating like a plant that has been neglected for too long. He moans in his pleasure and says things in Maori, in a different tone of gratitude. Cobbler doesn't pay him any mind, but quietly navigates the river with a placid grin. The locksmith certainly looks as miserable as I feel. He's even rocking in his seat, covering himself with himself which is all the shelter he has.

Soon, we pass around another large island in the middle of the river swinging wide away from the sheer cliffs, close to the roadside bank. Around this bend, I see a misty, enigmatic village appear, several buildings visible on the hillside above the sparse branches of the trees garlanding the river. Some houses dot the lower sections while, above, we are greeted by the front facade and spire of a little wooden church which seems to be waiting in the dark green hills to greet any travelers coming from the south.

There is activity too, the most human activity we have seen since the swimmers at Atene. Dozens of men are moving about, dark forms gliding here and there between the houses and up by the church. One man, an alarming figure dressed in bright purple robes, is running toward us on a bridge in a break between the trees. He is waving his arms frantically but he is too far away for us to hear anything he is saying. Is he cursing us? Welcoming us? Who could tell? Then he disappears behind some scrub and it is hard to know whether he has run down some unseen path or if he has fallen, his gait was so ramshackle.

Suddenly, the old man opens his eyes and whips his head around at Cobbler, and snarls, "Turituri!"

Cobbler says, "Yes Koro, I know," and, to my surprise, turns off the outboard motor. The locksmith stirs catatonically, looking to Cobbler for an explanation.

Cobbler has reached below his seat and drawn forth two oars. He hands one over his grandfather's shoulder toward the locksmith and says, "We'll need to paddle the rest of the way. The landing is just up ahead."

"What's going on?" I call out.

"We have to turn the motor off so we don't deafen the taniwha under the bridge," Cobbler calls back, just loudly enough for me to make most of him out, then he collects the tree branch from Ranana and tosses it into the water.

"The what?"

"The taniwha," the locksmith says, close enough for me to hear, as he starts to paddle behind Cobbler's leading strokes. Then he says in a lower voice, loud enough for me but not for Cobbler, "It's a Maori superstition. They believe spirits live in rivers and lakes," he looks over his shoulder, "apparently placated by foliage." He laughs, "Stories to scare children," and then intones even closer, "or a demonic presence."

At this, the old man erupts in a rage, standing in the boat and glaring at the locksmith and then at me. He's speaking a flurry of words in Maori, his eyes wide and his tongue darting out. He intersperses his words with hisses and grunts and his gesticulations cause the boat to pitch wildly. The locksmith half stands in protest or to calm him down, trying to explain himself in soothing tones that crack and whine as he fights with the noise of the pounding rain. As he shifts his weight and the old man drives his own foot harder into the floor of the boat to steady himself, I am thrown to my left and am forced to my feet as well. I try to correct the imbalance and step to my right but the floor is greased with rainwater. My foot kicks out in front of me and I careen out of the boat into the water behind us.

Shock.

I flounder, expecting my feet to touch sharp rocks or a sandy floor. I sink down what may be only seven feet before I feel the slimy bottom. With my first push off its muddy bed, I manage to regain the surface of the river and see the side of the motorboat with Cobbler reaching out to me with his oar, but he is too far away. The locksmith is trying to steer the craft back toward me, but I don't see any more as I sink again into the dark.

I splash my arms wildly and kick my legs with no effect. With a new breath of air stored, I find the bottom again and kick off but this time it is that much harder. One foot sticks in the mud and I lose a shoe as I kick at it with my free heel. Panicking, I try again for the surface, finding a rock beneath the mud that supports my push. I scramble high enough to push my face into the air, but there is no sign of the boat. My last view is of the village on the hill and the church steeple against the grey sky and I hear a bell tolling before I feel a pull on my leg below and I descend into the depths of the Whanganui, everything fading to black.

SUZANNE

When the sun rises again in the east, and the fog lifts, Io-wairoa shows us that Rangi-nui visits te wahine's land as well. Sheets of rain fall and we watch te wahine struggle to see as she pilots her iron waka through the pounding torrent.

She wipes her brow and shakes as if cold within her skin. She has tasted experience but she wants to pole her way back upstream. She has not found eternal bliss at the river mouth.

No tears fall on her hands or lap this morning. She needs to weave the experience into her life. It cannot be undone.

Still, pain calls out truth in us. We remember Moutoa, where brother killed brother and cousin mended cousin. Blood spilled that day but shocked our people enough to say, "Never again". The chord, though frayed, can be strengthened again.

~

"Nau mai, haere mai ki to tatou marare, e haere ma ra . . . ."

A woman's voice calls out to me and I see my mother's face. Her lips move in unison with the Maori chant, but it is not her voice that calls. She raises her eyes, her beautiful eyes skyward, pointing me toward something she can see that I can't; something she is familiar with but knows I will resist.

Then she's gone and another woman's voice says, "He's heard you Sister. He's still with us."

"Or he's come back to us," a third voice says with a French accent; an older voice, an ancient voice.

"Yes, Sister, you could well be right there," says the first voice, the one that called to me. Her accent is thick and Kiwi and sounds like Pio.

I open my eyes and everything is blurry at first, as if I've had a long sleep. I see the image of a woman in blue and as my vision clears, I recognize it is a painting on the wall across from where I am lying; a woman in blue kneeling at the foot of Jesus on His cross. Below the painting is a plaque which reads, "He died for us." There is movement to my right and I see another flash of blue as a woman lithely turns away from me and disappears through an open door. Her head is capped with a mass of white hair, short at the back.

I feel a hand on my left arm and I turn to see a younger Maori woman, dressed in a dark, fine lady's suit. She is smiling at me but looks sad. Behind her is the third woman who looks over her shoulder. Her arms are crossed and she wears a large medal around her neck, almost obscuring her white blouse under her suit jacket. On the table beside my bed is a collection of old brown bottles with labels you would only see at a garage sale or in a museum, reading "Natanata" and "Morphia". I feel so wonderfully dry.

The younger woman says, "Kia ora Conrad. Welcome to Jerusalem."

"Thank you," I say and my voice hurts. It feels thick and swollen and my words sound muddy. "Where is Cobbler?"

"He and the others are meeting with the kaumatua at the wharenui. He shouldn't be away long. He's shown great concern for you since rescuing you from the river."

"Nobody rescued him from the river Sister." It's a man's voice and I look to the doorway. It is filled with the man in the purple robe. He's standing with his arms folded and his face looks severe, his teeth bared of his large quivering lips. His eyes are manic and his streaked hair looks as if it has not been cut for several months. He looks Maori around his eyes and nose, but his skin is fair. "The taniwha spit him out," he says. "I saw it, down by the bridge. The taniwha pulled him down, swallowed him, then spit him out along the bank." Then he looks directly at me and says, "It's a sign. You are not meant to be here—you've crossed an aukati. The river doesn't want you here. You should be thankful you are not dead and leave this place."

He turns with a flourish of his robes and disappears in the same direction as the white-haired woman.

I look back at my two nurses for some sort of explanation, but my bedside maiden has turned her back on me and the older woman just shakes her head.

"Sister Lawrence! Sister Kalani!" It's the French woman's voice calling from outside the room. "Venez ici. We need to have a korero!"

The Maori woman pats my arm, standing to follow her companion out the door and I am left to listen to any sounds that might help me understand where I am and what is happening. I feel worn, and I have a severe pain in my hip, but I don't think it's so bad that I couldn't get up and follow. Still, I decide to wait and see what comes back to me through the door. I'm not waiting long before the woman with the medal returns alone and sits on a small wooden chair on my right. I wince as I sit up in the bed in hopes of a conversation.

"I am Sister Lawrence," she says. "We are the Sisters of Our Lady of Compassion here in Jerusalem. I understand from Ngarangi that you are from overseas so I expect you don't know very much about us or this place. You must feel very far from home. Are you feeling better after your time in the river?"

"Yes, thanks," I say, and I mean it. My voice doesn't feel as thick as it did a few moments ago. "I'm looking for my brother, Francis Murrihy. Do you know where he is?"

Her face, already somber, grows downward and she nods her head. "Yes, he is here. He has been with us since he arrived several weeks ago. I'm afraid your arrival has caused a stir in the village however, once Ngarangi told others who you are and why you have come."

"Who is Ngarangi?"

"Ngarangi is Cobbler. He is called Cobbler because he used to make shoes when he was in prison."

"I thought he worked at the prison."

"He does. This was before he started working there. He was well liked while he was a prisoner." She looks purposefully at me and says, "Ngarangi is very good at crossing lines. He means well—he tries to bring peace, but sometimes causes upset."

I feel disoriented. "Sister Lawrence, I heard a bell ringing when I went under the water." I try a little laugh. "I thought it was tolling for me."

She smiles and says, "That was the Angelus bell—a call to prayer, and . . . it would seem some sort of prayer was answered. There is no aukati here to bar your way. If indeed the taniwha did spit you out, it was because you are meant to live and possibly meant to be here. After all, according to the Cure D'Ars, only the friends of God know the fiend.'"

"Sister, I really just need to find my brother and take him home. Our mother is dying."

The nun puts her hand to her mouth and widens her eyes. "Oh," she says, rubbing her chin. She thinks for a moment and then says, "I should probably talk with the others," and stands as if to go back through that bloody door.

"No, wait Sister," I say, a little more forcefully than I should. "It's very simple. Just tell me where Francis is."

She doesn't sit down but looks at me with empathy. "It's not that simple Conrad. It's not up to me to lead you to him. There are others who must decide how far you can go." She stands as if to leave.

"Bloody Hell!" I shout, and my voice hurts this time. "He's my brother for fuck's sake. I've come all this way for my mother and I'm not going back without him."

I toss back the covers of the bed and yell again, this time in pain as I try and stand. I test my hip with a step and find that I'm still mobile, but realize I am wearing someone else's clothes—some jeans and a green t-shirt. Sister Lawrence walks out of the room without protest and without any attempts to stop me following her. I hobble through the doorway, expecting to encounter an army of Maori warriors standing between me and Francis, but see only a long hallway, simply decorated with small paintings and bookshelves. I'm in a rage as I follow in the direction of the nun. If she won't tell me where he is, I'll just keep going until I find someone who will. I want to find Cobbler. He promised he would take me to him.

At the end of the hallway I enter a sitting room. It seems to be situated at the front of the house as, through a small set of bay windows, I can see a front veranda illuminated by a simple porch light. Up until now, perhaps because I have just woken up after who-knows-how-much sleep, I had believed it was morning, but it is clearly evening as there are a host of mosquitoes dallying around the bare bulb. The sitting room is empty and lit by a lamp in the opposite corner from my entrance to the hall. I freeze enough to hear voices through another door leading out of yet another wall. I cross over to it and out into a porch area. I try the front door of the building and it opens out onto the veranda. Immediately, I am inundated by mosquitoes and other glowing night-flies and, out of habit, I close the door behind me so as not to let them into the house and feel the tight doorknob in my hand. I've locked myself out.

I rattle the knob, not sure how badly I want to get back in just yet. I step down the front steps of the convent and into the dark, away from the silent gnats, and survey my surroundings. There is no rain but the night beyond the porch steps is black as a tomb. I am in the village, evidenced by lighted windows of houses nearby, but too far away to measure any outlines of buildings. The streets, or pathways, are empty, with no signs of any of the activity I saw before falling in the river. It is so quiet, I can hear the river flowing somewhere in the dark, sounding full and heavy still, so I calculate that I haven't been asleep for days, but hours. Intermittently, an unusual-sounding owl echoes its call through the valley.

But it is too dark for me to go exploring on my own. The isolation of the place overwhelms me just now, with the understanding of how remote this place is in the world—this little village, buried deep along this mighty river amongst these massive hills and thick flora, in the middle of an island at the bottom of the Pacific ocean, just about as far removed from Nova Scotia as any place in the world. I need help.

I try the door only to confirm it is locked and then knock loudly, calling out, "Hello! Can you let me in?"

Instantaneously, footsteps trip along from the direction of the sitting room and the door is opened by the young Maori nun, Sister Kalani. "There you are," she says. "Sister Lawrence said you were up, and thought you were following her. Come into the kitchen."

I follow this lovely little woman back inside, through another sitting room to the right and out another door to a passage diverting into a well-lit kitchen. At a table are seated the older nun and Cobbler's grandfather. She is rubbing an ointment of some sort on his hands, from another old bottle—much larger than the ones in the bedroom and bearing the image of an elderly nun in black and white. She looks grimly from the label like a wrinkled apple-headed doll.

The label reads, "Parama." The old man is speaking, in English this time.

"Mother Aubert stole this treatment from my great Aunty Anehera, you know Sister." The stern face from the boat is still there, but with a twinkle in the eye.

"Non, Pakihiwi. You know as well as I do that's absolute rubbish. Suzanne Aubert never stole a thing—she merely used what was gifted to help the order and your people."

"Gifted, stolen, it is hard to tell the difference after so many years," he says, but he doesn't sound angry with her. "Either way though, I am glad it works." The nun dries her hands with a towel from the table and the old man rolls down the sleeves of his shirt.

"I saw old Hakia on the river today Sister, right where Haumoana used to be—the old pa tuna. He's still looking for eels I reckon."

The ancient nun replies, "Now, you remember what your wife keeps telling you—stop rousing those spirits. They've been there for hundreds of years and you need to leave them alone!"

The old man sputters, "I don't go rousing them, they come looking for me! Besides, they don't speak to me like they used to. We just see each other is all." He sighs. "Maybe they know this old kaumatua has had his day, eh?"

Until they finish their conversation, they ignore me, but now they both shift my way.

"Well, look at you," snorts Pakihiwi, "all dried out and no place to go."

The old lady stands and I appreciate just how old she is as she steadies herself with the counter top behind her. "No place to go," she repeats, "because he's right where he's meant to be."

The old man shrugs and says, "It doesn't matter to me anymore. I have come for the treatment. The rest of you can sort him out." He stands, pushing with his carved walking stick, and moves toward me as if to leave, so I step out of his way. As he approaches me, the face from the boat returns as he says. "A pakeha poropiti. Pfffft! He is not Te Mangai, so what of it? He's a driftwood. We have our poropiti at Mana Ariki. I'm so tired of hearing about the latest prophet." He looks back at the women in the kitchen. "Even I know the old ventriloquist trick to make people think I can speak to atua in the bush.

"Let him stay as manuhiri or let him return with you." He says to me, "Our ladies here are tangata whenua too, they can decide what to do with you." He shrugs again and pushes past me where he turns one more time to add, "But I'll tell you one thing—that man is tapu—he's sick and he needs to stay away from this kainga. Aue— you can't tell these young fellas anything though." He disappears around a corner and in a moment I hear the front door open and close and he is gone into the night.

"Come and sit down and we'll talk some more." It's Sister Lawrence again who has just walked through yet another doorway entering the back of the kitchen from behind the refrigerator. "Sister Kalani, can you please make us some tea? Sister Therese, I think it's time for your prayers. Are you OK to store the medicines away?"

"Sacre bleu—I've been doing this for sixty years," Sister Therese says. "Think I know what I'm doing alright." Then she says to me, "Listen to the sisters young man. Ecoutez bien. Listening's as important as talking, even when you're in a hurry—especially when you're in a hurry." She disappears behind the fridge and I hear her thick, high-heeled footsteps ascend some carpeted staircase deeper in the convent's interior.

"Please," Sister Lawrence says, indicating the chair recently vacated by Pakihiwi, "sit down."

I accept her direction and collapse onto the chair. I am so tired now; the rage and frustration of the last few weeks wear on me like a heavy coat. My hip aches and it feels good to sit. It feels good to be told to listen. It feels good to accept, even over a cup of tea, whatever it is that my nursemaids have to say. It feels like it will bring some measure of peace in all this confusion and turmoil.

Sister Lawrence sits opposite me while Sister Kalani waits by the stove and counter, having poured the tea. I look at this lady across from me and wait.

"Our order has been living and working in Jerusalem for almost one hundred and forty years. Our mission is one of compassion— suffering with others. We teach the local children and we bring God to all who seek him, through Mary and through any form of healing we can offer. We did not know about your mother until you told me tonight and we want you to know," here she casts a glance at Sister Kalani, "that we truly feel a terrible compassion for you."

I nod and listen.

"I mentioned that accomplishing your mission may be harder than you have already experienced and, despite what dear Pakihiwi said to you, this is beyond our control. We are tangata whenua, but we do not make the decisions here, and especially under such extraordinary circumstances.

"But, you have come for your brother and we have decided that we will assist you in at least finding him." She looks at Sister Kalani again, this time with a longer, more meaningful gaze. "After that, God's will must be done, regardless of our heart's empathy for you and Brother Francis."

"Thank you," I say, not wishing to interrupt her flow.

"Your brother was brought to us about two months ago. We were told that he was very sick, that he was dying, but we didn't know how severe his symptoms were until he spent some time with us. We have been allowed only one doctor's visit for Brother Francis—"

"That's not the way we normally do things here!" interjects Sister Kalani, who looks harshly at her superior and then at me in an attempt to persuade me out of some conclusion I wasn't drawing.

"No, that's true," Sister Lawrence continues calmly. "We work regularly with all aspects of the health profession in Whanganui, but there have been certain pressures on us to act as his sole caregivers. It is difficult to explain fully, but we were told that your brother was dying and that, if we could not cure him, we could at least provide palliative care for him in the form of prayer and Mother Aubert's medicines."

"What is wrong with Frankie?"

"The doctor doesn't know for sure. At first we worried that it was a return of ngerengere—leprosy—but he has suggested that it might be something called CJD—"

"It's very rare," says Sister Kalani.

"Yes, very rare. As rare as a man like your brother."

I feel panic for Francis now, a renewed sense of urgency; as if I could save him somehow if I could just find him. But I wait, and I listen.

"CJD is a degenerative brain disease," Sister Lawrence continues, easing into each word, obviously cautious about my possible reactions. "It causes parts of the brain to shut down, each patient experiencing symptoms of this in their own unique order." She reaches out and clasps my hand on the table and looks at me warmly and warily. "When you meet your brother, you may not recognize him."

I draw my hand back slowly from under hers and rub my fingers against one another, searching for the patience I had mastered at the beginning of our conversation. "But, you say you've been caring for him?" I ask.

"Yes, but it really has been palliative."

"That's not all we've done," says Sister Kalani, her voice trembling on an edge between excitement and fear. I look to her for an explanation, but Sister Lawrence intervenes.

'We have . . . limited the symptoms, but have not eliminated them and we have not stayed the course of the depreciation."

"Then, there is a chance he could be helped enough for me to take him home?"

Sister Lawrence sits back in her chair with a look of sympathetic exasperation and is about to speak when Sister Kalani interrupts again.

"No, he can't!' she exclaims and there's no hiding the fear in her voice this time. "He's a miracle! He can't leave, he's our miracle! He's Te Kaiwhakaoko!" Behind the voice are eyes of fire, eyes that burn at me in warning and jubilation.

"Look, I don't know what you think he is, but I know he's my brother. He belongs with his family. Now where is he?" I stand and stare hard, back at those fiery eyes, expecting them to flicker or faint like Jordan's when I put my foot down with her, but there is no flicker, no retreat. Instead, I turn away, not just from her eyes, but from her steadfast silence. I turn toward Sister Lawrence. "You told me you would help me, for my mother's sake, now help me!"

She is standing now as well and she reaches both hands out, one touching me on the arm, the other taking a firmer grip of Sister Kalani's shoulder. "We will," she whispers to me. "We will," she says again evenly and pointedly to her fellow, who, at the sound of these two words spoken twice over, steps back from both of us and says repeatedly, "Thanks be to God for what He has done and for what He is doing for us, thanks be to God for what He has done and for what He is doing for us" each time more quietly, more sedately than the last.

~

Good Friday 2000

> *While mowing the lawn, God gave me a new understanding about our situation.*
>
> *We do not invest enough in the people around us, buying a house, committing to community groups, etc. We have had an attitude of managing our life and what we have been given, rather than planting ourselves and our own seeds. Why? To plant seeds, to build, ultimately means we would have more to manage. We doubt our ability to be able to handle the growth God wants to activate in our lives. We actually don't trust <u>Him</u> to enable us to do so. We prophecy so much failure, avoid doing so much, that we end up just where we are: in an in-between place—between our past and our future; treading water between being Catholic and Spirit-led; in a garden and growing, but not striving for the highest places; too content to stay in the undergrowth and grumbling that others are blocking our sun. In order to break through to the canopy, and bear our richest fruit, we have to plant seeds and remove weeds, but also water and nurture, believing God, having courage and faith in Him that we can handle the trials and the successes.*
>
> *My lawn is not my own—I don't plant it, weed it, clear it of stones—I only mow it.*

~

There is a knock at the front door and Sister Kalani is dispatched to answer it while Sister Lawrence sits back in her chair and sighs deeply. From the front entrance come men's voices, then one voice responding to Sister Kalani's. They are arguing, sometimes in Maori, sometimes in English though we cannot discern the words from the kitchen. After several minutes, Cobbler appears, followed closely by the locksmith. There is no sign of Sister Kalani.

He smiles at me, but he looks strained, as if he hasn't slept for some time. Both men are covered in the same clothes they wore in the boat and they look rumpled, though dry now too. The locksmith is a picture of misery; his face is long and his shoulders are slumped but his eyes are alert and he seems to straighten up when he sees me.

"G'day mate," he says from behind Cobbler. I realize he is trying to sound like a New Zealander. "You're looking better. All dry and breathing again I see."

Cobbler walks over and gives me a friendly pat on the shoulder, nodding at Sister Lawrence. "Good work once again Sister," he says. "Thanks be to God, eh?"

"Yes, thanks be to God, Ngarangi. Are you OK? You've been gone longer than you thought. How is everyone?"

Cobbler turns his face downward slightly. "Oh, you know, not very happy with me. But I've been there before, though maybe not quite like this, eh?" and he laughs and looks at the locksmith who raises his head and lets out a low whistle. Cobbler adds, "Sister Kalani sure did give me an earful."

"She is young, and very enthusiastic about what's been happening. She doesn't understand that these things have their season, that God brings people into our lives for a time and then leaves us to carry on with what we've gained. Conrad here is quite upset too. I think it's good that you're back now."

Cobbler nods and says, "Well, I reckon we'd better just keep on keepin' on then." He looks at me and says, "I can take you to your brother now."

IN THIS VALLEY OF DYING STARS

Cobbler tells me that Francis is at Pati Arero. I ask him if it is far. He laughs and says, "It's here!"

We walk together, me on his left side, the locksmith on his right, beyond the light of the bulb above the front veranda. Cobbler is confident in his steps, even in this dark. The track under our feet is muddy and I step into at least two puddles, mindful of my hip, before we pass through a small gate. I feel drops of water landing on my neck, but these are not rain, but leaves draining from overhanging branches somewhere just above our heads.

I hear the lone owl calling again. Otherwise, all is quiet except for the sludgy tread of our feet. Cobbler takes us through a small grotto marked with a sign that says, "Rosary Way" in which we pass signs posted in the ground bearing religious images and a large white statue of Mary. He explains to us, "The women must stay out of it. We must work to keep them in their beautiful world, or ours falls apart."

We carry on behind the church, turning up the hill beyond a smaller, darkened house and enter a wooded track where the mud is thicker and we have to push through denser brush, further wetting ourselves in the process. We emerge into a small clearing and see a dimly lit white house in the dark. The house hums with baritone voices inside and several men are sitting on the front steps. Beyond them, just at the edges of the porch lighting are some small gravestones. We walk along the edge of a tree-line through some long grass, passing by the house quietly at a distance. The men watch us. They do not look happy. One folds his arms, but they say nothing.

"Most of those men are from the prison," Cobbler says, just above a whisper after we move out of ear-shot and down a long gravel driveway. "The house is filled with them, all men I know. That house has not been so full since the seventies when nga mokai were here, 'the fatherless' who lived on the pa in a kind of commune." They were led by a poet, who some say wrote with Biblical significance." The locksmith looks at Cobbler curiously. "It was before my time," he adds.

"Why are they here?" I ask, suspecting I know the answer.

Cobbler looks at me. "They come here for your brother, Te Kaiwhakaoko—the Listener. Most knew him when he visited them in Kaitoke, some have come after hearing about him. They are released men, they have done their time, but they come seeking forgiveness for what they have done, they come for the cleansing power they find in Te Kaiwhakaoko."

"Only God can forgive sins," says the locksmith.

"That is true and Brother Francis knows this. It is God who listens through him and who forgives their sins."

We come to the end of the driveway and turn onto a wider gravel road, starting our descent toward the river. Not far along, a figure approaches in the dark. It is another man, a young white man, walking with his hands raised in the air, alternating looks between the sky and the ground. As we near him, I see he is ridiculously happy, his teeth flashing and eyes wide and wet. He doesn't acknowledge our presence at all, as if he were walking through us as much as walking by us. He disappears into the darkness as quickly as he appeared.

"He has just come from the whare," Cobbler explains. "He has been heard."

"By Francis?" I ask.

"By God," Cobbler corrects me. "By God through and in Francis."

This is all too much. "C'mon, aren't we just talking semantics here? What is it really about Francis that makes people feel like that after telling him their sins?" I ask, remembering Pio's description of his encounter with my brother.

Cobbler pauses and looks at me in a way that makes me stop short and think I've asked the wrong question. "Conrad, I know you are not a religious man; I know you do not believe what we believe, but I think you will soon recognize that there is more going on here than just a good man listening to people in order to make them feel better. These men leave here touched—touched by God himself, and your brother is the vessel for this encounter."

The locksmith adds, "God has used many prophets in the past to speak to His people, to intervene in their lives and bring them closer to Him: Abraham, Moses, Jeremiah—"

"And he has used many prophets to speak to Maori people," Cobbler continues, "all who have passed on their mauri in a line of spiritual succession: Te Ua Haumene, his nephew Te Whiti, Tohu Kakahi, Te Kooti, Tawhiao, Te Kere, Mere Rikiriki and her nephew, T.W. Ratana. These men and women have had their own movements, speaking God's word, protecting our whenua and bringing healing to the Maori people. Some people believe these gifts ended with Ratana, but the mauri carries on. We believe it was the prophetess from Taranaki who blessed Te Kaiwhakaoko when they met in Australia. She is a descendant of Te Kere and a prophetess after Ratana.

"But He is not just speaking to us through Francis, he is listening. The Maori people need to be heard, not spoken at in these days. We have been spoken at by governments, foreign invaders, prophets and false prophets. But we are still not being heard. Our petitions to generations of governments fall on deaf ears, and we tire of having to speak the same message only to be sent away with little change. Our God, in His goodness, has sent us a different kind of poropiti, an ear who hears—with the promise that God Himself is listening, He is forgiving, He is moving, and He is leading us into a future in which our ancestors are honored and our children will once again grow and thrive."

A wind has picked up and I see in the dim that we are in a wide open space, free from any forest on either side of the road. We turn sharply again, still making our way downhill. The sounds of the river are much louder here. Cobbler has taken us out of the village altogether. The scene is clear—as the village lights dissipate, the stars say more. We walk in silence until we reach the paved road running alongside the river and we turn again.

"Cobbler, surely you could have taken us to this road by a shorter route."

He nods and says, "I wanted you to see the men your brother is helping."

"And you think Francis is more than a counselor. You think he's a prophet?" The words sound ridiculous coming out of my mouth.

"I do—others do not. Some say he cannot be our kaiwhakaoko because he is pakeha, not Maori. Others say we need another mouthpiece of God like Ratana or Alex Phillips; now that we know how sick he is, many are confirmed in this, that he cannot speak for the Maori people who need to be heard."

"But you say you still believe—why?" asks the locksmith.

Cobbler sighs and looks across the river at the unseen hills beyond. "Because of the miracles. They are enough."

The locksmith is intrigued. "What miracles?"

"My friend, we have three ways of acquiring knowledge—te mahiotanga, knowing through personal experience; te matauranga, knowing through being taught; and te maramatanga, knowing through illumination. You might call it revelation—when God reveals knowledge to you. You have the gift of tongues and it is truly a gift from God to be able to speak in the language of angels. But Brother Francis," he looks at him pointedly, "who does not fit with your theology, also has been given the gift of tongues. But when he speaks, it is not in the language of angels that needs interpretation by others in the Holy Spirit. When he speaks, he speaks in Te Reo, the language of my people."

The locksmith's eyes widen enough to capture all the light available in the night and he speaks excitedly. "I have heard about this! I've read about people who have been filled with the Holy Spirit and spoken in tongues for years and then moved overseas to do mission work, only to find that their tongues were an actual language. It's confirmation that the believer should be spreading the gospel to that people group!" He looks at me and blurts, "How would he have learned to speak Maori otherwise? Did he learn to speak it while living here?"

I shake my head. "I wouldn't have a clue, but he must have if what you're saying is true." I say to Cobbler, "He's lived here for seven years. Surely he picked it up somehow. How do you know he didn't have lessons?"

Cobbler stops again and is clearly agitated. "Because Francis told me he hadn't, and that is enough for me. He has gifts—the matakite and enokaia—he is possessed of the wise and understanding eye."

I stare back at him, dumbfounded. "So, you're saying that the supposed miracle is the reason you believe in him and the reason you believe in the miracle is because you believe him when he told you? That's circular reasoning. That's like saying, 'Jesus loves me this I know, for the Bible tells me so.' You believe in Jesus because of the Bible and you believe in the Bible because of Jesus. This is crazy."

"It's not crazy," Cobbler says and he steps toward me until our chests touch. He's right in my face and I can feel the energy emanating from him, volatile and threatening. "It's faith," he growls. "And it's not the only sign." He steps back again and the locksmith puts a hand on his shoulder which seems to relax him. "But you wouldn't believe that from me either. You need to see for yourself."

He allows the locksmith to steer him back on course and I follow the two of them further along the road. It feels very late now, though I have no idea what the time might be. No cars have passed us but surely this road is not busy at the best of times. Cobbler finally leads us off the road, down another track toward the river. The ground here is muddy again, but the path is clear of branches as if it has been pushed through regularly and recently. When we emerge from the short connector, we see a bridge, an old suspension bridge across the Whanganui.

And we can see the bridge and river clearly for, as we exit the track, both are bathed in starlight and we raise our heads to the sky. Whatever cloud cover had been present through this night has lifted and the canopy of stars offers a chorus of light. With no other light from houses or cars, I'm sure we can see every star in the universe above this remote jungle.

As we walk onto the bridge, which feels surprisingly stable, Cobbler continues to look above us. Somewhere nearby the same owl calls. "Nga whetu are the eyes of our ancestors in the sky," says Cobbler in his dreamy voice. "It was the stars of Matariki, you would call them the Pleiades, that guided our seafaring tupuna to Aotearoa from Hawaiiki. But it was not cold, dead constellations that guided them—it was our ancestors. We believe everything has a wairua, a spirit—our rongoa, our medicine, our carvings, the land. All of this is wairua." He drops his head and looks at me and the locksmith. "Our poropito are like the stars—they guide us to God."

~

Today, our heart broke for te wahine.

Women are sacred, sharing in the most creative parts of Io-wairoa's imagination. Like the earth, she can bring forth life and it is good. She is of the earth and she is of the heavens. When a woman gives birth, she buries the whenua—the after-birth—which must return to the whenua—the land. Ashes to ashes, dust to dust.

We watched as te wahine returned to the smoking house. She emerged with a little hine whom she hugged close to her breast and cheek.

Te wahine is also te whaea—a mother.

This hine is her lofty mountain.

Our grandmother's heart broke this day—for te whaea and for te hine; for the plaited chord of te whaea's whānau—her family—and for all those whose lives have been unraveled by infidelity. Above us, Rangi-nui wept and our waters raged against and beyond the banks, tearing our way down to our mouth to sweep our pain into the eternal ocean.

~

With the river's encouragement, we cross the bridge and continue on a track similar to the one on the other side. But this side of the bridge feels much older. We walk in silence for several minutes until we see another man coming from the opposite direction. He too ignores our presence and carries on by us, speaking under his breath, almost inaudibly, in words I don't understand. There is light ahead around a small stand of trees and as we round this bend, I see a small decrepit white building with red trim that looks like something between a house and a church. It is dimly lit from the inside.

"Stop here," Cobbler says indicating a spot just off the track and onto the edge of an open, grassy area between us and the building. "This is a marae," he says. "You must understand that you are manuhiri here—and you are most welcome—but there are protocols. When you enter the meeting house, you must remove your shoes. Our wharepuni is our ancestor and we must show respect. Your brother is inside."

Before he can continue, he is interrupted by a loud male voice calling out across the field. Emerging from the meeting house is the man in the purple robe. He is flailing his arms again, causing the robe to swoop and spin around him awkwardly. His eyes are turned upwards in his head and he sticks out his tongue while yelling something in Maori at us.

"Rawiri," says Cobbler, and sighs, staring at the harlequin.

"I thought he went to Palmerston North," I say, and Cobbler turns to me with a surprised look on his face.

"You know Rawiri?"

"No, not at all, but I was told he took Francis to Ratana and then went to Palmerston North."

Cobbler shakes his head. "No, he never went to the city. He left his job at the prison and came here. It was he who took your brother to Jerusalem . . . and he doesn't want him to leave."

Cobbler steps forward and starts to chant in Maori which causes Rawiri to pause and regard him from the distance. Our guide's voice is rich and sharp and fills the entire soundscape. It makes me think of winter storms and funeral processions.

Once Cobbler finishes, Rawiri descends the steps of the wharenui sideways and sidles ceremoniously toward us, emitting short grunts as he does so. From beneath his robe, he reveals a long pole, unlike a walking stick and more like a weapon. He brandishes it menacingly as he approaches and to my chagrin, Cobbler starts to advance across the field, motioning to us with his hands at his side indicating that we should follow him.

We meet Rawiri at the half-way point and he stops waving his stick, posing with it across the tops of his legs. Cobbler stares at him but says nothing. They seem to be sizing one another up and I can see that Rawiri is actually an unimposing figure. He is thin and below my height. There are tattoos on his face, but they don't look permanent like the ones on Cobbler's grandfather. His robe is a priest's robe, complete with a gold-colored trim. There are symbols of communion on the front: chalices, grapes and bread. The edges by his arms and feet are torn and frayed. He tilts his head back and eyeballs Cobbler.

"The kaumatua disagree with what you are doing. He should not be here."

"This is Conrad, brother of Francis, descended from the same line from his people in Canada. He shares the same blood and has a right to see him and take him home."

"The spirit is stronger than blood," Rawiri says, sage-like. "Te Kaiwhakaoko is whangai—an adopted son now. He is a child of God, no longer a child of man, descended from Abraham, Isaac and Jacob, from Jesse and David, from Te Kere and Ratana. He is tangata whenua. He has been grafted in. He is bound to this confessional which preserves for eternity the most beautiful secrets of love and grace. He needs to be with his people!" He thumps his breast with his fist and points at Cobbler's. He has not looked at me or the locksmith since we converged.

"His time has come Rawiri. He was sent for a season, but that season is ending. He is dying and so is his mother—"

"Te Whaea is his mother!" hisses Rawiri. "And here are his brothers," he says, stretching his hands out toward Cobbler and then wider toward the rest of the village across the river. "Anyone who does the will of our Father is his brother and his sister and his mother, and especially nga pani—the motherless who have been gathered by Te Whaea to this place. They were hollow men, but now they are filled! Remember the poet's prophecy: 'Men from the clink come to Hiruharama in the coil of the taniwha to get water for the thirsty, the burnt and the lame.' God will heal Te Kaiwhakaoko and the prophecies will be fulfilled."

"My brother," Cobbler says softly, "you know I believe with you in this. But other prophesies we believe are not to come to pass in this man. Remember what we thought about the words of Te Mangai: 'There will be no more prophets after this young man who will bring peace and get back our lands.' And you know the ways of our people—we adopt when we need to adopt, but when it is time, the dead must bury the dead, dust must return to dust, and Francis must return to his whanau and to his whenua."

Rawiri doesn't answer so Cobbler continues. "We can extend our korero here, but you know what I say is true. You have done your work well and God will reward you for it. I have come with another who knows our Lord well," he says, indicating the locksmith. "His name is Colin, descended from our people's friend, Richard Taylor. As such, he has mana here and is himself an adopted son through our

Lord Jesus Christ. He is filled with the Holy Spirit and speaks in the tongues of angels."

Rawiri looks at Colin and says, "Why have you brought him here? He cannot replace Te Kaiwhakaoko."

"But Rawiri, do we not believe that it is God in Francis who brings the healing? Why would God not do the same through another? I tell you brother, through Colin, I have met many others who host the gift, who bring power and life with their prayer and worship. Miracles are wrought and they believe the ministry is poured out for all who believe. What does it matter who is priest, who is confessor? We do not need to believe in just one anymore. There are more. There are many."

Rawiri remains silent for a long time and Cobbler allows him to have this. He looks at me, but now focuses on Colin with far more interest. Finally, he smirks and rocks his head back slightly. He says to Colin, "We have an old tradition here that your ancestor Taylor was familiar with." He looks at Cobbler and laughs, "Shall we lay down some hot coals for our two missionaries, eh?"

Colin and I share uncomfortable glances, but Cobbler laughs quietly and reaches out to put his hand on Rawiri's shoulder. The two men lean into one another and press noses twice while making soft murmuring sounds. When they separate, Rawiri says to Colin, "He's got something in mind for you. God's will must be done." Then he says to me, "Are you curious? Come."

MY LIGHT IS SPENT

12 November 2000

<u>*Questions*</u>

1. How can I remain pure?
2. How can I lead this family?
3. How can I help Kathy?
4. How can we get back to Canada?
5. Where do You want us Lord?
6. How can I develop my relationship with my family back in Canada?
7. How can I become more like Jesus?
8. How can we help others?
9. How can I feed Jacob and Kim your Word?
10. How can I glorify You Lord?
11. What is Your vision for us Father?
12. How do we handle Satan's attacks?

<u>*Answers*</u>

    Lord, we've had enough. Kathy is clinging to me again, Jacob is rebelling, I'm running—after new challenges but away from the ones that matter, Kim is stressing and panicking, our family seems to have forgotten us, we feel alone and lonely, lost with no certain direction, we've fallen away from your body, our finances have been struck a fatal blow by Satan, work pressures are intense, I'm losing my moral compass, I rarely listen for your voice. I need answers. We need answers.

You put this word in my mind tonight and reminded me that You made me good at finding answers—from authorities, from professors, from books, from computers, and now from You.

I pray, Holy Spirit, in the mighty name of Jesus, that You will guide me in identifying the questions we need answered in this season. Guide me on this journey as I seek out the answers in Your Word and through the people and circumstances You send. Let tonight be the turning point—a cornerstone to build upon.

<u>Places to look</u>

Remember Francis, to look, but allow Me to reveal answers to you. Do not try to create the solutions. I am not giving you a puzzle to solve. I want you to see. Open your eyes. Seek first the kingdom of God and the rest will be added to you. Trust me in this and seek.

~

Cobbler follows Rawiri up the steps of the meeting house and removes his shoes. Colin and I do the same, leaving them by a bench under one of the front windows. There are several other pairs of shoes resting there, all of them clean. I wipe the mud from my hands onto the jeans provided by the Sisters.

The front door is ajar. Rawiri pushes it wide and we all step inside.

It is dark. The light we saw from outside is coming from an oil lamp set on a small wooden table near the window to our right. In its glow, I see we are in a simple structure. There is no other furniture to be seen. The floor is carpeted but feels thin under my socked feet. What walls I can see are adorned with panels of Maori art work, symmetrical patterns of straight lines like thousands of eaves criss-crossing one another. We are standing in an open space under an apex—the ceiling has an intricate beam running length-wise starting from above our heads and disappearing into the darkness at the back of the building. Ahead of us is an equally intricate column like the cross in Taumarunui. It seems to act as a support for the roof but also sports faces with glowing, jeweled eyes and protruding tongues.

This place strikes me as part church—part community hall; a sparse museum with a life-force of its own.

From the back of the room, we hear voices. Two men are in conversation but their words are inaudible. One voice speaks in a continuous flow, like a small spring emptying into a roadside stream. The other voice responds only with affirming gestures, as if prodding the stream along. Then both voices stop and we stand in silence, and in a silence unlike any I've experienced. It is a silence that is full, not empty, though I wouldn't know how to describe the nature of its fullness. To speak at that moment would spoil something precious; it is like when my daughter was born and Jordan and I were left alone for the first time by the doctors and nurses. Jordan held her close while I sat on the edge of her bed and the moment was filled with our baby. Nothing else in the world mattered, everything else was gone and all time, space and our very lives were filled with the presence of new life.

There is a rustling sound from the back corner of the room as if someone were shuffling against the carpet and standing to their feet. Soft footsteps approach us and a young Maori man emerges from the shadow, teeth and eyes first. As he nears, I see tears on his cheek. This time, this man acknowledges us. He shakes each of our hands and presses his nose against ours, and I can feel the very breath flow out of his nose and into my mouth. He looks at me last and says, "I have never seen my sins so closely—a medley of sins—now gone. My head is empty—as empty as a basket and I cannot revive them. They are just a big blend, like thick plaster, but I can't see them." He stares into my eyes and I wait for his next words but he says nothing more, before he releases my hand and walks out the door and into the night.

Rawiri is looking at me too and I can't explain the way I am feeling. The silence returns and this time seems to be filled with a fragrance in the room of something familiar, like lilacs but even sweeter. He walks toward the back corner from where the young man appeared and we all follow him.

There is just enough light to see a figure in the corner. We hear him as well, as his body rubs against the carpet in sharp twitching motions. He is sitting up with his head resting against the paneled wall behind him. His face is a mass of hair, not long but wild and clearly unshaven for several weeks if not months. He is wearing a rumpled, dark suit complete with jacket, tie and vest. His eyelids are closed as if in prayer or in sleep and his mouth moves quickly amid the twitches in his face.

When the lids open, I finally see my brother's eyes.

"Frankie!" I exclaim in a whisper.

There is an explosion of activity as Frankie flings his head back and his body writhes flat onto the floor in convulsions and I fall to my knees to put my hands on his legs to stop them from kicking. His ankles feel skeletal beneath the suit pants. He's wearing no shoes or socks. Rawiri is on his knees too, supporting Frankie's head at the neck and speaking soothing tones in Maori. Soon, the legs stop kicking and his body relaxes and he is speaking to Rawiri with his eyes closed. His voice is strong, far too strong for this whelp of a man at my feet, and he is speaking Maori fluently and vigorously.

As he finishes speaking, Rawiri props him against the wall again with Cobbler's help. The locksmith is still standing but watching with fascination. Rawiri is weeping. I look at him for some kind of explanation.

He wipes his face and says, "It's the sickness that causes the fits. It's the Spirit that causes the korero."

I sit back and look at my brother again, now sitting still as he was when we came to him. I pick up an object by his leg. It's a broken thermometer.

"How can you leave him out here like this? He's sick. He needs medical attention, not hocus-pocus from some river witches and a wannabe priest. Who the Hell do you think you are doing this to him? And you expect him to stay out here for all these criminals, just so they can go away with a clear conscience?"

As I speak, my voice grows louder until I am shouting and I notice Frankie beginning to stir again and I worry I'll send him into more spasms. "Fuck," I say more quietly, "and then I come along and he freaks out when he sees me."

Rawiri looks at Cobbler as if to say, "He doesn't know?" To me he says, "Seeing you didn't cause this reaction. He can't see you. He is blind."

Blind? I lean closer to look at Frankie's face and at his eyes which are open again. They stare blankly back at me, with no motion and no emotion.

"Frankie?" I say and he takes a deep breath as if he expects me to strike him. "Frankie, it's me, Conrad. I've come to take you home."

He moves his mouth again, quickly and startling at first, but then his lips settle and he says, "I know Conrad. I know why you are here."

This voice is not the same as the one that just spoke to Rawiri in Maori. It's softer, less melodious and very tired. "How do you know?" I ask.

Frankie reaches out and finds my hand near his ankles. He holds it and it feels good to find him, to really find him, and I picture him holding Mom's hand at her bedside; but looking at him, how can I make that happen? He moves his eyes from my hand and up my arm until he seems to be looking into my eyes. He says, "I have seen you Conrad."

I look at Rawiri angrily. What sort of game is this? But Frankie continues.

"When you reached these shores, you found me; when you found my friends, you touched me; when you started up this river, you came to me; when you looked for me, I saw you."

I feel a hand on my shoulder—it's Cobbler. I look back at him and the tears in his eyes. "You see brother?" he says. "Miracles." Then he looks at Frankie and says, "Hello old friend."

"Ngarangi," Frankie breathes. "And who have you brought with you?"

Cobbler motions Colin forward. "I have brought another, Francis. His name is Colin and he is a man of God, a man who knows God and moves in His Spirit as you do. I have brought him here to receive your blessing . . . for you to pass on your mauri as Isaac did to Jacob, as Te Kere did to Mere Rikiriki and . . . to release you to return to your whanau."

Frankie breathes deeply and lets go of me, turning his body and full attention to Cobbler. "Ngarangi, what are you doing?" Cobbler takes him by the hand, but Frankie retracts it, his arm and legs twitching. "Ngarangi, I will die here. I am here for the iwi Maori and I will be here forever even as I pass into eternity with our Lord. Your people will hold my mauri and the Spirit of God that has been poured out through me. You do not need another. And I am not going home."

I want to cry out against all of this. I want to tell him to let go of all this nonsense and think of us, his family back in Canada, but Cobbler is not done. Undaunted, he says, "You don't understand Brother Francis. I believe the same and so does Colin. He has shown me that there are many others and there can be as many others as there are stars in the sky, just like in God's promise to Abraham." He is sounding excited now, preachy. "I've met them and they have their own miracles. They are filled with the Spirit and the joy of the Lord. They can show us the Way and you can rest, knowing you have served your time, and return to your people to bring them peace."

Frankie has not taken his thin eyes off Cobbler until now when he turns his head toward Colin. He speaks in Maori to him and his voice is clear and strong again, and direct. As he speaks, Cobbler lowers his head as in prayer.

When the flourish is over, Colin looks at Cobbler uncertainly, then at Frankie and says, "I'm sorry brother, but I don't understand the Maori language yet. I'm learning, but I don't know what you said."

Frankie replies, again in his faltering, faded voice, "Doesn't the Bible tell us that the Holy Spirit gives some the gift of tongues, and others the gift of interpreting those tongues? You say you have the Holy Spirit abiding in you. Can you not ask Him to interpret for you?"

Colin straightens up, as if preparing for battle, and says, "I do have the Holy Spirit my friend. The Spirit gives gifts to those He chooses like the wind which blows where it wants. I would say He has provided my interpreter in my friend here. What did he say Cobbler?"

Without taking his eyes off Frankie, Cobbler says, "It is one thing to have the gifts of the Holy Spirit as every true believer does. It is another to have the vocation from God to fulfill His purposes." Then he looks at Colin and finishes, "Have you been called by God to serve the Maori people of Te Awanui-a-Rua?"

"I sure have," Colin replies. "I have come from overseas as well, you know, called by God to bring His word to the Maori people."

"How do you know this?" Frankie asks. His voice sounds extraordinarily sad.

"I learned about the Maori people back in America, shortly after I was saved. I had a dream of introducing them to the Lord and setting them free from pagan ways. God has called me to be a missionary. That's why I am in New Zealand and that is why I've come up the river with Ngarangi."

"So, you are filled with the Holy Spirit?"

"I've told you, yes."

"And you've been called by God?"

"Yes."

"You've been called by God to spread the Word of the Lord?"

"Absolutely."

"To spread the Word of the Lord so that Maori might know the truth?"

"God's Word can only be true. They need to know the truth."

"And this will set them free from superstition, false religion and lead them to everlasting life?"

"Through our Lord Jesus Christ!" Colin exclaims evangelically.

Cobbler looks pleased too. "Do you see now Francis? He is here for us, sent from God just like you, just like our Maori prophets, just like Ratana and Te Whiti and the great missionaries, Taylor, Pompallier, Soulas, Lampila. The Spirit is in him and all we ask now is your blessing."

Frankie raises one hand above his head and Cobbler puts his own hand on Colin's shoulder apparently preparing to present the locksmith to him. But Frankie says, "Rawiri, help me," and his cloaked guardian comes alongside him, lifting him under his arms. It is still very dark and by the lamplight I can just discern the outline of Frankie's quivering legs and torso, but his eyes, his blind eyes are bathed in an invisible light, like flames in the night.

His voice is lecturous, scolding, seething in its intensity. He waves his arms as he cries into the little meeting house and the echoing walls seem to join in his recitation. The locksmith stands firm against the verbal onslaught and begins speaking in his own language with his own rich voice projecting words that bounce and glance off Frankie's like swords sending sparks into the darkness. But as he speaks, Cobbler begins to resign himself. At the same time, Rawiri begins to laugh and jump up and down on the spot in delight, clapping his hands and exclaiming his own words in Maori and English; short phrases—"Kia ora!" he cries and "the Spirit speaks to His people!"

Finally and suddenly Frankie stops. He stands silently; his eyes fade and the sadness returns. Colin carries on, speaking in his own unintelligible words, but Cobbler has left, exited the building entirely and the locksmith becomes aware of his absence. He continues for almost another minute, but his voice diminishes and power seems to drain out of him, until all that is heard is Rawiri's quiet laughter.

"Why are you laughing?" Colin demands angrily. "God will not be mocked."

Rawiri laughs even louder and says, "I'm not mocking God!" Then he steps toward Colin, pulling his robe close around him. He smiles at the locksmith and says, "Let's discuss interpretation. You tell us what you said, and I'll tell you what he said," pointing back at Frankie who is standing stock-still, unmoving and unflinching for the first time since I've seen him tonight.

"The Holy Spirit knows what I said," Colin mutters. "It is up to Him to speak into your hearts and up to you to listen to His small voice there."

"Very good!" chimes Rawiri as he swoops behind Frankie, putting both hands on his shoulders. "Whakarongo mai! Listen to me! Before the pakeha came to Aotearoa, I was here. I was with My Maori people and I was their God. I spoke with them and they spoke with me. The pakeha came, bearing My Word—the Word of My son who I sent to die on a cross for the forgiveness of sins and the redemption of all peoples. My Maori people heard this Word and many, many of them accepted it and it grew in Aotearoa. And even as this land was pillaged and polluted, they gave thanks for the Word. They knew that someday the chaff would be thrown into the fire but the wheat of the Word would be harvested.

"But, the chaff grew strong and choked the Word so that those who knew the Word could not be heard. They were strangled so that they could not speak—their language died out in many places and with it the mauri of the people that had been there before the pakeha came, the same mauri that recognized the Word and welcomed the Word and helped the Word to grow. While the Word was still preached, and the people heard from God through the prophets, the voices of the people were not listened to, not by governments, not by the prophets and, so they thought, not by God. Some gave up, some tried to access God's ear in other ways.

"I have chosen this little brother to show my people that I am still their God. I am still their father, a father who listens to His children. They come from afar, these prodigal sons, reeking of vice, stained with sin. I hear their confession and I come to the cries of my people who seek me, not to be told again what they already know, but to be heard. I do not say 'Whakarongo mai!' to my people. I say, 'Korero mai! Speak to me!' I am the Lord."

After Rawiri finishes, still smiling with delight, Colin raises his hand and points at Frankie, ignoring me and Rawiri. He speaks slowly and accusingly. "You . . . you are a false prophet. Your gifts are not of God, they are from the Devil! You teach a false theology that will save no-one. All these people will die in their sins believing they are free without needing faith in Jesus Christ. They'll think they can still follow their old gods and whatever prophet comes along."

Rawiri, furious now, steps quickly toward Colin, who falters back toward the lamplight by the door. "Get out!" he growls. "There is no blessing for you here. Haere atu koe!"

Colin turns on his toes and walks toward the front entrance. "Bless me? I wouldn't let him touch me. I cast you out in Jesus' name! May God have mercy on your souls!" He launches himself out through the door left open by Cobbler and is gone.

Behind me I hear an almighty thump and I turn to see Frankie has collapsed on the floor.

~

Our blessing, and our curse, is to welcome and accept strangers into our midst. We are quick to whāngai those who need a home, those who would join us as tangata whenua. Our waters then fill with the tares as well as the wheat.

Io-wairoa, forgive us—we want to expel te whaea in our pain. We want to flush her out. However, we have adopted her. She is ours now, even at such a distance. We don't understand it all, but it is our way, it is Your way.

We call out to her now as we call out to all our people who have left us and Your way. We rise again and karanga, "Haere mai! Haere mai!" to those of the diaspora. "Return, our people. Things will never be the same, but they can still be beautiful."

"Tihei mauri ora! Behold there is life!"

THE RAINBOW BRIDGE

"Hail Mary, full of grace, the Lord is with you, blessed are you among women and blessed is the fruit of your womb, Jesus. Holy Mary, Mother of God, pray for us sinners, now and at the hour of our death, amen."

Rawiri is praying, with a hand on Frankie's forehead. My brother is breathing, unsteadily, but without the awful spasming. Between each recitation of these words, Rawiri turns and addresses me.

"Mary is our mother, the patron saint of Aotearoa and all who would be led by her to the Son."

"Our Lady is the one who listens and takes our prayers to the Father."

"Like Mother Aubert, she brings healing to the river . . . and to our people."

"Her korowai covers both nga mokai and nga pani—the fatherless and the motherless."

"She is our tupuna, our ancestor who adopts us and gives us shelter with our older brother."

"Beauty has a face and you must make a friend of beauty."

He carries on like this for a decade and then stops and rests his hands, clasped on his lap. I reach my own hand out to touch Frankie's forehead. He is extraordinarily hot, so I work his arms out of his suit jacket, expecting Rawiri to protest, but he says nothing more until I tell him, "We need to get him to a doctor."

Rawiri shakes his head. "No doctor can mend him. Besides, there isn't one near for miles. He needs prayer and the Sisters."

"I need to take him home. I just can't believe he's got himself into this. I mean, look at where we are," I say, gesturing around the interior of this cave of a place. "He needed to be with his family, not here. He's hurt a lot of people."

"You judge Te Kaiwhakaoko. You don't judge Te Kaiwhakaoko like an ordinary man."

Frankie moans and shifts his head toward the two of us and opens his unseeing eyes. He begins to shake again as he says, "Where are you from?"

I look at Rawiri questioningly, but he offers no response.

"Frankie," I say hesitantly, remembering the shock I caused the first time I spoke to him, "it's Conrad here with you."

No convulsions this time, just a deep sigh and perhaps a small smile?

Rawiri asks, "Brother Francis, kei te pehea koe?"

"I am dying Rawiri."

Rawiri shifts uncomfortably, quickly. "No brother, your time is not yet. Let me go and fetch the Sisters and their medicines. Our Lady will see you right."

Frankie smiles again, almost imperceptibly, but with a definite gesture to both of us. "Rawiri, it is my time. Ngarangi was right—the mauri needs to be passed on—the mantle of one who will continue the work amongst God's people. All that counts is what God wishes for us. If He desires to speak to us as He did to Elijah in a fresh and gentle breeze, do not demand that He speak in the flashes and clouds of the burning bush as He spoke to Moses. Receive this blessing Rawiri."

Now it is Rawiri who shakes as he bows his head to meet Frankie's outstretched hand. His voice changes as he speaks slowly in Maori, deliberately and calmly. Rawiri sobs quietly, "Thank you, thank you," until Frankie stops and holds his hand above Rawiri's head, suspended there while Rawiri crosses himself, saying, "Ki te ingoa o te Matua, o te Tamaiti, o te Wairua Tapu." We sit in silence for several minutes after Frankie has lowered his hand. I can no longer hear his breathing and am about to check on him when he says something else, something shorter to Rawiri, this time in Maori but in his weaker voice.

Rawiri raises his head. His shaking has stopped and his face is dry. He stands tall with his shoulders drawn back, crosses his arms to gather his purple robe and raises it above his head, before letting it slip to the floor. He stands above us bare chested, his skin emblazoned with a fiery tattoo above his heart and long thin scars on his forearms, which he flexes like a prizefighter. He reaches into the back pocket of his shorts and extracts a fern leaf which he lays on the floor beside the robe. He does this without taking his eyes off me, walking backward toward the door, growing clearer in my vision as he enters the light of the lamp at the front.

"Ka kite ano au i a koe," he says with great dignity. "I will see you again." He steps further back until he reaches the doorway which is now allowing the first rays of the morning sun to enter the wharenui. "Ka kite ano au i a korua. I will see you both again. Take him home, with our blessing. Haere ra," he says, and is gone.

Beside me, I hear a whispered echo of his words. Frankie breathes deeply. I don't know what to do.

"Frankie," I start, but he interrupts me.

"Most of those boys were victims before they were criminals. They didn't have a chance."

"Frankie, I don't want to hear an explanation."

"We need to have hearts big enough for everybody to find room in them."

"Frankie, I don't—"

"It is judgment that defeats us. We need not be hollow men—"

"Frankie, Mom's dying."

His breathing stops and I worry I've done it again until I hear him say, "I didn't know that."

"It's why I'm here. She's asked for you." I hesitate. What's the point in telling him this? It's too late—I'm going to lose a brother as well as my mother. Why leave him with this? But I want him to know. I want him to feel the hurt we've felt—the pain of separation and the helplessness of knowing there's nothing you can do to mend a relationship with a person who has distanced himself.

"You left her to come and find me?" he wheezes.

"Yes, I did!" The pain-fueled anger is there again. I want to lash him with it, to pull out every bit of the hatred I have for him and beat him to death with it and leave him here to rot so I can go home and deal with my own shit. "You left us Frankie, right when we needed you—when she needed you the most. You fucking left us to go chasing after . . . I don't even know what this is! It's not family Frankie. It's not blood. Do you know Dad came all the way down here looking for you? He had to go back when he found out about Mom's cancer. That's right Frankie—a brain tumor. And now here I am, chasing you down, missing the last days I can spend with my mother, just because she would rather see you."

I'm standing now. I want to leave him where he is, just like he's wanted it all these years—alone in this God-mad country, with these crazy people and his disease and filth.

"You left Jordan and Jade to come and find me?"

"Yes!"

"Do you love them Conrad? Do you love your wife and daughter?"

"Of course I love them, Frankie," I say, exasperated.

Then he asks, "Then when do you intend giving up this abominable life?" stressing each syllable.

I retreat from him, feeling . . . I don't know what. Angry? Confused? Unmasked. I walk toward the other end of the meeting house by the column standing lonely in the room. I lean my forearm against it and rest my head, looking down at the floor. I can see the pattern in the carpet now. It is old and dust-covered. At the base of the column I see carvings of feet and as I lift my head, I stare straight into the eyes of one of the faces carved on the pole. This face is atop another pair of legs and there are others above and below him. I say "him" because these are people. In the darkness of the night I had thought these were fantasy figures, images to frighten strangers or intruders. But they are people, people in a line, one descending from another. These are family.

I turn and look at my family, lying in the corner, alone with no-one above him or below him. My big brother who was supposed to be with me, supposed to be with us, supposed to be with his own family. I walk over to him and kneel beside his head. His eyes are closed but he knows I am there. His lips move and I hear him whisper, "I have something I need to tell you."

Detective Daniels appears in my mind. I steel myself for what comes next. "What is it Frankie?"

"I prayed that God would take my family."

"What do you mean?"

"Kathy and Jacob and Kim. When God called me—when he chose me, I couldn't handle being their husband and father. I prayed that I could be set free, to live my life for God, with God, in God. God answered my prayer—and I have not deserved to have a family since."

I am stunned. "You didn't choose this Frankie. It happened to you. You didn't cause the accident."

Frankie sighs and looks somewhere past me and in me. "No matter how you might interpret it, God answered the prayer of my heart. Was it for good or for evil? I still can't tell."

It was for evil. He chose his God and all of this over his family—not only Kathy and the kids, but all of us in Canada. All this time, all this anxiety, all this travel—and my mother. All of this over a guilty conscience? I cannot get my head around it. But then, images swirl through my mind—images of me volunteering for stories that would take me away from home over nights, leaving Jordan alone with our new-born baby; images of me returning home drunk from friends' and missing dinners and appointments; images of me arguing with Jordan about my family, my continual siding with them and undermining her.

I look in my brother's eyes, and for the first time, he seems to see me. He peers into me with a look of recognition, of me perhaps or of something he sees in me. I want to turn away from those eyes; turn away so that he can't see whatever it is he is seeing and blind him further so that he will never look at me that way again.

But I don't turn away. Instead I say, "I have sabotaged my marriage Frankie. I have not loved Jordan as a husband should. I drink, I work overtime, I stay out with friends, I still love Mom and Dad more than her. I have never given my all to her."

At this, his eyes change again, never wavering from mine, but absorbing all the light in the room. Everything around us goes dark except for those eyes, and I continue to feed them with my faults, my flaws, my sins. I tell him about my dishonesty in dealing with co-workers, my impatience and negligence with Jade, my callous remarks to Jordan about her own family and my refusal to support her when she has been mistreated by mine. I pour it all in, I leave nothing out.

Time passes and I feel the sun's warmth on my back as it must be streaming into the house, but the room remains dark. Only as I finish speaking does the darkness lift and I see all of Frankie in the full

211

morning light. He closes his eyes and the light returns to the world. "Thank you Conrad," he says, "thank you."

I put my face in my hands and I weep for the pain I have caused but I also weep for the magnificent cleansing I am feeling. It feels like someone has poured a white liquid into me and it has spread to every pore, every tip so that I feel whole, connected, eternal.

"Conrad?" Frankie asks and I look at him, lying prone in front of me, his arms at his side, his eyes closed, his moving chest the only sign of life. "Conrad?" he asks again.

"Yes Frankie?"

"I worry that our father will not understand what I have tried to be. Tell him what I have tried to be."

"I will Frankie."

"I will see my mother Conrad. I will go to our lady. Remember Conrad, the sins of men are mountainous and mutinous. But . . . once removed . . . oh the beauty." He breaths slowly. "The beauty."

These are his last words. For the next hour, I sit listening to his breathing. I look up only when his breathing stops. Without air passing between his lips, my brother forms words with his mouth but there is no sound, only motion and then stillness. I close his eyes, then stand and walk out of the meeting house.

The sun is brilliant this morning and a vivid rainbow arcs across the sky. The stars are gone. Never before has this land, this river, this jungle, the very arch of the blazing sky appeared to me so hopeful and so bright, so welcoming to human contact, so respectful of human dignity. The front grass is covered with dozens of people. I pick up my shoes and carry them down the steps, past Sister Kalani, past Cobbler who turns and follows me through the rest of the crowd of ex-prisoners, unknown villagers, children, and the other sisters. There is no sign of Colin, but as I reach the back, Rawiri greets me silently, again taking my hand and leaning in to press my nose. "Kia ora," he says, loud enough for only the two of us to hear.

He follows me too, as I walk across the suspension bridge, onto the track and down the hill. We are joined by a small bird with fan-shaped tail-feathers who flits in front of us between the trees on either side of the track. I don't stop until I am in the river, Rawiri and Cobbler at my sides.

Above us, I hear a wailing woman and then a thunderous eruption of men chanting and stomping. As the ground shakes, I allow Rawiri to mark a cross on my forehead with a small stone and immerse me in the river where I listen to the sound of a tree falling and the taniwha singing.

~

Today, te whaea is crying. We cannot see her eyes, but we can see her tears fall on an image of the man in her hands, the face of a man we now know. The tear washes over the image until it reaches her ringless finger causing the skin to glisten under the dim light. She returns her ring to her finger and rests it, along with the photo at her knee-side. She is floating forward—to a time of purpose, to a time of mystery—to follow her tears and see what might yet be.

HAERE RĀ KI HIRUHĀRAMA

Flying into Nova Scotia, I see evidence of winter's approach canvassing the ground. Pine needles litter the floor of every wooded area beneath us on this clear, autumn day. I have missed Thanksgiving while I was gone, but not Hallowe'en and I wonder if Jordan has worked out a costume for my little girl. I'll be back in time to see if the Red Sox will break the curse of the Bambino and win their first World Series in eighty-six years and to see the remainder of the election campaigns of Bush and Kerry. Of course, this flight is taking me back to my wife, my daughter, my mother and all my family.

The land below me seems different from when I left just a few intense weeks ago. It seems to have a voice of its own, not an audible voice, but one that speaks to my heart as we land.

Leaving Jerusalem was not instantaneous. The people insisted they take care of all Frankie's funeral arrangements in something called a tangi. They invited me to stay, but I declined in order to get back to Mom. I told them that there was no point in me staying for my dead brother when I had a living mother to attend to. But I was grateful to them and am confident that a burial in Jerusalem is what is best for Frankie. They showed me where he would be buried, in a small lot next to the prisoners' house, next to the poet's white headstone marked, "Hemi".

Cobbler arranged a drive back to Upokongaro for me and, after I had a day's sleep back in my motel, I left Whanganui for Auckland.

From there, I finally rang Dad to break the news to him that Frankie was dead. This truly was the hardest phone call I've made in my life. I didn't tell him about all the circumstances, but told him that I had seen Frankie alive and that things had ended for him as well as they could and that he would be at rest here; that his new caretakers would welcome a visit from Dad at any time in future. I will never tell him of the charges laid against his son.

Despite hearing the news of a recent cargo plane crash back in Halifax, I felt no fear of flying. I left New Zealand and arrived back in Canada without incident, recapturing the day I lost. Somewhere under the night skies of the Pacific, I opened a note from Rawiri who had given it to me with instructions to wait until I left his shores to read it:

He aha te mea nui te ao?
He tangata! He tangata! He tangata!
What is the most important thing in the world?
It is people! It is people! It is people!

It is cold here, much colder than when I left and far colder than New Zealand, but I open my jacket to receive the air as I walk from the airport to my truck. The accents of the people are enough to warm me. It is good to be home.

I am the caretaker of my brother's memory now. Or at least, I carry his last words, the last contact my family will have with him. Of course, I've failed really haven't I? Mom will not see him. But she will see me and I can tell her my own story of what happened to her oldest boy. I've had some days to think about it now and will give her as much peace, or at least as much satisfaction as I can.

Driving home on the highway, snow begins to fall, most certainly the first snowfall of the season, and a premature one at that. It is only a light dusting, but in the grey of this day, the white flakes perform a light dance for a driver's entertainment. New snow always provides that sense of freshness even as it marks the end of growth for a time.

I only make one stop on the way home, for some gas at the new station in Millbrook. This area has changed so much in recent years since the development of Truro Power. A vast complex alongside our twinning highway is growing—lots of concrete, more convenient gas and yet another Tim Horton's which I eagerly rush over to after filling up. Nothing like a taste of home to make you feel at home.

Growing up, this side of the highway only had one building—the Mi'kmaq craft shop, "Glooscap's". Then, we'd called it the "Micmac" craft shop. It's taken a long time for us Canadians to listen to our First Nations people, even just to learn how to pronounce their names. I only remember us stopping in here a couple of times as a kid. Mi'kmaq people were strangers to us and this shop was as much a tourist attraction to us as it would be for an American or Australian. Glooscap was a figure of the visiting troupes of actors to our elementary school, nothing more significant than a comic book character.

I'm curious after my experience in New Zealand, so I walk over to the little white building with the red trim to look inside while I drink my coffee and maybe find a gift for Jade. The shop is pretty much as I remember it—filled to capacity with all sorts of colorful things: beading and embroidery using dyed porcupine quills for moccasins, shirts, snowshoes and tobacco pouches; Canadian flags with pictures of Indians in the center, dream-catchers of all sizes, baskets with brightly colored rings and diamond patterns. I walk through the shop, sipping my large double-double, flipping through books, rifling through cards with romantic images of men on horses with giant feathered headdresses. I select a book to read about early French Catholicism in Nova Scotia.

I finger through a basket of dolls until I find one that Jade might like, a lively-looking Indian woman with a long flowing tan dress and a rainbow-colored headband that can be removed and used as a tie for the doll's long, thin black hair. It's not the latest Barbie, but maybe this will give her something different from the rest of her friends. Seven-year-old girls like to be different from their friends don't they? We can call her Keri Tekakwitha.

So far, I haven't seen another person in the shop and it is not until I approach the counter at the front that I see a small, round Mi'kmaw woman. I didn't hear her move so it's quite possible she has been standing there this entire time. She's sitting, weaving a basket, camouflaged by the myriad of trinkets on display on, around and over her counter.

"Hi there," I say.

She doesn't say anything, but responds with a nod.

I hand her the doll and book and she rings them through on her register. I pass her a note only to realize I've given her a bill from

New Zealand. "Oh sorry, I've given you the wrong money," I say. She doesn't hand it back however, but stares at it without acknowledging me. "I've just returned from New Zealand," I say, hoping to break an awkward moment.

"What is this?" she asks, pointing at a picture of a wharenui behind the figure on the $50 note.

"That's a meeting house. I was actually just in one before I left. They're owned by Maori people—on their marae."

"Is that like a reservation?"

"I don't think so actually." I hadn't thought about that—were there reservations in New Zealand? It didn't seem like it.

The woman shrugs her shoulders and returns the note to me and I offer her two Canadian twenties instead. I thank her and she says, "Welcome home," and I walk out of the shop and back to my car with my book and the gift for my girl.

As I drive home, I think about the woman's question. I think about the marae and what I know about reservations; I think about home and place and belonging; I think about original dwellers and conquests and colonialism; I think about this idea of tangata whenua and how close I feel to the land that surrounds me now, this land of my forefathers, a land taken by them from the forebears of the woman in the shop who so generously welcomes me home.

To the southeast from here, near Musquodoboit, is Murrihy Mountain, named after my father's ancestors. To the north-west, near Tatamagouche, is a cemetery filled with my mother's family, my family. Our names for places mix with the names of the places occupied by the Mi'kmaq people. Our blood mingles with the soil as theirs does. We can never undo the conquest, but at what point do we all claim original status here? I was born here. I have no other homeland. The mountain, although I rarely visit it, is my mountain. The northern shore is my coastline. The brook behind my grandparents' house is my river.

The snowfall must be moving southwest as the blanket on the ground grows thicker as I near home and the exit off the Trans-Canada. I say home, meaning my parents' place. It really is time I started calling my own house my home. I plan to check on Mom first before carrying on to Sutherland's River to see Jordan and Jade.

The trees aren't holding much of the snow, just the dusting of the evergreens, the spruces and pines. I imagine it will be gone by tomorrow afternoon, but for tonight it is slick and I have to drive carefully as I didn't put winter tires on the truck before going to New Zealand. A few skidding turns through town and I'm at my parents' drive-way, just as the day is turning to dusk. Smoke from the chimney blends with the greying sky. It looks like I won't have to wait to see Jordan as her car is in the driveway. This is unusual, especially as she doesn't like driving any distance in weather like this, nor does she like to visit my parents without me, but I suppose she wants to see me when I arrive.

I park beside her car and as I get out, I spot headlights behind me. Getting out of their truck are Clio and Daniel. They don't have their kids with them. I wave to them and smile before turning to see Jordan in the front doorway. Jade is standing beside her. I call out to them, "Don't come out in the snow, I'm coming right in."

Jordan greets me with a kiss on my cheek, but I kiss her on the lips and hold her there, with one arm pulling our daughter close to my leg for a hug. Jordan doesn't pull back as she has done lately and it feels good to re-connect as she squeezes my hand until my wedding band digs into my finger. There's something different about her—I want to show her how I can be different for her too. We separate and I look into her eyes. She's crying and I wipe away a tear before dipping down to give Jade a proper hug.

"I missed you Daddy," she says.

"I missed you too sweetheart, more and more each day."

Clio is behind me now. "Hi Jordan," I hear her say and the tone of her voice tells me something is wrong.

I stand up and look at her and for the first time in our lives, Clio hugs me and holds me tight. She is crying and saying, "I'm so sorry Conrad. I'm so sorry."

My mind reels with thoughts of Frankie and Mom and I pull away from her embrace. I look her in the eyes and I know. I rush into the house. "Dad!" I cry. "Dad!"

Dad meets me at the top of the stairs, coming out of the kitchen. He's wearing his jogging pants and hooded sweatshirt. I have to tell him more about Frankie; I have to tell *them* more about Frankie. "Dad?" I say again, and he shakes his head, speechless and looks toward his bedroom.

"No . . . No . . . No," I groan and cover my face, but still walk into their room, needing to move, needing to see. Mom is lying in her bed, much as I left her, but the stillness in the room is stifling, as if no new air has entered for days. I walk slowly over to her, Dad close behind me. I sit down on the edge of her bed and look at that face with its thin, straight lips, its lovely defined nose, and its closed eyes, the ones I know better than any photograph. The face is beautiful. Someone has untied her hair and let it reach out full length so that it covers both of her shoulders. She is fully dressed in her best evening gown, a summer dress even on this autumnal night.

Dad sits beside me and places his hand on my shoulder. It seems cold to the touch, and I'm unsure how to feel about him.

"Conrad, I'm sorry," he says. "I sent you away. I caused you to miss your last moments with her."

I nod my head and whisper, "Yeah, you did Dad, you did," and I feel his hand tremble before he removes it. I reach my own hand out and touch Mom's ankle, half-expecting a twitch, a reaction, but there is nothing but that awful stillness.

"I need to let some air in here Dad," I say, getting up and going over to the window. I open it and feel the cold wind enter with gusto, eager to steal some warmth for the outside. I turn to see Clio and Jordan in the doorway, both with tears in their eyes watching me, waiting for some response and I wonder what is expected of me in this moment.

"When did it happen Dad?"

"Two days ago. Not too long after your phone call from New Zealand. We didn't try to contact you—we didn't want you to be alone out there . . . with this."

I nod my head, still thinking, still feeling, still torn. I look at Jordan and remember. "Dad, I failed. She wanted to see Frankie and I couldn't get him back here. I . . . I found him, but it was too late. He was sick and . . . he couldn't come back. I failed—she's gone without seeing him again." My own tears fall like raindrops—large and heavy—onto the carpet and onto the bed as I kneel beside it looking up at Mom's face.

Clio starts to say something. "Conrad, she . . . she . . . ." Then she settles her voice enough to say, "Dad, I don't know what to tell him. I don't know how to say it."

"It's OK," Dad says. "We just tell him as she told us."

"What are you talking about?" I ask, looking through tears, between my sister and my father.

Dad walks over and pulls a chair to the side of the bed and takes Mom's hand, looking at her lovingly. He speaks without looking at me.

"Three days ago, the day before your mother died, I was sitting out in the living room watching T.V. I heard voices coming from in here. At first, I thought they were background conversations in the show I was watching, but the voices continued when it went to commercial." He stops for a moment, then says sincerely, "It was your mother's voice and a man's voice.

"The other voice was low and indistinct through the walls. I got up to check on your mother and as I walked toward the room, I heard your mother say, "I'm ready." I opened the door to find her lying down, much as she is now, her eyes closed and her breathing the most peaceful I had seen in weeks.

"Of course, I checked all through the room and all through and around the house, but I found no-one. I decided to let your mother sleep the night and wait until morning to ask her about it. I thought she must have been talking in her sleep, but I couldn't explain the quality of the other voice.

"The next morning, the morning of the day she passed away, I brought it up. Clio was here." He briefly looks at Clio and smiles, then looks back at Mom. "I asked her if she remembered talking in her sleep the night before.

"She told me she knew what I was talking about but that she hadn't been talking in her sleep." He turns to look at me, determination in his eyes. "She said, 'I've been talking with Francis.'"

~

In the beginning of our world, Te Ao Mārama spurt like a ray of light from the thought of Io-wairoa. She is our world of light who shines like the morning star over the whole of creation. She, too, is our source from which all creation flows. She alone is capable of capturing the streams of love which pour from the heart of God.

But not all see her even when they live in her. Hine-nui-i-Te-Po guards the threshold between light and dark. Only some glimpse through māramatanga, through illumination, like a child moved from the womb of Te Po—the night— into Te Ao Mārama, now suckling at mother's breast.

Kia ora Io-wairoa, He who reigns above and in all things. Your thoughts are not our thoughts, Your ways are not our ways, but now we see.

Haere rā te whaea whose eyes we now see, weeping tears for her returning husband.

Haere rā brother of our son, who now remembers and paddles forward.

Haere rā.

Haere rā.

~

It has been three months since Mom's funeral and Jordan and I have since moved closer to Westville. This allows us to check on Dad regularly. I've left the newspaper and am now working as a real-estate agent in New Glasgow. I help people find a house they can call home.

Jordan has picked up a job as a teachers-aide at Jade's school. Both are happy with this arrangement—for now. After my experiences, I watch the closeness of their relationship carefully, but am thankful that both are happy in the now.

Dad is still walking in a shadow of a shadow, but he delights in our girl and in Clio's children. He's decided to retire instead of returning to work. He can help me build a new deck come summer. He and my dear aunt Mavis have a flight booked for New Zealand in the Spring.

Tonight is our eighth anniversary and we managed to score an evening of free babysitting from Dad while we went out for dinner. Returning home, it's my job to prepare Jade for bed while Jordan prepares something for the two of us. Teeth are brushed, PJs are on and it's story time.

"How about tonight, Daddy tells you a story instead of reading one from a book?" I ask Jade.

"No, I want a book. Grampie promised me you would read the one about Glooscap."

"That's a very good story, but we'll save that one for another night," I say gently.

"Grampie promised—"

"I know sweetheart, but you don't have to keep promises that others make for you—only the ones you make for yourself," I say, not really thinking through whether that's a good message or not. "I promise you I'll tell you a really good story, a story that will give you wonderful dreams."

She smiles and gives three exaggerated nods of her head. "OK!" she says.

I tuck her blankets up under her chin and begin.

"A long time ago, when the world was very different from the one we have today, the sky was called Rangi-nui and the earth was called Papa-tū-ā-nuku. Rangi, the sky, was like the father and Papa, the earth, was like the mother. Isn't that funny? The one called 'Papa' was the woman."

"That is funny," she says.

"Well, Rangi and Papa loved each other very much—so much that they wanted to hug and kiss each other all the time and never stop."

"Ewww!"

"Haha, I know. Moms and dads can be pretty gross, eh? Anyway, they had lots of children, all boys and no girls. And these boys had to live in the cramped space between their parents. Can you picture that? The sky and the earth are hugging, so how much space is left between them?"

Jade puts her fingers to the side of her mouth, raises her eyes to one corner in a thinking pose and then says, "None!" in her best "Aha" voice.

"That's right. All their big strong boys had no place to play or to run around or to wrestle or go snowmobiling or anything. Not much fun, eh? So they made plans to try and get their Mom and Dad to stop hugging each other all the time.

Would you believe that one son wanted to kill them?" Jade looks shocked. "That's right, but none of the others agreed, especially Tāne-mahuta, who thought it would be better if they just pushed them apart. So that's what they did. Lots of their children tried to do it, but it was only Tāne-mahuta who finally did it. He was like the big tall trees and he pushed his father up into the sky so that his mother was below where she could nurture her children just like the earth does. What do you think Rangi and Papa thought of that?"

"They wouldn't like it," Jade says in a sing-song voice.

"That's right. In fact, Rangi still gets so upset that he cries all over everybody just like the . . . ?"

"The rain!"

"Good girl. But you know what? Tāne tried to make his father feel better by dressing him up with millions of stars. He did a good job didn't he?"

She nods.

"And Papa-tū-ā-nuku tries to reach out to Rangi and some people feel this when there are earthquakes. But for the most part, even though she misses her husband, she still makes sure she looks after all her children here on earth.

"Just like your Mommy and Daddy will always look after you. Now, was that a good story?"

"Yes, Daddy. But can we read about Glooscap tomorrow night?

"Absolutely darling," I say, putting one hand on her cheek. "Now, close your eyes."

ACKNOWLEDGMENTS

Redeeming Brother Murrihy existed as an idea and as a working title for over thirteen years before the story was written and published. The author needed three things to happen in order to turn the idea into a novel: shut up, write it and get help.

Many thanks go to my first readers, Dale and Fiona Thomas. Your feedback and input was sincere and touching.

I appreciate all the people, past and present, that I have worked and worshipped with in Taumarunui's Immaculate Conception parish and especially in St. Patrick's school. This sentiment extends to the people and places of Taumarunui and area — including the inspiring rivers, bush and mountains.

There is a significant amount of Maori content in the book, inspired and informed by my experiences in New Zealand. I was not brave enough to conduct personal interviews though I have reflected on conversations and observations over the years with kaumatua and kuia in my circles.

At its core, *Brother Murrihy* is about family as much as it is about the theological themes. John Steinbeck advised novelists to write with one person as an audience — for me, this was my brother Aaron, but all my family in Canada were in my thoughts.

However, as in the story, it is my immediate family who need recognition — my wife, Mary, and my children, Sam and Katie, who put up with a tired and distracted husband and father who chose his word processor over time with them. I hope you are proud of the work I've done.

I invite readers to provide feedback to inform future revisions via my website: antonymillen.wordpress.com

Kia ora,

Antony Millen
June 2013

FURTHER READING

There is a tremendously rich spiritual and cultural backdrop located in the people and places of New Zealand. Capturing just some of that through research was immensely daunting and rewarding. While my preparation involved more than listed, I recommend these texts and links for any who are interested in finding out more about these and other topics in the book.

Barr, Hugh. *The Gathering Storm over the Foreshore and Seabed: Why they must remain in Crown ownership*. Wellington: Tross Publishing, 2010.

Baxter, James K. *Jerusalem Daybook*. Wellington: Price Milburn and Company Limited, 1971.

Cody, Philip. *Seeds of the Word: Nga Kakano O Te Kupu: The Meeting of Maori Spirituality and Christianity*. Wellington: Steele Roberts Publishing Limited, 2004.

Dyk, Jonathan and Cornelius Buller. "Toward an Aborigiinal Biblical Theology of Land." *Journal of North American Institute for Indigenous Theological Studies* 2 (2004).

How Far is Heaven. Dirs. Christopher Pryor and Miriam Smith. 2012.

Munro, Jessie. *The Story of Suzanne Aubert*. Auckland: Auckland University Press, 1996.

Waitangi Tribunal, New Zealand. *The Whanganui River Report*. Wellington: GP Books, 1999.

Winoska, Maria. *The True Face of Padre Pio: A Portrait of Italy's 'Miracle Priest'*. London: Souvenir Press, Ltd., 1961.

Young, David. *Woven By Water: Histories from the Whanganui River*. Wellington: Huia Publishers, 1998.

ABOUT THE AUTHOR

Antony Millen is a Canadian living and writing in New Zealand.

He is an avid reader who spends far too much energy on less important things. He has won no awards for his unpublished short stories and poetry.

Antony's healthy addictions include watching ice hockey on the internet and writing. He has seven bad habits: three are mundane misdemeanors, two exasperate his wife and one should be against the law but thankfully isn't. His seventh is forgetting items in a list.

In his spare time, Antony leads a High School English department and bumbles his way through family life.

Redeeming Brother Murrihy is his first novel—a labour of love for almost fifteen years.

FOR MORE INFORMATION:

Website & Blog: antonymillen.wordpress.com

Twitter: @antony_millen

Facebook: Antony Millen author page

MAPLE KORU PUBLISHING

ALSO BY ANTONY MILLEN

TE KAUHANGA

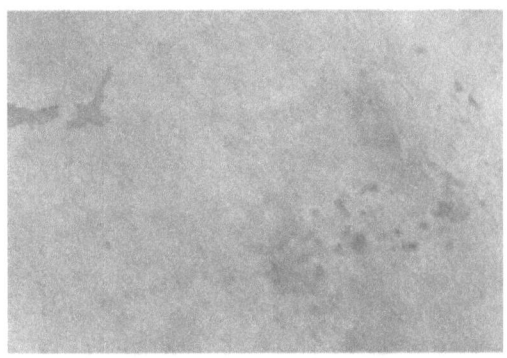

A Tale of Space(s)

ANTONY MILLEN

www.ingramcontent.com/pod-product-compliance
Lightning Source LLC
Chambersburg PA
CBHW050038180626

46810CB00002B/783